The Chinese businessman had been a long time dying

The knife work his body bore wasn't particularly artistic and most of the gashes were small, but it had obviously been effective. Wei's face was frozen in a rictus of pain.

Suddenly Bolan shoved Katz aside and triggered a short burst from the Beretta. A black-clad man staggered under the impact, then crashed to the floor.

Bolan strode forward and removed the hood from the corpse to reveal Oriental features. The sleeve of the black ninja suit had been pulled up the arm, baring a tattoo of a realistically drawn Chinese dragon emerging from a cracked egg.

"That doesn't look like any Triad badge I've ever seen," Katz remarked. "They're usually more formalized. But I don't think it's a personal marking."

"Me neither," the Executioner agreed. "This is getting complicated."

DON PENDLETON's
MACK BOLAN®
CAGED

A GOLD EAGLE BOOK FROM
WORLDWIDE®

TORONTO • NEW YORK • LONDON
AMSTERDAM • PARIS • SYDNEY • HAMBURG
STOCKHOLM • ATHENS • TOKYO • MILAN
MADRID • WARSAW • BUDAPEST • AUCKLAND

First edition November 2002

ISBN 0-373-61487-X

Special thanks and acknowledgment to
Michael Kasner for his contribution to this work.

CAGED

Who but shall learn that freedom is the prize
Man still is bound to rescue or maintain;
That nature's God commands the slave to rise,
And on the oppressor's head to break the chain.
                                    —John Quincy Adams
                                        1767–1848

Animal Man has always preyed on those too weak
to help themselves, and I'm almost never surprised
to find out just how low some men can sink to take
advantage of the helpless. The bastards should
keep looking over their shoulders, because I'm
right behind them.

                                        —Mack Bolan

CHAPTER ONE

Los Angeles, California

L.A. wasn't exactly one of Mack Bolan's favorite places. The new millennium was still young, but so far it hadn't made much difference to America's most loved or reviled megalopolis. It was true that attempts were being made to refurbish some carefully selected, high-profile, downtrodden areas, but that was just headline grabbing, L.A.-style eye candy for the liberal establishment. The city fathers could point to those projects and pat one another on the back for having done something for the "less fortunate," who couldn't afford to live in their trendy neighborhoods. That way, they wouldn't feel so bad when they drove their SUVs past the burned-out yards, layered graffiti, deserted buildings and derelict cars that decorated too many of L.A.'s suburbs.

L.A. might not have been on Bolan's top-ten list of the most livable cities in America, but he didn't try to avoid it, either. As with everything in his life, it was the mission that was important, not where it took him. The mission that had brought him to California this time wasn't one of the Executioner's crusades, though. It was merely a favor he wanted to do for a man he had once known. To him, favors were duties, and he was a man who took his duties seriously.

Since he was "off the clock" professionally, as it were, he wasn't packing heavily this time. That didn't mean, though, that he was unarmed. His standard weapons were loaded in the trunk, but under his jacket a Beretta Model 92 rode in armpit leather. The part of L.A. his duty was taking him to wasn't a place one wanted to enter without a gun. The sun hadn't yet sunk into the Pacific, but already the emergency and police sirens were wailing.

He'd gotten a tip that the man he was seeking might have been seen in a drug house, and Bolan had even been able to get a street address. It was a long shot, but this entire gig fell into that broad category.

He parked his rental car in a secure lot and set the alarm. According to the map he'd picked up at the airport on his way in, the street he wanted was only five blocks away. Moving as a man with a purpose, he breezed past the district's inhabitants waiting out the setting of the sun unmolested. None of them wanted to try their luck with him in broad daylight. It might be a different story come dark.

Rounding the corner, he spotted the address he'd been given. The exterior of the building wasn't all that different from the others along this side street, a dilapidated wreck that should have been pulled down long ago as a hazard to passersby. It did, however, have bars on the windows—a dead giveaway that it was a shooting gallery. The door was thick, the most substantial part of the entire structure, and was banded with iron bars, but that was to be expected.

What he hadn't expected to find was a door not locked and barred from the inside. Rather than knock and get into a beef when he was denied entrance, Bolan opened the door and slipped inside.

The interior of the building was filthy, semidark and it reeked. A medley of stale vomit, feces and urine shared top billing with the harsh smell of chemicals and hit him like a hammer. The only thing missing was the indescribable stench of dead ODs. Whoever was running this particular shooting gallery was at least properly disposing of his casualties.

Bolan paused to let his eyes adjust to the darkness.

"What the fuck do you want?" a hoarse voice rasped.

Turning toward the sound, he saw a hulk of a man lumbering toward him. Bolan wasn't a small man, but this guy was huge, at least six-six and easily three hundred pounds of fat layered over muscle. From his size alone, the soldier guessed that this was the proprietor of the establishment, which made him the man Bolan had come to see.

"I'm looking for a man named Nguyen Chu Lee," Bolan replied. "He usually goes by Tommy."

"Never heard of him," the thug growled.

The fact that the hulk had answered without even bothering to ask what Tommy looked like told Bolan one of two things. The first was that he knew exactly who Tommy was and was covering for him. The other was that this self-appointed hardcase was just being a butt-head.

Bolan opted for the second circumstance.

"If you do see him," Bolan said, "you might want to tell him that his father's dying of cancer and he wants to see his son before he dies."

"Right, man," the hulk said, sneering. "I've heard all that shit before. Get your sorry narc ass outta here before I stomp on you."

Bolan wasn't looking to start anything this evening, but he didn't care for the guy's attitude. He'd always had a low tolerance for butt-heads, and the fact that he wasn't on an official mission hadn't changed that one bit.

He stepped closer to his target, keeping his hands in plain view. "If you happen to see Nguyen Chu Lee, I recommend that you pass the message on."

"Fuck you, asshole," the thug snarled. "And fuck your message."

That wasn't the response Bolan had come for. But it was the one he'd been given, and he knew how to deal with it.

Snapping out his right leg, Bolan drove the toe of his boot into the guy's crotch. Even taking his bulk into consideration, the testicle-crunching kick didn't move him that much. But the man mountain did fold at the middle. When his beefy neck came within range, Bolan hammered his fist on the base of his skull with measured force. The thug hit the floor face first and didn't move.

Since the response had been a well-calculated effort, Bolan didn't bother to check to see if the hulk's heart was still beating. Had he intended to kill him, he would have been dead.

"I still need to talk to Tommy," he called out to the shadowy audience that had silently gathered from the darker recesses. "Is he here?"

"I'm Tommy," a voice came from the back of the room. "Who are you?"

"That's not important," Bolan replied as an emaciated crack addict approached him. "Your father helped me once, and I'm trying to repay the favor. He doesn't even know that I'm here. I do know, though, that he wants to see you before he dies. You're his only son."

Tommy hung his head. "I know he doesn't want to see me this way."

"He knows your situation," Bolan said kindly, "and it no longer matters to him. He's dying, and he's a father who wants to see his son one last time."

"I don't know if I can do that." Tommy shook his head.

"That's entirely up to you," Bolan said. "I'm not here to kidnap you and drag you back. I just wanted you to get the message."

"Thanks."

Bolan glanced at the unconscious body on the floor. "You guys might want to help that bozo brush up on his social skills. His manners suck."

The thug groaned, but Bolan refrained from kicking him again. The hulk wouldn't be bothering anyone for quite some time.

WHEN BOLAN STEPPED back out onto the street, the sun had sunk below the horizon and the blanket of L.A. smog had brought instant twilight. And with the darkness, the inhabitants of the area started to surface.

The collection of addicts, late-stage alcoholics, crack whores, low-level pushers, pimps and petty thieves who called this place home weren't any different from the derelicts of any other major American city. California was supposedly a Garden of Eden, but it didn't necessarily attract a better selection of social rejects.

Bolan was halfway back to where he had left his car when a woman's scream cut through the background noise.

A cry of pain, male or female, wasn't all that unusual in this environment. Screams, shouts and curses were almost a formal language among the population here. Life could be painful when you were on the street. What caught Bolan's attention was the terror all too evident in that particular scream.

When a second terror-laden scream sounded, Bolan loosened the Beretta in his shoulder rig and turned in that direction. He had been off the clock when looking for Tommy, but one of his most deeply ingrained responses had just kicked in. He had an old-fashioned notion that women hadn't been put on Earth to be hurt.

Rounding the corner, he spotted the source of the screams right inside the next alley. Under the only working streetlight on the block, a woman was sprawled on the ground with half a dozen men clustered around her. In the weak light, the woman appeared to be of mix-blood Asian descent. Her attackers, though, could have been street-gang scum from any of a number of Asian cities, as well as L.A.

Their exact ethnic identification didn't really matter to him. What they were trying to do to the woman did. Rape was never excusable.

The thugs were so involved in what they were doing that they'd failed to post lookouts, which indicated that either they were extremely stupid or far too arrogant to care who stumbled onto their activities.

Resolving this incident involved instantly prioritizing the threat. The guy with the knife at the woman's throat came up as number one in Bolan's target-selection process. Number two was the rapist. Since no one was showing iron at the moment, targets number three through seven would be selected as the scenario played itself out.

Bolan cleared leather, and his first 9 mm round slammed into the head of the thug holding the knife. The resulting blood and brain splatter on the wall behind him wasn't as spectacular as a slug from his .44 Desert Eagle would have produced, but it served its purpose.

Before the muzzle-blast had a chance to echo away, Bolan's second shot caught the man kneeling between the woman's legs. The 9 mm slug ripped through both the carotid and jugular, shutting down his brain in a split second. Clutching his neck, the rapist had the good grace to roll clear of his victim before he died.

With the woman out of immediate danger, Bolan paused momentarily to give the thugs a chance to get smart and break contact.

No such luck.

One of the men facing Bolan reacted fairly quickly for a guy whose eyes had been fixed on the action playing out at his feet an instant before. The thug's right hand dived to his belt, but he wasn't fast enough.

Bolan's third shot punched through the gunman's heart, shredding the muscle and ending its beating. His hand never made it to the butt of his weapon.

That shot had given the surviving four rapists another chance to reconsider committing suicide, but they went for their iron anyway.

The Executioner's next three shots were on rapid fire, but the range was well within the realm of sightless snap shooting. All three empty 9 mm cases were in the air at the same time.

One of his targets actually managed to get off a shot as he went down, though. The round cut through Bolan's jacket, stinging his right shoulder and causing him to pull his fourth shot. He got a hit, but not an instant kill. The punk didn't let the round drilling high into his shoulder slow him as he took to his feet and slipped around the corner.

Bolan allowed him to get away so he could remain with the woman. Dropping the almost empty mag from the butt of his Beretta, he slammed a fresh one in place and unlocked the slide. He didn't expect any more trouble, but he'd learned not to put too much faith in expectations.

The soldier leaned down to offer the woman his hand. "Are you okay?"

She looked up at him blankly, one hand trying to hold her blouse together. Considering her ethnicity, whatever it was, he realized that he might have a language problem.

"Let me help you up," he offered, extending his hand. "We need to get out of here."

She took his hand and he effortlessly stood her on her feet. Slipping out of his jacket, he placed it around her shivering shoulders.

"Do you understand English?" Bolan asked.

She glanced down at the bodies and shuddered. "You saved my life. They were going to kill me. I…"

Her English was faintly accented, but so fluent that he figured her for an Angeleno.

He took her arm and she didn't pull away. "Miss, we need to leave here quickly before the police show up. Come with me, I won't hurt you."

"I..."

The woman was going into shock and the only thing he could do for her was to get her walking and hope she didn't slip into unconsciousness.

"We have to go."

With a last glance at the bodies on the ground, the woman let herself be led away.

He didn't run, but held the woman's arm to hurry her along. The neighborhood was no stranger to gunfire and most of the inhabitants wanted no part of whatever had gone down. But someone was sure to have called the cops.

With the woman wearing his jacket, Bolan shrugged out of his shoulder rig and stuffed it in his pocket. The Beretta went into the back of his belt. That wouldn't help him if he got stopped by a cop, but this was no time to ditch his hardware.

CHAPTER TWO

Los Angeles

The final few blocks to the parking lot passed quickly. The woman was still in shock, but she gave Bolan no argument as he unlocked the passenger door of his car, helped her inside and buckled her in. When he stopped at the booth to pay his ticket, he caught the sound of the first emergency siren approaching. The half-stoned parking attendant didn't even look up as he took Bolan's money.

Easing out into the street, Bolan watched his rearview mirror for several blocks before turning his attention to his passenger.

"It doesn't look like anyone spotted us," he said.

The woman closed her eyes for a moment before turning to him. "I don't know how to thank you, sir."

"I'm Belasko, Mike Belasko," Bolan replied. "And you are...?"

"I am Jasmine Farjani."

That was clearly a Middle Eastern name, but he

couldn't quite place it. Thick black hair hung to her shoulders and was accented by golden skin that spoke of an Oriental heritage. Her eyes, however, were almond-shaped green, and her nose was straight in the heart-shaped face of an Indo-European. It was an interesting combination, but he didn't need to know her ethnic particulars any more than he needed to know how she had ended up in the hands of an Asian street gang. She was safe now, and that's all that mattered.

"Where can I take you?" he asked.

"I don't know," she said dully, her eyes fixed on the windshield of the car. "I am far from home."

"Where's home?"

"Calcutta," she answered.

Bolan was surprised. "What're you doing here in L.A.?"

"I was supposed to take a job here with an American export company," she said. "I'm a translator."

"What happened?"

Farjani shuddered. "Once I boarded the ship to come here, I was kidnapped. They put me and the others into the metal boxes in the ship's hold and explained that we would be working for them from then on."

"What were you supposed to do for them?"

"They had me go to the job I had come for," she said, "but I was supposed to be a spy for them not a real employee. I was to tell them when certain ships came in so they could hijack the cargos. When I learned what they wanted me to do, I just couldn't do it. I told them I would repay the costs of my passage, but they wouldn't release me.''

This was a new one for Bolan. The modern incarnation of slavery usually provided warm bodies for the sex industry or sweatshops. When these naive "workers" arrived at their destinations, they were told that they had to work off the costs of their transportation, usually tens of thousands of dollars. If they didn't agree to the terms, their families at home would be threatened.

Bolan hadn't heard of this new twist of placing slaves in companies to be spies.

"How did you end up in that alley?"

"They were going to punish me because I hadn't done what they had wanted. They said they'd do the same thing to my sister if I didn't obey them in the future.''

"Your sister is here?" Bolan asked. "I thought you said your home was Calcutta.''

"She came with me, and she's still on the ship. They said they'd hurt her if I didn't do what they wanted.''

The woman turned to him. "Please, sir, can you help her, too? She's only fourteen.''

Threatening to harm family members was stock-in-trade for slavers. The desire to save a family member almost always overwhelmed a person's sense of self-preservation, and the smugglers counted on that.

"Where's this ship?" Bolan asked. He was still on

his own time, and lending a hand in this kind of situation was a reflex action for him.

"I'm not sure," she replied. "It's docked at one of the cargo piers."

Since Greater Los Angeles was the West Coast's largest cargo port, there were hundreds of piers with hundreds, if not thousands, of ships docked at them. If a fourteen-year-old girl was being held in one of those ships, he didn't have time to conduct a ship-by-ship search.

"Do you know the name of the ship?"

"It's called the *Singapore Queen,*" the woman said.

"Let's find it."

With time a critical factor, Bolan went to information central to locate the ship. And that was just a phone call away to a small farm in rural Virginia. Pulling up to a phone booth, he got out and dialed Aaron Kurtzman's number. In the age of cell phone intercepts, a land line was always more secure.

"Bear," Bolan said when Kurtzman picked up his private line, "Striker. Look, I'm in L.A. and I need you to locate a ship that's supposed to be docked somewhere around here."

Kurtzman had no idea what Bolan was doing in California, but he knew that tone of voice and responded appropriately. "What am I looking for?"

"The *Singapore Queen*. I don't know the flag."

"Gimme a second here."

It took a little longer than a second for Kurtzman

to call up the shipping register for the California ports and get a listing for her.

"I have her at pier 230B," Kurtzman responded. "It's a cargo-handling area by San Pedro. And if you're thinking of checking her out, I suggest you do it right away. According to this, she's scheduled to pull anchor real soon."

"How soon?"

"Oh-dark-thirty."

That was military jargon for sometime after midnight and before dawn.

Bolan jotted down the address. "Thanks. I'll get back to you tomorrow."

Kurtzman also knew better than to ask what Bolan was after. If he needed to know, he'd be told later.

"I FOUND THE SHIP," Bolan told the woman as he slid back behind the wheel. "It's not far from here."

"Thank God," she said. "She's been in there for almost a week now. They haven't let me talk to her, and I know she's scared. She's never been away from home before."

Bolan still didn't have enough information to know what he was getting himself into, but he did know that the chance of the sister still being alive and unharmed was razor thin. Slavers weren't known for the humane care of their human cargo.

It was fully dark now, but dock work was around the clocks. The piers were lit up as the cranes and longshoremen moved cargo from ships to trucks and warehouses. While the level of activity was something he'd have to take into consideration, it could also keep him from standing out.

Bolan parked his rental in the dockworkers' lot. "We'll walk from here," he told his companion.

Going around to the back of the car, he opened the trunk. If he was going to work tonight, he needed all of his tools. It took but a moment for him to slip into his blacksuit, put on his gear and grab his weapons.

"Come on," he told the woman.

The two made it to the warehouses and stacks of crates along the dock without being spotted. As Bolan had expected, the foot traffic served to make them less noticeable.

"That's it." She stopped and pointed. "There at the end of the pier."

The *Singapore Queen* wasn't the rusting hulk Bolan had expected to find. In fact, it was the last ship in the port he would have suspected as a being slaver. This was a modern container ship, and her white paint was fresh. The red-and-white banner of Singapore proudly flew from her stern, and he could see the uniformed night crew standing watch on the bridge.

"You sure that's the right ship?"

The woman shuddered. "That's the one, sir. They kept us inside in metal boxes like the ones over on the dock. They let us up on deck for fresh air a couple of times, so I know it's the one."

By metal boxes, Bolan knew that she meant the cargo containers the ship was designed to carry. He'd heard of illegals being smuggled into European ports in cargo containers, and if it worked there, it would be tried here. A container ship could carry hundreds, if not thousands of the standard-sized containers. It would be only too easy for the smugglers to mix a couple of containers full of humans in among the other import goods.

"Okay," Bolan said, pulling her into the shadows behind a stack of crates. "You stay right here. I'll go and see if I can find her."

"Let me go with you, please," Farjani pleaded. "Roxanne's frightened and I know she needs me."

"No way," Bolan said flatly. "If that ship is what you say it is, I won't be able to protect you and look for your sister at the same time. If I do this, I have to do it my way or not at all."

Her heart urged her to ask again, to plead to join him. But she knew this strange man was right. She was thinking like a woman, an older sister, and he had the hardened, practical mind of a man of action. She didn't know anything about him beyond the fact that he had rescued her from the alley, but that alone was enough to trust him. She would put her faith in him and hope that, like a hero of the old folk tales, he would again perform a miracle.

"I will stay hidden," she agreed.

"You have to," he said. "I won't be able to do anything for you if you're discovered."

BOARDING THE SINGAPORE QUEEN turned out to be easy. The dockside lights left the ship's bow in deep shadow, and Bolan went up the mooring rope. Since the *Queen* was in port, all of her vents and hatches were open to catch the air. The Executioner easily slipped past one of the two men walking the deck and found an open passageway leading into the hold.

Bolan's rubber-soled boots made little sound as he went down the ladder to the cargo decks. The instant he entered the main cargo hold, he caught the acrid scent of cordite laid over the sweet, coppery smell of fresh blood. He was too late.

And it was his fault.

The wounded would-be rapist in the alley he had failed to chase down had obviously come back and alerted the slavers that the woman had escaped them. Rather than risk discovery, the crew had written off the rest of their human cargo.

Even knowing what he was going to find, Bolan continued his search. This had now become his business. There was nothing he could do to bring back the slaughtered victims, but he would insure that this particular crew of slavers never did this to anyone again. And when that debt was paid, he would look into the rest of those who trafficked in human misery.

He moved into the dimly lit, crowded hold, his night-black combat suit hiding him in the shadows. The tools of his trade, the .44 Desert Eagle and his silenced Beretta 93-R, were in his hands, ready to got to work. And this time no one would escape. He wouldn't make that mistake again with these people.

Four crewmen were working in the rear of the hold, moving containers with a forklift. They appeared to be unarmed, but that didn't deter Bolan; he wasn't taking prisoners. As his first target, he selected the guy who looked to be giving the orders.

The Executioner had come calling, and the roar of the Desert Eagle announced his presence. The .44 slug exploding the crew boss's head was his calling card.

There was an instant of stunned silence, rather like when a light was snapped on in the kitchen and the roaches froze before they scrambled for cover. Unlike the startled housewife, though, Bolan was prepared and gave these human roaches no slack.

Flicked over to burst mode, the 93-R snapped out silenced 3-round bursts. The first two crewmen were still trying to figure out what was happening when the 9 mm slugs punched holes through their chests. The fourth guy had been a little more mentally nimble, but his feet weren't as fast as his brain. He was still turning to run when his share of silenced rounds caught up with him.

Knowing that the roar of the .44 would have alerted the rest of the crew, Bolan went proactive. Rather than remaining where he was and letting them come to him, he headed up on deck after them.

One crewman shouted down an open hatch, but when he had no answer, he started to climb down to see what had caused all the noise. He was halfway down the ladder when Bolan nailed him with a well-aimed single shot. Since he didn't know the size of the target field he was dealing with this night, he didn't want ammunition supply to become a problem for him later.

The inquisitive crewman wailed as he dropped off the ladder and landed with a sodden thud on the deck plates. But Bolan didn't mind. He was taking his act up on deck, and drawing more of them down to where he had left would help contain them until he had cleared the upper levels. They wouldn't escape, though. They were all going to die for their part in this outrage.

He was almost at the top of the companionway when a beam of light swept overhead. He ducked to let it pass before climbing the last three feet up to the deck. A man behind a powerful searchlight on one wing of the bridge had just put himself at the head of the target list.

The Desert Eagle roared and the man fell back against the bulkhead behind him before slumping to the deck. A second round turned off the light.

As he had expected, the entire crew had turned out for the party. They were armed with what looked like AKs or local copies, and that was okay with him. The old Kalashnikov was a fine assault rifle, but this particular close-quarters battle zone favored handguns.

The two crewmen racing toward him hadn't spotted him yet, but that was their problem. The .44 sent one of them crumpling to the deck, and the Beretta took care of the other.

Bolan was lining up another target when the clatter of an AK on full-auto sounded from his six. Now that he was on deck, his night-black fighting suit had turned into a disadvantage. The dock wasn't brightly lit, but it was lighted. And that light, bouncing off the *Queen*'s gleaming white paint, made him a silhouette target.

Too late to duck, he spun to face his attacker as the long burst of 7.62 mm slugs chewed up the nice white paint to his left.

Close. But close only counted in horseshoes and hand grenades.

The bark of the Desert Eagle insured that he wouldn't have to worry about that particular AK again. The crewman folded at the waist, his back shot out.

Ducking behind a man-sized ventilator, Bolan reacquired the guy he'd been tracking earlier and sent a short burst after him. That cleared his path to the bridge, and he paused to drop the empty mags from his weapons and refresh. No point in running short when there was still work to do.

Top on his list of those due to have their tickets punched were the officers of the ship. A defense lawyer might be able to make a case that some of the crewmen might not have known about their human cargo. He doubted it, but anything was possible in L.A. The officers, though, had to have known full well what they were doing.

He also knew that if he was going to deliver ret-

ribution, he had to get it moving. With this firefight
taking place dockside in a busy port, it wouldn't be
long before someone called the cops. The harbor-
security guys probably wouldn't be up to getting involved with anything that had to do with full-auto fire,
but they could call for someone who made that their
line of work. Going up against the LAPD SWAT
units wasn't on his schedule. He had to be long gone
by that time.

As he raced for the bridge, an Oriental man in black
pants and white shirt with gold epaulets stepped out
of the wheelhouse, a submachine gun in his hands.
When he leaned over the railing to track Bolan, he
collected a trio of 9 mm rounds, as well as a .44 slug.
The impact slammed him off his feet.

Taking the companionway two steps at a time, Bolan reached the bridge deck just in time to intercept
two men racing around the corner. They spotted him
at the same time, but were a split second too late
deciding what to do. Firing decisions came instantly
to the Executioner, so he simply blew them away and
moved on.

The man on bridge watch had a ringside seat to the
bullet-spitting whirlwind that had just come on deck.
He also had no options. The door from the bridge led
into the path of death. Opening a locker, he emptied
it, stuffed himself in and pulled the door shut.

Seeing no one on the bridge itself, Bolan turned to
the wooden door on the opposite side of the corridor.
A boot slammed the door back, revealing a stateroom.

From the fancy cap on the desk, it was obviously the captain's quarters. A man wearing an undershirt and black pants spun when the door crashed open, a semi-auto in his hand. But Bolan gave him no chance to use it. A single .44 slug sent him sprawling on the carpet.

Hearing voices in the corridor outside the state-room, Bolan snatched a flash-bang grenade from his harness, thumbed the fuse and tossed the bomb through the door. A few shots sounded before it detonated.

The men in the corridor were still trying to get their retinas working again when Bolan stepped out of the captain's cabin, guns blazing. When he let off the triggers, another four men were facedown on the deck.

He paused again to change magazines before checking the rest of the bridge. Finding it empty, he started planning his egress.

Back outside, he slid down the companionway and was headed for the ship's bow when a crewman came out from behind a ventilator, his AK blazing.

Bolan went flat on the deck plates, rolling out of line of the Kalasnikov's muzzle. As he rolled, he swept the Beretta in front of him. A burst stitched the crewman across the belly, and he slumped backward over the railing.

His way now clear, Bolan sprinted the last few steps to his exit. He slid back down the mooring line and disappeared in the shadows.

CHAPTER THREE

San Pedro

Hiding behind the crates on the dock, Jasmine Farjani had her fist jammed in her mouth to keep from crying out at the gunfire coming from the *Singapore Queen*. Her imagination was running wild, flooding her mind with images of Belasko fighting his way through the ship's crew to reach Roxanne. He would snatch her from the dark and bring her out unharmed.

Her rescuer appeared in front of her suddenly like a jinni from the shadows, but he was alone. He hadn't saved little Roxanne.

"Where is she?" she gasped even though she knew the answer.

"She's dead," Bolan said as gently as he could. "The smugglers killed all of the people still on the ship before I got there."

The woman choked back a cry of grief. She knew that giving into her pain would reveal them to the people who had been drawn to the gunfire. The sound of approaching sirens only reinforced the need for her to stay silent.

"Come on," Bolan said as he assisted her to her feet. "We have to hurry before someone spots us."

Once more the woman let the warrior lead her away. This time, though, sobs racked her body and tears streaked her face.

ONCE MORE, Bolan was able to simply drive away from the carnage he had created. Since a person was never too far from a freeway in L.A., he took the first entrance ramp he came across and headed south.

Several miles down the road, he turned to his passenger, who was huddled against the door, sobbing quietly. There was nothing he could do for that right now, but he could get her situated for the evening.

"Jasmine," he said, reaching out to touch her shoulder, "I need to get you somewhere safe so you can sleep. In the morning, I can contact the police and have you taken into protective custody until you can be returned to Calcutta."

"No, please!" she said through her tears. "Not the police. And I can't return to Calcutta. There is nothing for me back there now. My family is all dead, and if I return, I'll be in danger from the people who sent me here."

"Okay. I'll get us two rooms in a motel and you'll be safe there tonight at least. In the morning, I'll see about getting you the proper paperwork so you can stay in this country legally."

"You can do that?" She turned her tear-streaked face to him.

"No problem," he said. "I have some friends in high places and I'll call in a favor."

The longer she was with this man, the less Jasmine understood who or what he was. His casual offer of legal immigration clearance was a gift without price. The only way she would ever be free again would be to become a real American.

"Who are you that you can do something like that?"

"Let's just say that I'm someone who doesn't like to see people like you and your sister get hurt. I was too late to save her, but I can see that you aren't bothered while you try to get your life back together."

At the mention of her sister, fresh tears flooded the woman's eyes again. Little Roxanne was dead and it was her fault. She was the one who should have died, not her sister.

BOLAN DROVE to Ontario before stopping at a Red Roof Inn. His Belasko credit card got him two rooms on the second floor. Since Farjani had nothing more than the clothes on her back, he got her a toothbrush pack from a vending machine and a comb. It wasn't much, but it might help.

He saw her up to her room and stood in the open door.

"Are you hungry?" he asked. "I can get you

something if you want. There's a couple of fast-food places down the street. It would be just a minute.''

''Thank you,'' she replied. ''But I couldn't eat now.''

''In the morning, I'll get you some new clothing. Or if you'd like, I'll go to your apartment and see what's there.''

Farjani sat on the edge of the bed and studied the American. He was a big man, but he moved like a cat. His bravery was unquestioned; he had gone into unbelievable danger twice and had emerged unscathed. That he was an experienced fighter wasn't in doubt. Perhaps he was a professional of some kind; she had met men like him before.

What she hadn't expected from him, though, was his concern for two women he hadn't known before that day. The look in his blue eyes told her that it was genuine. Another man might have done what he had done, but she had never known one who would have done it apparently without expecting payment of some kind. All he had spoken of so far was helping her. She was ashamed that she really didn't understand.

''Please stay a while and talk to me,'' she said. ''I know I cannot sleep yet. My mind is in a jumble. I'm so grateful for your saving my life. I don't know what they would have done after they were finished with me.''

''I don't think they would have killed you,'' Bolan told her. ''From what you said, they needed you to work for them more than they needed you as an example to the others.''

''I've never been so frightened,'' she replied. ''I didn't know that I could feel so helpless.''

Since she wanted to talk, Bolan thought this would be a good time to get to the bottom of what was going on. Since he had decided to take this to its conclusion, he needed information.

''How did you and your sister get hooked up in this?'' he asked. ''If you can, take it all the way from the beginning, everything you did, everything you were told, every detail you saw as best as you can remember it. If they were going to make you work for them as a spy, I know there have to be other people being forced to do the same, and maybe I can help them, as well.''

''But I don't understand what you can do about this.'' She frowned. ''They're organized and very powerful.''

''I'm a soldier,'' he said simply.

''You're in the Army?'' She was surprised.

''No, I work by myself.''

''As some kind of secret agent?''

''Something like that.''

''Okay,'' she said, taking a deep breath. ''I'll tell you everything I can remember, but I want a promise first.''

''What's that?''

''Promise that you will let me help you with whatever you do,'' she asked.

Bolan hesitated. If this venture took him where he saw it heading, it wouldn't be a walk in the park. Slavers had no use for human lives beyond the money they could bring them. The slaughter of the people on the *Singapore Queen* had been merely a business decision for those who were behind this.

"I know it'll be dangerous," she continued. "But this is something I feel I have to do. Roxanne would still be alive if I hadn't made a mistake, and I don't want any more young women to die if there's anything I can do to help put an end to this business."

"There will never be an end to slavery," Bolan said bluntly. This was no time to spout moronic, idealistic slogans. "As long as there are people who are willing to traffic in human misery, it will continue. All I can do is try to take out those who were behind what happened to you and your sister. I owe you that much at least."

"If you really do feel that you owe me," she said, "and I have no idea why you should think that you do, let me come with you. I'm not from a warrior family, but I know the world these men operate in. My father and his family before him were export-import merchants. They never trafficked in slaves, but they were associated with those who did."

She looked Bolan squarely in the face. "Since my father, in his own way, contributed to this trade, he also shares responsibility for my sister's death. The only way I can make amends for my family's sins is to help you."

Bolan saw the flash of dedication in her deep green eyes. The dedication to make amends for what she had unwittingly brought about, as well as for her family's peripheral involvement, was plain. It was there now, but there was no way to tell how long it would last when the bodies started to fall.

"When I said that I was a soldier," he explained, meeting her gaze with one of his own, "that doesn't mean that I operate in the way the soldiers you may know about do. When I find these men, I won't arrest them and turn them over to the authorities to stand trial. When I find them, I'll kill them."

Farjani didn't flinch from the reality of his words.

"Just as they killed my sister and the rest of the people on the ship," she said softly. "And it is good that they will die, because I know that if they're turned over for trial, they will just be freed. The governments of the Asian countries they operate from are corrupt. That much I know."

"I have a feeling that this will take me to more places than Asia," Bolan said.

"It is all connected," she said. "In my country, it is widely known that young women are sent to Europe to work as prostitutes. But, since they were always poor women, before this I didn't feel that it concerned me. Now it does, and I'm ashamed that I didn't care before. My family are Persian and Chinese and we were a prosperous, happy family until a plane crash killed my parents and my brother. With my father and brother dead, my uncle was heir to the business, and by our custom, he also owned my sister and me because we weren't married."

Her eyes flashed. "His idea of how to deal with this tragedy was to marry us off as soon as possible so he wouldn't have to share anything from my father's business with us. In fact, he wanted me to marry one of his in-laws, a horrible old man. When I refused, he threatened to throw my sister and I out of our home. I had to do something and, since I had worked as a translator for my father, I thought to do that in another country."

"How many languages do you speak?"

"English, French, Mandarin, Farsi, Arabic, Japanese and Hindi," she said proudly. "The major commercial languages in the Pacific Rim."

"Go on."

"I went to an employment agency run by a man my father had known and asked for work. He arranged for an interview with a company that provided linguists to foreign companies trading in the Pacific. I was offered a job, and like I said, it was supposed to be legitimate work so I could make a home for my sister. Even though the job was in America, the recruiter said that I could take her with me. I thought it was odd that we would travel by ship, but I didn't expect anything like what happened. How could I have known what they had in mind. I knew that girls were forced into prostitution in other countries, but I had never heard of it happening to women of my class. And not through an employment agency.

"When we got to the ship, I recognized that it was a cargo ship, but I knew that cargo ships sometimes carried passengers. We were shown to a bare cabin, but as soon as we were at sea, we were taken down below and put in one of the containers. It was then that I learned what my real work was to be. I was to betray my employer and be a spy. That was the last thing I wanted to do, but since I could only stay in your country if I kept the job, I knew that I had to do what they wanted.

"When we arrived in America, I was told that my sister would stay on the ship until I had proved myself. They put me in a small apartment and had me report to my new job. I was afraid, but I went to work and, the next night, one of the smugglers came to my apartment with a list of cargoes due to come in. But when the time came for me to let them know exactly when they arrived, I just couldn't do it. I was afraid that the company would catch me, find out that I was illegal and have me deported or sent to prison.

"Anyway, when the smugglers learned that I hadn't done as they'd wanted, they took me to that alley where you found me. They said they were going to show me what would happen to my sister if I ever disobeyed them again.

"And now she is dead." The woman's eyes teared up again. "I must see to her body. Can you help me?"

"I can take care of that for you," Bolan offered. "Do you have a picture of her?"

Farjani reached for her purse, pulled out a folding gallery of family photos and handed them to Bolan. "That's her," she said.

Bolan saw that had Roxanne lived, she would have been the same kind of exotic beauty Jasmine was.

"I'm not in this completely alone," Bolan said as his mind shifted to planning his new operation. "I have friends I can call. One of the things they can do is to take care of her body however you would wish."

"When my people die away from home, we are cremated."

"I can have that done."

"I don't know how to thank you."

"Your offer to help me is enough."

WHEN BOLAN WOKE early the next morning, he didn't bother to turn on the TV while he made his motel coffee. He knew what would be on the news, and he had work to do. Even though he wasn't on an officially sanctioned mission, he could still call upon the assets of Stony Man Farm to do some of his footwork for him.

Aaron Kurtzman picked up on the first ring, as if the call had been expected. "I need you to do something for me," Bolan said.

"Is it by any chance related to the *Singapore Queen?*"

"More or less."

Kurtzman chuckled. After the call the previous night, he'd had no idea what in the hell Bolan was up to, but he knew he wouldn't have asked him to locate the *Singapore Queen* on a whim. Something was going down in L.A. Since Bolan's track record often included spectacular outcomes that made the evening news, he'd switched one of his monitors over to L.A.'s Channel 6 to see what was shaking.

The first indication that the Executioner had been on the job in L.A. came with the late-night report that six Asian males had been found shot to death in a bad part of town. When one of the cops on the scene mentioned that the men had been killed with single shots, Kurtzman had instantly recognized the Executioner's signature handiwork.

It was only that morning, though, that the TV cameras started showing the carnage that had been discovered on the decks and in the cargo holds of the ship Bolan had asked about. Kurtzman knew that Bolan wasn't responsible for the dozens of bodies of the women and children who had been found gunned to death in the containers. The bodies of the black-clad crewmen many with weapons at their sides, though, were another matter.

"What are you into this time?" Kurtzman asked.

"I've come across a new twist on white slavery."

"What's that?"

"Using slaves as spies for industrial espionage to set up hijackings."

"Of what?"

"I haven't gotten that far yet."

"What can we track down for you?"

Stony Man Farm was more than just the operations center for the nation's most secretive convert-action teams. To be able to send Phoenix Force and the Able Team against a threat, the Farm had to know exactly who, what and where the threat was. And the bread and butter of that requirement was information gathering, which just happened to be what Kurtzman's Computer Room crew did best.

"I need a number of things," Bolan said. "First off, I need a rundown on recent large-scale hijackings of high-ticket commercial goods. Check on military hardware while you're at it."

"That's easy enough. What else?"

"See what you have on recent white slavery incidents. Not only the ones that have made the news, but the intelligence agency summaries, that sort of thing."

"I'll get Hunt working on that, too, and get back to you tomorrow."

"Good," Bolan said. "Also, what's Katz up to?"

"Our last report has him toasting his buns on the French Riviera. He's got a little villa right on the beach outside of Cannes."

"Is he bored yet?"

"More than likely." Kurtzman laughed. "You know him. He can take only so much fun in the sun."

Bolan did know Yakov Katzenelenbogen well. Very well. They had a long history together, and even though the gruff Israeli had retired from leading Phoenix Force, he still kept his hand in the game by filling the role of the Farm's tactical operations officer.

If Katz was as bored with too much fun in the sun as Kurtzman thought, he might be open to playing tac officer and backup for Bolan's current project.

"Give me his contact number."

CHAPTER FOUR

French Riviera

Yakov Katzenelenbogen had always enjoyed staying at Cannes. It offered a good combination of Mediterranean climate, great cuisine and comfortable modern accommodations. He was kicked back on the veranda of his rented villa, a Campari aperitif in hand, when his phone rang. He punched the speaker button.

"*Âllo,*" he answered in French.

"Katz," Bolan said, "I've got something going you might be interested in, and I could use a little help."

Katz chuckled. If Mack Bolan was interested in whatever it was, the odds were good that he'd be interested in it, as well. And if this was an invitation to the dance, it had come at the perfect time. He'd thoroughly enjoyed his vacation, but he was weary of seeing young Frenchwomen in minimalist bikinis parade past his veranda in an unending stream. The eye strain was killing him.

"What's the story?"

"Come to L.A. and find out," Bolan said. "Your tickets are waiting at the Air France ticket counter.

If Bolan couldn't talk about it over the phone, it had to be something he wanted in on. "When's the flight?"

"It's open-ended," Bolan said. "There's a domestic from Nice leaving for Charles de Gaulle in two hours."

"I'll be on it."

"I'll be waiting for you."

Los Angeles

BOLAN WAS at the Air France gate at LAX to meet Yakov Katzenelenbogen's nonstop flight from Charles de Gaulle International Airport.

"You're looking fit," Bolan said, greeting him.

"Tanned, fit and rested," the Israeli replied. "Ready to go to work."

"Good, because we've got work to do."

The two men said little as they worked their way down to baggage claim, retrieved Katz's single bag and headed toward Bolan's rental car. From long habit, they said nothing until they were well away from the LAX complex and back on the freeway.

"This one's nasty," Bolan said. "The media and the Feds are all over it like flies on ripe roadkill."

"If it's about that slave ship that got shot up," Katz replied, "it's the flavor of the month in Europe, too, particularly in France. The old bash-American crowd is getting a lot of mileage out of it. The French have been fighting the new slave traffic for so long that they're overjoyed to be able to point at us and say that they're not the only ones who can't handle it.''

"It is about that ship," Bolan said. "And I know we can't put an end to slaving. But I think we can thin them out and make sure that the survivors get into the habit of looking over their shoulders for a long time to come.''

"That's not a bad idea. What's the plan?"

"I'm just in start-up phase, no specific targets as yet. I've got the Farm crew doing the legwork for me, and the Bear thinks they can come up with something for us to work with real soon. And we'll have a third party with us this time.''

Anytime Bolan brought an outsider into one of his missions, there was a good reason for it. Katz raised one eyebrow in question, and Bolan continued.

"Her name's Jasmine Farjani, midtwenties, from Calcutta, and she's my main source on this. She and her sister were brought here supposedly for legitimate jobs. Instead, the woman was placed as a spy in a large export company, and her young sister was held as insurance. When the woman balked at what her masters wanted her to do, they decided to show her what was in store for her and her sister if she didn't play ball. She was being gang-raped when I happened to stumble onto it. The rest, you saw on the news.''

Seeing the look in Bolan's eyes, Katz knew that

there was more to this story than he was being given at the moment. Something that had impacted Bolan on a personal level. He also knew, though, that if he needed to know what it was, he'd be told at the appropriate time.

"How far are you planning to take this?" he asked.

Bolan got a look in his eyes that Katz knew well. "As far as it takes."

"Sounds interesting."

"I'm not sure that's the word I'd use for it," Bolan said. "But I'm pissed."

"I can tell."

JASMINE FARJANI WAS startled by the knock on the door of her room, but went to the peephole. Seeing Belasko and an older man, she unlocked the door to let them in.

"Jasmine," Bolan said, "this is my friend Lev Bronski. He's going to help us."

"Enchanted," Katz said in French as he bowed slightly over her hand.

"Shalom," she answered in Hebrew.

"You didn't tell me you spoke Hebrew," Bolan said.

"I don't speak it very well, but it's a useful trade language."

"My people have been known to buy and sell on occasion." Katz laughed.

"I didn't mean to insult you." The woman lowered her eyes in shame.

Katz smiled. "You didn't, my dear. We Jews have been a mercantile people for thousands of years."

"Lev's one of the best planners I know," Bolan told Farjani, "and he's going to be a lot of help on this. To bring him up to date, I'd like you to go over everything you've told me with him again. I'll go get us takeout for lunch while you're talking, and we'll go over what we're going to do when I get back."

WHEN BOLAN RETURNED with several containers of steaming Chinese takeout, Katz had his battle face on and looked ready to strangle someone.

"What do you think?" Bolan asked.

"I think we need to get serious with someone."

"Any idea who?"

"A couple," Katz replied. "Jasmine was given a contact number, and I've got Aaron running it right now. I think that's as good a place to start as any."

Bolan laid his fragrant paper bags on the table. "Let's eat."

Lunch was barely over when Kurtzman called back. "Your number belongs to a local import-export firm, Global Imports, Inc.," he said to Katz. "Or rather to another small company whose phone bills are paid by them."

"Great," Katz said. "What are the particulars of the parent firm?"

Kurtzman read off what he had learned while Katz made notes. To no one's surprise, Global Imports mainly worked the Pacific Rim, but dabbled in the

Middle East. It also wasn't surprising that the company was owned by a Chinese American who did a great deal of business with the old country. The American Chinese were big in the import-export business, and who better to deal with the growing economic giant of the Pacific Rim than a native son?

"What are they moving?" Katz asked.

"Industrial electronics and machine tools that are very useful in military manufacturing," Kurtzman said. "The kind of thing that China needs and has trouble getting the most."

"Any contraband busts?"

"Nothing written up so far, but that doesn't mean anything. As you know, the Federal Trade Commission goes out of its way to give its blessings to shipments that we're likely to get back sharp end first, and you have to be blind to get a job as a customs inspector."

"What about the company that answers the phone?" Katz asked.

"It's called Sunset Electronics," Kurtzman said, "but they don't seem to do much business, if any at all. That's why I checked to see who was paying their bills."

"A front, then," Katz said.

"That's sure what it looks like."

"Great," Katz said. "We'll start working on Global, but I'd like you to keep digging on both companies. And if this turns out to be what I think it is,

I'm going to need a referral when I try to place my order.''

"What kind?''

"Since I'll be going in as a Middle Easterner, give me someone from the Islamic Brotherhood who's in hiding.''

"How about Amal Zawa,'' Kurtzman suggested after a moment. "He's Egyptian and hasn't been heard from in a long time. He may actually be dead.''

"Perfect,'' Katz said. "I do a real good Egyptian.''

KATZENELENBOGEN WALKED into the lobby of Global Imports holding a fat leather briefcase. His linen suit had that look of not being American made, and it was out of style for L.A. but it would have been right at home in Beirut. His coloring wasn't as dark as the popular expectation of an Arab, but his face passed as Middle Eastern.

Since the Chinese weren't known as Arabic linguists, he didn't bother with trying to put on a fake Arab accent. He did, though, bring out his Hebrew to color his English and knew that it would pass. Arabic and Hebrew were both Semitic tongues.

Walking up to the obviously native California girl behind the lobby desk, he reached into his jacket and brought out a business card identifying him as an Egyptian engineer, Ali Hadan, of Cairo.

"May I see Mr. Wei, please?'' he asked. "Mr. Amal Zawa suggested that I talk to him.''

"I'll go see if he's in," the perky blonde replied. "Have a seat."

"Thank you." Katz sketched a bow before taking a seat on the couch.

As he had halfway expected, Zawa's name insured that Mr. Wei, Global's owner and CEO, was in. The receptionist was back before he had time to warm up his seat. "Mr. Wei will see you now."

"Thank you."

The woman led him into a finely furnished but understated office. A middle-aged Oriental man strode across the carpet to greet him.

"I am Chu Wei," he said, extending his hand.

"Al Hadan," Katz replied as he shook the businessman's hand.

"Tea?" Wei asked as he guided Katz to a chair.

"Please. That would be nice."

Wei keyed his intercom and spoke rapidly in Cantonese. The answer was one syllable.

In moments, a young Asian woman walked in bearing a silver tray with two silver cups. Katz could smell the cardamom and knew she was bringing Arabic tea. The subtleties of the marketplace were being observed.

Both men were silent as the woman poured and left the room without a word.

Wei took a delicate sip of the hot, fragrant brew. "How may I be of assistance to a friend of Mr. Amal Zawa's?" he asked.

"As I'm sure you are aware," Katz replied, "the

political situation in the Middle East often makes it difficult for a small businessman such as myself to do business.''

"Sadly, that is true," Wei agreed. "If more politicians were businessmen, these difficulties would not exist.''

Katz took another sip of his tea.

"How may I help your business?" Wei asked.

Since the Chinese was forging ahead with this without wasting more time on small talk, Katz did, as well. "I was told that you might be able to help me with a supply problem I have been experiencing.''

"And what would that be?"

"My company makes testing equipment for the Egyptian electronics industry," Katz said.

Wei would have to know that no electronics manufacturer in their right mind used anything other than Western or Japanese testing equipment. Not if he wanted to produce a quality product. But if Wei bought that one, Katz would know he was talking to the right man.

"An exacting business," Wei said, stringing him along.

"Exactly," Katz said. "And that is the problem. Certain Western-made components are difficult for me to obtain at times. I can import them on occasion, but have not been able to secure a reliable source of supply.''

"As I'm sure you are aware," Wei said, "my company prides itself in making critical components read-ily available to small foreign customers. Maybe I can help you.''

Katz calmly said, "I need laser exciters made to the LS-2304K specification.''

LS-2304K exciters had absolutely no application in any kind of testing equipment used in any industry. They were, though, the heart of laser guidance systems for missiles and other guided ordnance. And they were on the Department of Defense's and Department of Commerce's list of items prohibited from export.

Anyone with any expertise in electronics had to know that, but Wei didn't even blink. He tapped on his keyboard and studied his monitor for a moment.

"It so happens that we have two dozen LS-2304Ks in stock at the moment.''

"Excellent," Katz replied. "And what is their availability in the future?''

"If you have a standing order," Wei said, "we will be able to meet it.''

"Excellent." Katz beamed. "And at what price?''

Laser exciters were expensive, but when Wei quoted a price at twenty times the fair market value, Katz frowned. He'd have gladly paid the asking price to nail this guy, but he was playing a Middle Easterner, and not to bargain for a better price would make Wei suspicious.

"I only have a small company," Katz stated. "And as I'm sure you know, the recent financial instability in the region has created uncertainties for businessmen such as myself. I have to watch my bottom line very carefully.''

"I understand very well.'' Wei sounded sympathetic. "The powerful can make it very difficult for honest men like us to make a living.''

"My people say that 'when the king scratches, everyone has an itch.''' That was a Katz original, not an Egyptian proverb, but it sounded good.

"All too true. Since you are looking for a reliable source instead of a one-time purchase, I can supply what you need at a twenty percent discount.''

"I have a pending contract that will require me to greatly expand my facilities,'' Katz replied, getting into the game. "And, of course, when that happens, I will order all of my components through you. But to make the numbers work for me right now—'' he shrugged expressively "—I would have to have a forty percent cut.''

Wei glanced back at his monitor for a long moment. "I am sorry, but I can offer only a thirty percent discount.''

"If you make it thirty-five,'' Katz pressed, "I can make the payment in cash.''

Like all Middle Easterners, Asians liked cash almost as much a they did gold and diamonds. The Chinese had invented paper money, so folding green was okay with them and was preferable to an electronic transfer.

Wei took another sip of his tea, and Katz did the same. He wouldn't want to get into a high-stakes poker game with this guy. But then, he was an old poker player himself and knew the game well.

Wei emptied his cup, looked at his monitor again and smiled. "I can do that," he said.

"Excellent." Katz smiled back.

"HE'S DIRTY," Katz said when he reported to Bolan in the motel room they were sharing. "Real dirty. He didn't even blink when I told him I wanted to buy Mil-Spec laser exciters. He just looked to make sure that he had them in stock and then priced them according to how badly he thought I wanted them."

"When do you pick them up?"

"I'm to examine them at his offices tomorrow, pay for them and arrange for their shipping."

"He offers that, too?" Bolan was surprised.

"Oh, yeah, he's a hot one, a full-service dealer in contraband electronics and God knows what else."

"We need to find his warehouse."

"I've got the Bear working on that right now," Katz said. "He's running phone intercepts on all Global's numbers."

"I'll get our kit together."

CHAPTER FIVE

Stony Man Farm, Virginia

Aaron Kurtzman was a little surprised that his phone intercepts had paid off so quickly, but he had the readouts in his hands. One would have thought that a man in the electronics business would have known how easy it was to eavesdrop on phone conversations. But despite the recent controversy about the government's Carnivore Program, many people still thought that their conversations were their own. Thankfully Mr. Chu Wei was one of those deluded fools.

The conversations they'd taped were in Chinese, but the translation program quickly broke them down. And like most phone calls, the content was fairly innocuous to the casual listener. However, there was nothing casual about the way the Farm crew dug into the information the minute the first call came out of the translator.

A glance at the clock bank over the big screen on the wall told Kurtzman that the sun was just going down over L.A. when the results were in and he reached for the phone.

"Striker," he said when Bolan picked up, "congratulations, your number's a winner. It turns out to be in a warehouse in Riverside run by Chinese. Better yet, the rent is being paid by Wei's front company. I'd say that it's your next likely target."

"Good work," Bolan said. "We'll cruise out there tonight and have a look."

"I thought you might. Good hunting."

"Don't really know what we're hunting for yet, but it's worth a look."

CHU WEI'S WAREHOUSE in Riverside bore no sign indicating its ownership, its facade bearing merely a street number. It was brightly lit, though, and Bolan could make out security cameras mounted on the corners of the building and the tops of the light poles in the parking lot. Interior lights were on, indicating that the night shift was on duty.

"Someone doesn't want people breaking into that place," Bolan said as he surveilled the warehouse from their parked car a block away.

"Not very hospitable of them," Katz said. "We'll have to do something about that."

"Such as?"

"Power outages are still a popular event around here," Katz said. "So why don't we manufacture one? It will save us the trouble of dodging the cameras and sensors."

"Good point," Bolan said. "What do you have in mind?"

"Well," Katz replied, grinning, "since we don't have Gadgets handy to rig up one of his remote-controlled toys for us, we'll just have to do it the old-fashioned way."

"Some things never go out of style," Bolan told him.

Driving back to the entry to the industrial area, Bolan stopped by the power pole feeding the warehouses. Stepping out, Katz looked both ways to make sure they were unobserved before taking aim at the transformer with his silenced mini-Uzi and cutting loose half a dozen rounds.

A shower of blue-and-orange sparks rewarded his efforts, and the lights went out.

With the entire area in darkness, night-vision goggles were in order for the approach to the warehouse. If the gods of war were with them this time, the opposition would have left their NVGs at home.

Parking their ride out of sight behind the adjoining building, the pair crossed the almost empty parking lot to the side of the warehouse. Rather than go in through the office in the front of the building, they tried the side door. The power outage had sent the electronic locks into the default, locked-down setting, sealing the occupants inside, which was precisely where Bolan wanted them.

The soldier could hear men shouting back and forth in the darkness inside and opted for the quick entry. His titanium pry bar made short work of the lock, and any noise it made was lost in the commotion. His Beretta silenced and ready in his hand, he slipped into the building.

The interior of the warehouse was even darker than outside. Flashlight beams cut through the darkness, so he crouched inside the door, his blacksuit rendering him all but invisible.

"Go," he whispered to Katz over the com link. "But keep low, they're using flashlights."

Katz entered and knelt low against the interior wall. "Shit!" he said. "They're trying to start a generator."

The gruff Israeli turned toward the sound, and his NVGs showed him two men standing by a boxy piece of equipment at the rear of the building.

"Do it," Bolan whispered.

Katz's silenced mini-Uzi spit flame from its short barrel, and the generator team went down.

At the same instant, Bolan acquired his target, a man who looked to be talking on a cell phone. A silenced 9 mm round put him down, sending the phone skidding across the concrete.

Their weapons were silenced, but someone spotted their muzzle-flashes. The chatter of a subgun sent a burst slamming into the concrete-block wall to one side of Bolan.

He rolled off to his right and returned fire. Muzzle-flashes worked both ways. His target grunted and went down hard.

Katz had also managed to put down another pair.

Two more brief exchanges brought silence, and the two men moved out to check their results.

"No one left to talk to," Katz announced as he paused by the last bodies.

"Let's see what they were so willing to die for," Bolan said.

"I'll check from the front while you're doing that. Someone might have heard the shots."

Grabbing a flashlight from beside one of the corpses, Bolan opened the beam and swept it over the shelves. Most of the goods were still in their original containers, which bore military markings and classification labels.

Bolan clicked in his com link to Katz. "We've got a nice collection of things here that belongs to either NASA or the military."

"Maybe Wei is in the Salvage business?"

Bolan grunted. "This isn't outdated MREs or dented mess kits and tent poles. We're talking about top-drawer gear here, and a lot of it is wearing classification markings."

"We've got a couple of guys with flashlights heading our way," Katz announced from the front office. "I think we've worn out our welcome."

"Some welcome."

The two men exited by the same door they had entered and kept to the shadows until they reached their rental car. Sliding behind the wheel, Bolan took the back way out to avoid the people drawn to the warehouse.

As he drove, Katz pulled out his cell phone and

speed dialed the Farm. "Bear," he said, "we need a little favor."

"You need a little long-distance cleanup?"

"Kind of. Call the L.A. FBI field office and tell them that there's a warehouse of stolen, classified military hardware out here. Also let them know that eight corpses are guarding it, so they'll get here quick."

"You guys clear?"

"Yeah. We're on the freeway heading west."

"Keep me informed."

"Will do."

"Let's go have a chat with your Mr. Wei," Bolan said. "I've got a few questions to ask him."

"Good idea," Katz said, whipping open his field notebook to get the address.

THE PANICKED phone call from the chief of his warehouse security stunned Chu Wei. When the sound of the man choking on his own blood sounded clear over the cell phone, he became angry. This could only be a raid on his goods, and he was above that. He ran an organization that preyed on other businesses, so having someone attack him was an outrage.

Wei was dirty, but his first instinct was to call the cops. He hesitated, his hand poised on the speed dial before pulling back.

Suddenly cautious, he thought about the *Singapore Queen* incident. He wasn't directly involved in bringing the ship's "cargo" into the country and placing the people in the target firms. Slaving was something he didn't want to be associated with in any way. It was bad enough that the system in place required that the spies report to one of his subsidiaries. It was a risk he had to endure, but there was no way he wanted to be connected to it any closer than that.

Nonetheless, the raid on the *Queen* had affected his operation in a big way. One of the women smuggled in was to have been placed in a company he was interested in. In fact, the buyers were waiting for their goods, and now he would have to wait until her replacement could be found before he could move on that company. This raid, if that's what it was, on his warehouse following so closely to the attack on the ship worried him.

Turning to the woman next to him in bed, he unceremoniously rolled her onto the floor. "Leave me!" he snapped.

She blinked to focus her mind. "But—"

"Go now!"

Pausing only to scoop her clothing from the floor, the woman hurried out of the room and closed the door behind her. After hearing his bodyguard start to make a pass at her, Wei dialed his cell phone.

"Lee," he said abruptly, "this is Wei. What are your people saying about the *Singapore Queen?* Who do they think attacked them?"

"We don't have a clue," the Chinese American cop on Wei's payroll answered. "And now it doesn't look like we're going to get a chance to find out. The Feds have completely taken over the investigation. They're busting balls down on the docks trying to find out why the customs morons or the Coast Guard flun-

kies didn't find those containers when they inspected
the ship. They're looking into everything from the
payoff angle to organized crime and drug smuggling.
Everybody except maybe the goddamn EPA is involved.''

"Is anyone talking about our organization?" Wei
asked.

"I did hear one of the Feds mention something
about Hong Kong," Lee replied. "But that's all I
heard. They think the LAPD's in on this up to their
belt buckle, too, so they aren't saying dick around
us."

"Keep me informed," Wei said.

"Of course, Uncle," Lee responded.

When Lee rang off, Wei checked the digital clock
on his nightstand before dialing a number in Hong
Kong. It was daylight there, and the colonel should
be available.

"Honorable Colonel," Wei said in Cantonese
when the phone was picked up, "this is Chu Wei
calling from the Land of the Golden Mountain. I believe we have a problem."

Hong Kong

RED ARMY COLONEL Gao Dong clicked off his cell
phone. As the head of the Special Economic Project,
he had been informed of the raid on the *Singapore
Queen* in detail almost before the shooting had ended
that night. One of his operatives on the ship had survived the gun battle and had made an immediate re-

port. He had also taken his own life when ordered to do so. Dong couldn't risk the man's being captured and interrogated by the Yankees.

The Dragon Egg teams, as the Special Economic Project operatives were called, were handpicked not only for their linguistic abilities and intelligence, but also for their rigid obedience to orders. They knew the risks that were involved in their work, but for the chance to catapult the motherland boldly into the twenty-first century, they were willing to take them and die when the fates went against them.

The perks, as the Yankees called them, of the job also kept his people deeply loyal to Dong. Few Chinese of the People's Republic ever had a chance to live as they did. Only the highest Party officials had ever experienced the contact with the West they enjoyed on the Dragon Egg teams. The colonel had wisely chosen his men from the sons of the merchant and Tong families of old Hong Kong. Such families were "tainted" by their years under British rule, and these young men would have never been able to rise in the Communist Party hierachy otherwise. If they were successful with the colonel, they would receive instant full Party status, which would open a world of privileges to their families.

Even though all of the Dragon Egg operatives lived well, there was constant competition on the team to be assigned to the "cargo transfer" units. These were the men who actually moved the slaves into the target countries and handled them once they were placed on the job. Since most of the slaves were young women, his operatives had unlimited sexual access they could have never enjoyed in the rather puritanical Marxist motherland.

Using sexual favors to insure obedience was a decadent tool unworthy of the People's Republic, but it was effective. The colonel was a loyal follower of the Great Leader, Mao, but he had the deep-rooted pragmatism of the peasant class he had fought his way up from. Idealism was a good trait only as long as it brought the desired results, and results were the only thing that mattered to Dong. There was nothing he wouldn't do, and no one he wouldn't expend, to attain them.

Speaking of expendables, Chu Wei had been the linchpin of his American operation for years now. In fact, when he was honest with himself, Wei had been instrumental in giving him the idea of using slaves as spies to steal technology shipments from the West. Wei was a valuable man and would be hard to replace, but sadly, he'd made a mistake. And if there was anything the colonel wasn't flexible on, it was mistakes. He simply didn't tolerate them.

Clicking his phone back on, he dialed a number in L.A. "I have an immediate mission for you," Dong said. "Your uncle has saddened me."

Los Angeles

CHU WEI'S HOUSE wasn't a typical L.A. mansion, but it was a large, well-landscaped house. Set on a hillside well off the road, it gave Wei complete privacy at the price of obstructing fields of fire and offering good covered avenues of approach. Obviously the Chinese businessman didn't have much of a military background.

After a drive-by recon, Bolan and Katz parked their vehicle at a turnout a quarter mile away and made their approach on foot. The decorative lights on the grounds were turned down low enough to allow them to use their NVGs as they made their way to the darkened house. Rather than trying the front door, they headed to the back. Finding a sliding door already open, they readied their weapons.

The door of the first room they came to was cracked open, showing a light inside. Katz provided cover while Bolan investigated with his silenced 93-R leading.

On the far side of the small room, an Asian couple was lying motionless on the single bed, the woman naked and on top of the man. She was petite, but still covered much of the larger body under her. He was naked from the waist down, but wore a loaded shoulder holster over a tank top. A Colt M-4 carbine near the edge of the bed further identified him as a bodyguard.

The woman had been dealt a single gunshot wound to the back of the head. The man had also been shot in the head, but twice and from the front. His face bore an almost quizzical look.

Since there was no sign of a struggle, except on the mattress, it was obvious that the couple hadn't been confronted. Merely caught off guard. A professional had been at work here, and Bolan knew what he was going to find when they located Wei.

They found the master bedroom down the hall, and the door was open. The bed was empty.

When Bolan shrugged, Katz motioned for them to check the front of the house. Another opened door led into a dark office, but Wei wasn't behind his desk. Instead, he was in the middle of the room bound to a chair with duct tape. Another strip of tape covered his mouth.

The Chinese businessman hadn't died as suddenly as the woman and the bodyguard had. In fact, from the blood pooled under the chair he was taped to, he had been a long time dying. The knife work his body bore wasn't particularly artistic, and most of the gashes were small, but it had obviously been effective. Wei's face was frozen in a rictus of pain, his eyes bulging and his tongue bitten through.

"I wonder who got angry at him?" Katz asked.

"That's what we need to find out."

Suddenly Bolan shoved Katz aside and swung around his Beretta, triggering a short burst. A black-clad man staggered under the impact, and Katz heard a silenced round sing past his head.

"Damn," Katz swore.

Bolan stepped forward and pulled the hood off the corpse, revealing an Oriental face. "I'd say that someone felt that Wei had done something wrong."

The right sleeve of the body's black ninja suit had pulled up past his wrist and revealed part of a tattoo.

Bolan slid the sleeve up to his elbow and saw a tattoo of a realistically drawn Chinese-style dragon emerging from a cracked egg. The image was small, only an inch and a half across, but looked a little like the Triad marks he'd seen in the past.

"Take a look at this," he said.

Katz did. "Doesn't look like any Triad badge I've ever seen. They're usually more formalized. But I don't think it's a personal marking."

"I don't, either," Bolan said. "I wish we had a camera."

"I can sketch it when we get back."

The Smith & Wesson 39 that had fallen from the man's hand was fitted with a sound suppressor. Bolan knew the ballistics would match the slugs that would be taken from the bodies in the other room.

"This is getting even more interesting," the soldier stated, "but I think we'd better evaporate. As soon as the Feds hit the warehouse, they'll be coming here next."

"I'll grab the computer on our way out," Katz said. "Maybe Aaron can get something out of it."

CHAPTER SIX

Los Angeles

The next morning, Bolan, Katzenelenbogen and Jasmine Farjani sat over their breakfast coffee and planned their next move. The night before, Katz had faxed his sketch of the dragon-and-egg tattoo to the Farm. But even after running it through all of the Asian gang task forces, both state and federal, it hadn't yet been identified. Both men were certain that there was more than one guy on the West Coast wearing that tattoo, but with Wei dead, their leads had died with him.

It was time to take the action back to the source, and that's where Jasmine was going to come in.

"There's the man in Calcutta who set up you and your sister," Bolan suggested to Farjani. "Don't you think he knew what he was sending you into?"

"He must have known," she replied firmly. "I don't see how he could not have." Her eyes misted over. "And he was supposed to have been one of my father's friends."

"Do you think you're up to facing him again?" Katz queried. "We would be close by to back you up, of course, in case something went wrong. But I think that you could get more out of him than we could. Maybe…" He hesitated. "You could even ask him to find you another job."

She was outraged. "You mean give him a chance to sell me again? Why would I want to do that?"

Katz shrugged. "It would give us an instant contact with the smugglers."

"But I don't understand. He would know what had happened to me before. He would instantly suspect me if I asked that of him."

"To him you're just a woman, and men like him don't consider women to be very intelligent," Katz said confidently. "I'm sure we can come up with a story he'll buy."

"But what?"

"Let's see, now." Katz thought for a moment. "We'll need a reason why you had to leave America in a hurry and don't want to go back there. I know. You don't want to go back because of your sister's death. And, of course, you don't suspect that he had any role in what happened after the two of you boarded the *Queen*. That's something I'm sure he'll buy in a flash."

He grinned. "After all, you're just a woman."

Farjani steeled herself. She had told these men that she would do anything she had to get vengeance, and this was no time to let them, and Roxanne, down. "If it will help you get those men, I will do it."

"Good girl."

"I'll tell Aaron where we're going," Bolan said, "and have them start getting her a passport and any paperwork we might need."

Farjani had been with these two men long enough to no longer be surprised at the things they could get done with a phone call. She wasn't completely comfortable about going back to Calcutta, even with them guarding her, but she had vowed to avenge her sister.

WHEN BOLAN WAS pursuing a private venture, he was under no obligation to keep Stony Man Farm informed of his doings. His informal arrangement with Hal Brognola, the head of the Farm's Sensitive Operations Group, gave him complete freedom to do what he'd always done without interference. Even so, it was usually to his advantage to give the Farm a heads-up once he got into action. That way the aftermath of his activities didn't end up on the threat board and kept his back clear of federal interference.

Also, since he often tapped into the Farm's information-gathering capabilities, it made good operational sense to at least let Aaron Kurtzman know where he was going and what he was thinking about doing. That way, along with Kurtzman's Computer Room crew feeding him intelligence, he could tag along in cyberspace and keep his eyes and ears open as an early-warning system.

"You guys still in L.A.?" Aaron Kurtzman asked when Bolan called later that morning.

"We plan to take off soon," Bolan said. "We've done enough damage here to get the ball rolling for someone else to take it over."

"I have to agree." Kurtzman chuckled. "There's half a dozen federal agencies swarming over that warehouse right as we speak."

"They finding what I thought they would?"

"That place is a veritable treasure trove of missing electronic and high-tech goodies," Kurtzman replied. "Mostly of a military nature and many of them highly classified, as well. They're finding stuff in there they didn't even know was missing. Someone's going to go to Leavenworth for sure over this."

"Have they started asking questions about how this cache was uncovered?"

"Not a word. With the kind of material they're finding, I think they're so glad to get it back under control that they really don't care who discovered it. There's going to be so much cover-your-ass going on that they won't have time to mess with anything else. The cops are racking up your body count to that old California standby—gang-related violence."

"That's always good to hear," Bolan said. "I don't want to have to look over my shoulder as we're leaving."

"Speaking of," Kurtzman said. "Where are you going?"

"Katz and I decided to go to India and follow up

on the Calcutta connection. Jasmine knows who set up her and her sister, and we're going to talk to him. We'll need a passport for her, and Katz is sending the photos.''

''I'll have the guys get right on that,'' Kurtzman replied. ''Do you want me to prestock any gear for you?''

''Let me get on the ground and have a look at what we're dealing with first,'' Bolan replied. ''But you might want to alert Cowboy that we'll be calling on his services.''

John ''Cowboy'' Kissinger was the Farm's armorer and go-to guy for hardware and operational supplies. If it went bang or did harm, he had it or could get it on short notice.

''No problem,'' Kurtzman replied. ''He's been sitting on his thumbs lately and driving Buck nuts with plans to update the blacksuits' entire arsenal. He's even after him again to give up his old .45, and Buck told him that the only way he'd get it was to pry it from his cold, dead fingers.''

Bolan laughed. Buck Greene and his old Colt went back a long way, and Cowboy knew better than to separate a man from his favorite piece. ''You'd better send him to me to keep Buck from skinning him alive.''

Kurtzman laughed.

''Patch me in to Akira,'' Bolan said, ''so I can give him the flight information.''

''Good hunting.''

Stony Man Farm, Virginia

BARBARA PRICE STRODE out of the elevator onto the main floor of the Annex, the heels of her worn cowboy boots clicking softly on the floor. With the threat board clear of hot topics for a change, the atmosphere in the command center was laid-back.

That didn't mean, though, that the Computer Room crew was slacking off. The air carried the faint scent of ozone from the mainframes as they churned through the megabytes at blinding speed. The situation map was up-to-date with the latest worldwide incidents of man's inhumanity to his fellow man. And the printers and faxes were spitting hard copy into the overflowing trays.

The only thing missing was the overlay of adrenaline and stale sweat that not even the air scrubbers could remove, and that was just fine with her.

Being the mission controller for Stony Man Farm SOG was a 24-7 job, and it was nice to have a chance to stand down and catch her breath every now and then. Along with seeing that the nation stayed safe, she did have other, more mundane things that made demands on her attention every now and then.

She walked over to the availability board to see where her action team commandos were enjoying their time off. The Phoenix Force commandos were scattered to the winds as usual, but it looked as if the members of Able Team were cooling it together in the Caribbean. Strangely enough, Katzenelenbogen was in L.A. for some reason. And Bolan? According to this, he was in L.A., as well.

It wasn't unusual for those two to spend time together, but not in L.A.

Sensing something more than mere coincidence, she made her way over to the small-sized refuse heap that Kurtzman claimed was his workstation. The debris field surrounding it actually looked a little smaller than usual, another sign that Stony Man was in a hiatus. When things got busy, she needed a backhoe to get past it to talk to him.

"How's Striker doing?" she asked.

Kurtzman unlocked his wheelchair and spun it to face her. "He and Katz should be leaving L.A. right about now for Calcutta."

"What's in India?"

"A slave trader who snatched a woman and her sister and sent them to California."

"Is this by chance tied in with that ship thing in L.A. that was on the news?"

"That's the one," he replied. "The *Singapore Queen*. The crew killed the people they were trying to smuggle in, so he killed the crew."

"I thought that looked like his work."

During this downtime, Price had been taking care of her other full-time job, keeping the Farm running. While she immersed herself in the day-to-day supply, management and accounting chores, she relied on Kurtzman's crew to keep her informed of potential areas of interest. Apparently someone had dropped the ball this time, and nothing angered her more than not knowing what was going on.

"Why didn't you let me know about this, Aaron?"

He shrugged. "There's nothing to tell you. Really. Striker just happened to stumble into a situation...."

"And...?"

Kurtzman sighed. He really knew better than to try to shortchange her, but he really hadn't thought that she needed to know about this one, since the Farm wasn't going to get deeply involved.

"Okay," he said, "grab wood. This is going to take us a while."

She glanced at her watch. "I've got all day."

"I ADMIT THAT'S a new twist on an age-old story," Price said when Kurtzman finished explaining. "Putting good-looking slaves to work as spies instead of hookers."

"That's what I thought," he replied.

"What's the deal with the woman?" she asked. "Why's he taking her along?"

"From what he said, she's an asset in that she's a multilinguist in the regions he expects to have to go into. Also, she's apparently looking to get a little payback for her sister's death."

Price frowned. Bolan usually went to great lengths to keep noncombatants out of the line of fire when he was on the job, particularly when they were women. But if he'd opted to get this woman involved, he had a damn good reason.

"And you're bird-dogging for him again, right?"

"Nothing major." He shrugged. "We're just running some background information on the slave trade and recent commercial hijacking incidents. It's not taking all that much time."

"Since the board's clear," she said, "go major on this. Keep his ass clear and keep him informed."

"I kind of thought we'd do that."

"I kind of thought that you might," she replied. "And Aaron..."

Here it comes, he thought. "Yes?"

"You know better than to try to keep me in the dark on something like this."

"I'm sorry."

"Oh, no, you're not," she said.

MOST AMERICANS TENDED to think of slavery as something that had gone out of style right after the American Civil War. Nothing, however, could be more wrong. The scourge of buying and selling humans had never really gone away. In the past 150 years, it had waxed and waned subject to economic and political realties, but had never died. It was true that for most of the late twentieth century, it had been mostly an African and Arabic traffic in people snatched for manual labor or sexual purposes.

Since the end of World War II, the UN had even had a standing committee on slavery. But beyond issuing bland annual reports, it had done little about the trade because it wasn't a significant factor in the modern Western World. Then came the fall of the Soviet Union and the freeing of the subjugated nations of Eastern Europe.

Freedom in the old Soviet Bloc hadn't brought the Western-style prosperity their populations had hoped for. In fact, the collapse of the tightly controlled Communist economies had actually made things worse. Their industries had been obsolete to begin with, and their products couldn't match more sophisticated Western goods. Even East Germany and Russia, the stars of the old Soviet system, found it hard to compete.

The result was that hundreds of thousands of people had been thrown out of work. The cradle-to-grave social systems they had counted on were gone, as well. The result was that unemployed men turned to criminal activities, and women, particularly young women, went into the sex trade. Since the wages of sin were better in the West than in the East, those who could manage it left their poverty-stricken homelands to practice their new trade in the EU.

Organized crime had always dabbled in the sex trade, particularly where it had been illegal. Running protection rackets on bordellos, producing porno and shaking down pimps had long been a staple for crime bosses. It didn't take long for the Russian Mafia and their Eastern counterparts to see that they had an untapped gold mine in their own backyards.

The 2001 report from the EU Justice Commission estimated that over five hundred thousand young women were being smuggled into Europe each year to work the legal sex trade alone. That was a lot of warm bodies, but the business burned them out quickly. That and the attrition from working for brutal Mob bosses rather than themselves. In some urban areas, the Euro mobsters even chased the local hookers off to reduce the competition.

In fact, the French prostitutes' union had gone on strike to protest that their government wasn't doing enough to keep these new girls from cutting into their trade. The painted ladies had carried signs and chanted their demands, blocking the street in front of the offices of the French labor commission, but to no avail. The government did nothing, and their customers had taken a fancy to the younger, more exotic, Eastern European women now working the streets. Hundreds of French-born hookers went into early retirement.

That was an old story, but putting slave spies in industry was entirely new.

GETTING THE INFORMATION Katzenelenbogen had wanted on recent hijackings and theft of sensitive material and equipment turned out not to be easy. A company that ''lost'' a shipment of sensitive material destined for a government end user usually wasn't eager to publicly announce it. In fact, doing so could easily cost that company its lucrative military contract. The Defense Procurement Agency didn't like to deal with firms that couldn't guard their own wares.

Plus, admitting the loss could result in a security investigation that could cause even more grief with civilian customers.

Looking through the scheduled delivery dates of such material, however, showed that in particular, deliveries of classified electronics had a nasty habit of showing up late. Often the companies claimed that internal problems or suppliers had held up their production lines and paid a nonperformance penalty without taking it to court. The fines cut into their profit margin, but that was better than undergoing a federal investigation and risk losing their contract.

After finding a number of such delayed deliveries, Hunt Wethers whipped up a home-brewed program that identified them and set it to work on a number of categories of military and aerospace procurement contracts. The fact that the contracts themselves were classified and had to be hacked into kept him from getting bored.

It didn't take long before he had a list of things for Bolan and Katz to go over. He also added a longer list of shipments of critical raw materials that had also gone AWOL. Manufactured components weren't the end-all and be-all of the modern technological world. All too often, the raw materials needed to make them were even more critical and harder to obtain.

It was just background material, but sorting through it might let them find the one key thing they needed to know.

CHAPTER SEVEN

Calcutta

Mani Mohandi made a good enough living at his employment agency to live quite well for a man of his low social status. Calcutta's economy had recovered from the Asian meltdown of a few years earlier and was forging ahead again. It was true, though, that many of the vaunted Asian economic tigers had turned out to be overinflated house cats, and not very well fed ones at that. Businesses were more cautious than they had been before, but that had turned out to be a windfall for him. Many talented people were desperate for work.

Everyone who came to his agency looking for a job went through a triage according to how much money they would bring him. The uneducated and the not so well favored went into the low-wage, home-market pool. There wasn't much money there, but he had to keep up a front business, and they served to do that for him. Good-looking young women were chosen to be dragooned into the better-paying sex trade. The skilled and educated, both men and women, who had been turned out by defunct businesses were now going into a third category that brought him a great deal of money.

He really didn't know who was behind the organization he worked for, and he wasn't sure that he wanted to know. All he knew was that he had a place to sell every well-educated young woman he came across and most of the educated young men, as well. As was always the case in his line of work, the more beautiful the woman, the higher the price he got for her. Should the woman not work out as a spy, if she was a beauty, she could always be sold into a brothel.

That line of thought reminded him of Jasmine Farjani and her younger sister, Roxanne. He had gotten the highest price he had ever been paid for those two beauties. He regretted not having held out for even more, but he feared pushing the Chinese too far. Under their calm faces lurked the minds of beasts when they were thwarted.

On the other hand, Mohandi's real regret was having even offered them to his contacts at all. Had he been a wealthier man, he would have kept them for his own private use. Jasmine had been a rare beauty in full bloom, but her sister would have become even more beautiful. And with Roxanne, he would have had the pleasure of initiating her himself.

Thinking about what he couldn't have was a waste of time. All it did was make him even more unsatisfied with his current mistress. He vowed that the very next time a suitable young woman came through his front door, he'd keep her for himself instead of giving into the money she would bring him. He vowed that, but he really knew that he craved the money more. The only way he could rise in Calcutta's society was through his displays of wealth, not through his cloistered mistresses, no matter how desirable they were.

Mohandi reached for the stack of résumés with attached photos that had been collected that week. He quickly sorted out the handwritten ones, stopping only if a photo caught his eye. Nothing special this time. He then sorted the men and women into two stacks and started working through the female applicants first.

He was lingering over a photo of a sloe-eyed, mixed-blood beauty who reminded him of Jasmine when his intercom buzzed. "Yes," he snapped at being interrupted.

"Mr. Mohandi," his receptionist announced, "you have a visitor. Miss Jasmine Farjani."

Mohandi was speechless. Something had gone seriously wrong. Jasmine was supposed to be in America. The Chinese had paid good money for her, and they weren't going to be happy when they learned that she had somehow slipped out of their hands. For the briefest of moments, he considered calling them immediately.

Curiosity stayed his hand at first, then he realized that if he could get her under his control again, he could sell her again. Not to the Chinese, of course, but there was always Europe or the Arabs. Not before, of course, he allowed himself to spend a few days with her.

He hit the button on his intercom. "Please show her in."

He stood to greet her and was dismayed to see that she was in mourning. "My dear Jasmine," he said, rushing forward. "Whatever is the matter? Why are you not in America?"

Farjani allowed herself to be hugged as if she were a family member, not a mere acquaintance. But she didn't fail to feel his pelvis pressed against her. What a fat swine!

"My sister died," she said as she gracefully disengaged herself from his clutches.

"I am so sorry to hear that. What happened?"

"She was killed in a traffic accident," she said, tears welling in her eyes.

Mohandi knew that American traffic was legendary for its dangers. But he was surprised that the Chinese had let Roxanne out of their direct control long enough for something like that to happen. His understanding was that once Jasmine was fully compromised and unable to back out, her sister would have been sold into the sex market.

"Your employers don't know where you are?" he asked.

"No," she said, lowering her head. "But I just

couldn't stay in America a moment longer. I had to leave and flew out.''

This was the only part of Bolan's plan that they had been concerned about. The news about the slaughter on the *Singapore Queen* was a hot topic in the international news, and the chance that Mohandi had heard about it was a risk they had to take. Farjani said that he didn't speak much English and wasn't likely to be a CNN watcher, so they decided to chance it.

''I understand entirely,'' he said. ''That must have been a terrible shock.''

''It was.''

''Is there anything I can do for you, my dear?''

She looked him full in the face and used the full force of her green eyes on him. ''I am hoping that you can find me another job overseas. Not in America, though. I can never return there. But maybe in Europe?''

''I do not see a problem,'' Mohandi said, fairly beaming. ''A woman of your rare talents will never need to be unemployed for very long. There are hundreds of companies that need a woman such as yourself on their payroll.''

''I am so happy to hear that.''

''HE IS A GREASY, fat pig,'' Farjani almost spit when she reported back to Bolan and Katz. ''I don't know how I could have ever trusted him before. What was I thinking?''

"Did he fall for it?" Bolan asked.

"Oh, yes," she replied. "Completely. He says that he has the perfect opening for me with a British export company that needs a translator."

"You realize, of course," Katz said, "that since you no longer have family to threaten, the slavers wouldn't have a way to control you."

"You're right. But why did he make the offer, then?"

"I'd say that it is merely to get you interested, and he really intends to market you for another purpose."

She was smart enough that she didn't have to ask what that purpose would be. "He wants me to come back tomorrow evening to meet with a representative of the company."

"And so you will." Katz smiled. "Eager and ready to start a new career."

When she looked shocked, Katz quickly added, "But you won't be alone. Mike and I will be close at hand and ready to step in as soon as we're needed. We're hoping that he'll take you to his confederates, and we can bag the whole lot of them at one time."

She was concerned about being along in a room with Mohandi and a slaver at night. But she had told Belasko that she would do anything necessary to get to the men who had killed Roxanne, and a Farjani's word was good.

"I will do it," she said.

"Good girl."

MOHANDI DIDN'T want the Chinese to know that Jasmine Farjani had returned, but had no idea that his receptionist was double-dipping. Lin Liu, the leader of the Dragon Egg cell in Calcutta, had recruited Rani Bargava a long time ago to keep an eye on her employer.

Bargava had also realized what the reappearance of Jasmine Farjani meant. The Chinese slavers never allowed anyone to escape them. If threats to family members didn't work to keep a slave in line, they killed him, or her, without a second thought. Too much was at stake for any mercy to be shown to anyone who threatened them. If they learned that the woman had returned to Calcutta and Bargava didn't tell them, her own life would be endangered, as well. Working for the Chinese was lucrative, but it also carried risks.

As soon as her boss left the office to visit his mistress, the receptionist took out her cell phone and placed a call to a memorized number.

"This is Bargava," she said. "I have very important information for you."

"At the south gate of the park in an hour."

"I will be there."

JASMINE FARJANI WAS more than a little apprehensive as she walked through the door of Mohandi's employment agency that evening. Belasko and Bronski had told her that they had everything under control and she was wearing one of their miniature radios, but her heart still pounded. She knew that she was going into a bad situation and if the Americans were killed, she would be kidnapped and enslaved again.

Mohandi had a smile on his fat face when he saw Jasmine walk in. The man with him, though, was stunned. He had been told that she was a rare beauty, but Mohandi would have said the same about a female water buffalo he was trying to sell. This time, though, he had understated the woman's appearance.

"My dear," Mohandi said, trying to press himself against her one last time as he greeted her.

The woman dodged adroitly and turned to face the other man.

"Jasmine," Mohandi said, "may I introduce Mr. Hassan al Hassan. He has the contacts in England I mentioned, and he will interview you."

"I am honored." Farjani bowed her head as she spoke in Arabic.

"We can speak English," Hassan answered in Arabic, his palms in a sweat as he handed her his card. "After all, it is the language you will be using on your new job."

He didn't bother to mention that her job would consist of her serving foreign visitors to one of the oil emirates. But that would be only after the emir and his sons had grown tired of her. Considering her exotic beauty, though, she might end up in the palace's private reserve stock and never make it into the general entertainment pool of Western women.

Either way, even at what it was costing him, Hassan stood to make a great deal of money from handling this transaction. And he would make sure that she remained untouched until the emir could take possession of her. That would be difficult, but he vowed that he would restrain himself and tell his men that anyone who touched her would be castrated with a dull, rusty knife.

"Very good," she replied. "What will my duties in England be?"

Hassan launched into his spiel. "My client is a large import-export firm that does business in the Middle East and Asia. They are looking for..."

"THE OTHER GUY'S an Arab," Katz said as he monitored the conversation over the concealed com link Farjani was wearing. "And I don't like how that smells. I got a thousand bucks that says he's a harem broker."

Even before the most recent flood of white slaves into the European sex trade, beautiful women of all races had a habit of disappearing into the Middle East. It was the stuff of movies and romance novels, but it was a practice that went back for centuries. In the sixties and seventies, it had been blondes vacationing by themselves in the Mediterranean who had turned up missing. Now that every wealthy man, it seemed, had a private jet at his command, the reach had widened considerably.

"That's not exactly what we're after here," Bolan said, "but we can deal with him, as well."

"We'd better or we're going to lose her."
"That's not going to happen."

BOLAN HAD WARNED Farjani against eating or drinking anything during the interview for fear of being drugged. Even so, she was surprised when Mohandi brought out a silver serving tray with an Arabic tea set. The pungent aroma could have hidden anything.

Mohandi poured for all three of them, but Farjani noticed that neither he nor the Arab did more than touch their small cups to the lips. She did the same and caught an underlying bitter scent over the cardamom and almond.

The Arab was in eloquent midsentence when a shocked look came over his face and he slumped forward.

Mohandi was halfway out of his chair when his knee exploded in blood. He screamed, clutched his leg and rolled to the floor.

Farjani screamed and tried to run, but was grabbed from behind.

HEARING THE SCREAM, Bolan and Katz wasted no time. They entered the front door of Mohandi's agency, weapons in hand.

Four black-clad men wearing hoods were in the reception room. One of them was leaning down to put a bullet in the back of Mohandi's head, and another had his pistol to Jasmine's temple as he tried to back out of the room.

Bolan's Desert Eagle roared in the close confines. The .44 slug exploded the head of the gunman holding the woman splattering her with blood and brain. His second shot went into the heart of the thug targeting Katz as the Israeli killed the men executing Mohandi. When the fourth attacker hesitated between his two opponents, Katz sprayed him with his mini-Uzi.

It was over in a flash.

Farjani had been shocked by the suddenness of the attack and her protectors' response, but she had come a long way from the woman who had been rescued from the L.A. alley and recovered instantly. "Who are those men?"

Katz knelt beside one of the bodies and pulled up the right sleeve of the corpse to reveal a dragon-and-egg tattoo on his forearm. "Bingo. Someone didn't want you to get away from them."

Farjani had been given a sanitized briefing on what they had found at Wei's house in L.A. after the warehouse raid. She'd not been able to shed any light on why the Chinese American had been killed and couldn't remember having seen the dragon-and-egg motif before.

"But who are they?"

"That's what we're still trying to figure out," Katz said.

"Get her out of here," Bolan told him as he glanced at the late slave trader's desk, "and take his computer with you, too."

"Where're you going?"

"Out back to see if they have any lookouts posted."

"You sure you want to split up?"

"Get moving."

BOLAN KEPT to the shadows as he moved into the fifty-yard-long alley behind Mohandi's building, his rubber-soled boots keeping his approach silent. A four-door sedan was parked at the far end, its lights out. With all the noise of traffic in the area, he couldn't tell if its engine was running.

Snapping down his NVGs, he scanned it and got a return from someone sitting behind the wheel. He was moving toward the vehicle when a shadow detached itself from a garbage heap.

Bolan dropped against the base of the wall as a hail of slugs from a subgun slammed into the wall close enough to send grit into his face.

The shooter had to have thought he'd scored, because he broke cover to move in.

Bad move.

A long burst from Bolan's 93-R stitched the gunman from crotch to Adam's apple, and he staggered back into the shadows.

In that instant, the driver of the sedan slammed into reverse and shot backward out of the alley into traffic. By the time Bolan got his Desert Eagle clear of his holster, he'd lost the shot.

"How's Jasmine?" Bolan asked when he returned to the hotel room he shared with Katz.

"She's okay. I've got her tucked in for the night, and she'll be a hundred percent in the morning."

He reached out and handed Bolan an automatic pistol he'd taken from one of the bodies in Mohandi's office. "Ever seen one of these?"

"Not in a while," Bolan said. "It's a Red Chinese special-ops Type 64, fires a 9 mm Kurtz. The slide locks for each shot, and you have to crank it back yourself to reload, but it's completely silent."

"That answers one of our questions," Katz said.

"But are they Triad or Chinese special-ops?"

"I guess we'll find out sooner or later, won't we?"

Bolan reached into the side pocket of his pants and pulled out a set of night-vision goggles. Flipping them over, he saw a triangle with the number 67 inside. "State Factory 67," he said as he handed them over. "They used to make AK ammunition and RPGs."

"Not bad," Katz said as he examined the goggles. "They're basically the new-issue Russian optics, which makes them another mark in the government-sponsored column."

"I don't see the Chinese government getting into the slave trade," Bolan stated. "Too much bad publicity if it was discovered."

"But they're in it for a new reason," Katz pointed out. "They're using their slave operatives to loot and plunder high-tech material. My take is that they're wanting to push their new weapons programs. The

Russians have backed off on selling them the latest hardware, and I think they're trying to beef up their home-grown programs.''

"That would fit,'' Bolan agreed.

CHAPTER EIGHT

Stony Man Farm, Virginia

Hal Brognola was in the habit of making the short flight from his D.C. cover job at the Justice Department to the Farm at least a couple of times a week. Not only did it keep him up-to-date in a way that a scrambled fax couldn't, it got him out of his office. Some days there was only so much Washington BS a man could take.

When he walked out of the Annex elevator into the Computer Room, the crew didn't exactly look like it was running a mission. The stale pizza crusts and cups half full of dead coffee were only at the normal level, and the big-screen monitors weren't lit up. Nonetheless, the guys were intent in a mode he knew well, and it told him that they were backing some kind of operation. Since he knew that Able Team and Phoenix Force were both still on R and R, that could only mean that Mack Bolan was running again.

He didn't try to get in Bolan's road when the sol-

dier was in the field. For one thing, it simply wouldn't
have worked. For the other, that wasn't their agreement and he was a man of his word. The deal that
had brought the Executioner in from the cold to work
with the Sensitive Operations Group had hinged on
his retaining his complete freedom of action. It had
been the only way Brognola could have gotten one
of the world's most dangerous men involved with the
nation's most covert strike force. However, their
agreement didn't mean that he had to completely ignore what his old friend was up to.

Spotting Aaron Kurtzman in the middle of his clut-
tered workstation, Brognola decided to start with him.
"What's Striker working right now, Bear?" he asked.

"Funny you should ask." The big man turned his
wheelchair to face his boss. "I just got a message
from Katz you need to read. He and Striker are in
Calcutta working on a white slavery thing."

While the slave trade was an abomination by any
standard, it usually didn't fall into the category of
things that SOG got involved with. Unless, of course,
it bled over into becoming a matter of national security, which wasn't too likely. But if Bolan was interested in it, it behoved him to at least take a look
at the situation. Striker didn't waste his time on things
that didn't have a larger impact.

"What's the angle?"

Kurtzman quickly read Brognola into the sequence
of events starting in the alley in L.A., through the raid

on the warehouse, Wei's death and on to their activities in India.

"The take from the L.A. warehouse raid alone makes this more than worth our looking into," he concluded. "I couldn't believe the list that came out of that."

"Can you get me a white paper?" Brognola asked. "I know the Man's going to want to know about this. Contraband electronics with military applications have been a real hot topic at briefings lately. The Trade Commission and the Pentagon have been going at it hot and heavy, particularly about keeping that stuff away from the Chinese."

"It's in the works already," Kurtzman replied. "Do you want me to include the Chinese special-ops weaponry they came up with in Calcutta? Anything that makes a direct connection to Beijing has to be of interest in the Puzzle Palace, and I've got Hunt working on that aspect of it right now."

"Put all of it down."

"Thought you'd feel that way."

"I take it that you're backing Striker's play?" Brognola asked.

Kurtzman shrugged. "Nothing else was going down."

"Has Barbara been informed?"

"Is the Pope Polish?" Kurtzman grinned. "I got caught trying to hold out again."

"You know better than to even try that." Brognola

grinned. "But keep on it and give Striker and Katz everything they want."

Kurtzman didn't bother to tell him that he already was, but it was nice to have it official.

"I've got a hardware resupply loading up for them right now. Kissinger's making the delivery."

"And Cowboy's going to hang around over there and lend a hand, I assume?"

Kurtzman grinned. "There wasn't all that much going on around here to keep him occupied. He was getting the idle-hands syndrome big time, and Buck was about to brain him, so I thought it would do him good to get him outta Dodge while he still could walk."

"Have Buck send one of his blacksuits down to the armory to cover for him."

"Already taken care of."

"You bucking for my job?" Brognola asked.

"You gotta be joking." Kurtzman looked offended. "The only way you're going to get me anywhere even near D.C. is to bury me in Arlington."

"I can manage that."

"You do and I promise I'll haunt your sorry ass." Brognola laughed.

Hong Kong

COLONEL GAO DONG wasn't pleased at the report he had received from his operatives in Calcutta. It disturbed his *wa*, his personal harmony. Coming as it did after the disastrous raid on the L.A. warehouse and the death of his operative in Wei's house, it could mean only one thing. He was facing professional opposition and they were tracking down his operation. It was also easy to see that the centerpiece in these setbacks was that damn woman, Farjani. His people had handled that poorly and those responsible had paid the price. The Dragon Egg Project couldn't tolerate errors of that kind. And never more than now.

The lords of Beijing were putting great emphasis on advanced-weapons development, the Long Leap Program as it was being called. Much had been accomplished already, particularly in the aerospace applications. But much was still left to be done before the mother country would be at a military parity with the Yankees. Rehashed, monkey copies of out-of-date Russian technology had served China well for many years, but no nation had ever achieved greatness by arming its military with weapons made with obsolete technology.

The technology that China needed to become a real world power had to be built around the absolute latest inventions, and that meant mainly American and Japanese developments. But since the new Yankee administration had shut down the old conduits for semi-ilegal advanced-technology transfer, the Long Leap Program was suffering greatly and his Dragon Egg teams were under even more pressure to produce.

Dong had never understood how the Americans could have been so stupid to allow their defense contractors to operate as they had done for so long. For years, corrupt Yankee businessmen with close contacts to the White House bought with campaign financing had been allowed to freely sell military critical material to China as if they were mere trinkets. Any Chinese businessman who sold classified material to a potential enemy would have been executed slowly over several days. Even though it was unfathomable, it had been a great boon to the People's Republic.

He'd once spent months getting a Dragon Egg team in place in Russia to steal a Russian MRV warhead to copy when the American Loral Company had freely handed that critical piece of missile technology to China on a plate as a gift. Now the mother country's ballistic missile arsenal carried multiple nuclear warheads that increased its threat many times over. And Loral wasn't the only greedy Yankee company that had betrayed its nation's security in hopes of gaining future profits.

It wouldn't be long before all this advanced technology would be returned to the Yankees attached to state-of-the-art weapons ranging from ballistic missiles to stealth bombers and missile-launching nuclear submarines.

Western historians had taken to tagging the twentieth century as having been the American century. The twenty-first century, though, would wear the red banner of the People's Republic as she expanded into the Pacific Rim and beyond to fulfill her destiny. That the United States of America would be destroyed in the process was inevitable. No empire lasted forever, and certainly not one as corrupt and decadent as the Yankees.

He had no particular hatred for the American people, but for the mother country to achieve her rightful place in the world, loyal Chinese such as him had to do their jobs with diligence and devotion. And right now his job was to track down and destroy the enemy team that was disrupting his operation. And to do that, he would call on China's most unlikely allies.

It was ironic that a nation who's founding father had taken such great efforts to destroy the foreign religions that had taken over so much of early modern China was now teamed up with the God-mad. But as the Arabic peoples themselves said, "The enemy of my enemy is my friend." In this war of technologies, China needed all the friends she could find.

The Dragon Egg teams were allied with several similar operations in the Islamic world. Egypt, Iran, Iraq, Syria and Pakistan were all joined in their burning desire to build advanced weapons able to punish the Great Satan of the United States, and China was willing to help them in return for their aid. The colonel didn't really understand why the Arabic peoples were so radically opposed to the West, but he really didn't care. Their insane hatred made them play right into the hands of the Chinese in their quest for world domination.

The radical Islamic movements were also danger-

ous to China's long-term goals; there was no doubt
about that. Their dreams of a completely Muslim
world wouldn't mess with China's plans. At some
point in the future, China would have to eradicate
them with the technology they were helping steal. For
now, though, they were useful tools.

In the Middle East, the Dragon Egg Project worked
through Islamic operatives to place many of its slaves
at their targets. The Arabs also provided many well-
trained women for the project, which was welcome.
Dong always tried to match his spies carefully with
his targets. The French, for instance, were particularly
susceptible to Arabic women, as the Japanese and the
offshore Chinese were to Western blondes.

Being a man who didn't have much time to spend
on women, any woman, as long as she was young
enough, served his purposes. He didn't understand
why some men became so stupidly focused on a particular type of woman. Nonetheless, that they did was
central to his operation.

MUHAD FUAD of the Islamic Brotherhood wasn't surprised when Colonel Gao Dong called. Fuad had a
nice package in Cairo waiting to be moved to Europe,
and he needed the Chinese to make that happen. His
own organization wasn't inexperienced at moving
goods from Europe to the Middle East, but they were
usually more lethal cargoes—weapons, ammunition
and explosives. Even though the Brotherhood controlled the docks in Alexandria, transporting people

took more resources than he could call upon. The security forces of Europe were more than alert to infiltration by Islamic groups.

Fuad was surprised, though, when the Chinese officer wanted to talk about something totally different. When Dong gave him a carefully edited version of the events that had impacted the Dragon Egg teams over the past week, it sounded very familiar to him.

"For many years now," Fuad started out, "there has been a shadowy figure who has haunted our own operations," he said. "There is much debate about who this man is, if he even does actually exist. He usually works alone, but he can have as many as half a dozen men with him. They come in like smoke in the night, kill like rabid wolves set upon a sleeping flock and then vanish like jinn."

Dong was accustomed to working with Arabs and let the man tell the story in his own rambling manner. The Islamic peoples were hopelessly superstitious and mired in their own fears and mythology. Men didn't move unseen like smoke in the night. Even the Tong assassins or the legendary ninja could be seen if you knew what to look for when they attacked.

"I for one," Fuad concluded, "have not seen this man, but I do believe that he exists. Men who I would trust with my life, some of them who have survived his attacks, have seen him."

Dong controlled himself. "Does this man have a name and a country?" he asked.

"He is often believed to be an American com-

mando and my people call him Al Askari, 'the Soldier.'"

"Do you have any idea what this man calls himself?"

"Sadly no," the Egyptian admitted.

There were tales in the Orient of such a man, as
well, a man said to be a evil spirit, but Dong put little
faith in them. The people who told these tales were
usually trying to cover up their own mistakes, and
what better way than to blame an enemy superhero
when something went wrong? The Yankees had many
well-trained covert-action units and they used them
far more often than was ever reported in their infa-
mously propagandist media. Their counterterrorist
and antidrug strike teams were particularly active, and
he put the stories of the invincible, lone warrior into
that category.

However, if the Arabs could help him get a lead
on this man, he would look into it.

"I need anything you may have on this 'Soldier,'"
Dong said. "What he is reported to have done and
where he might be now."

"I will call my contacts in the Brotherhood,' Fuad
replied. "They have been watching for him for a long
time and know much about him."

The Islamic Brotherhood claimed to go back to the
centuries of the Christian Crusades. Dong doubted
that seriously and had seen nothing to back up the
claim. He did, though, know that they had been very
active for the past twenty years or so and might have

collected something of value during that time. He also knew better than to depend on it, though. In his dealings with the Arabs, he had found them long on talk and short on facts.

"I can use anything at all you can get for me."

"We will have it to you as soon as possible," Fuad promised.

WHEN DONG CLICKED off his cell phone, he placed a call to the lone survivor of the raid on Mohandi's office in Calcutta. He felt there was almost no chance that this so-called Yankee Soldier would still be in India, but it would still have to be looked into. He already had a second, reinforced Dragon Egg team on its way to take over the decimated operation and start searching for him.

The reason Dong was willing to invest so much manpower in finding this man, or men, wasn't just because Farjani had gotten away from him. Were that the case, he would have freely let her go. He had to secure the integrity of his Calcutta operation at all costs.

Not only did Calcutta provide many educated, multilingual women as spies, but also much valuable raw material available only in the Indian subcontinent and the Middle East was shipped through her port. China was a vast country, but there were still raw materials vital for high-tech industry that couldn't be found within her borders. Since most of these materials were also on the trade restriction list, the easiest way to obtain them was through dock theft or high-seas piracy.

Right now tungsten was at the top of the Dragon Egg list of priority-materials targets. The Chinese aerospace industry was desperate for the rare metal to make the exotic, high-temperature alloys necessary for its work. A large shipment of high-grade tungsten ore was due to be sent to Japan in a few days, and it was scheduled to be hijacked on its way through the South China Sea. He had to make sure that whoever was dogging his operation didn't learn of that particular mission and involve himself in it, as well.

"A replacement Dragon Egg team is coming in from Singapore tonight," Dong informed his operative. "As soon as they report to you, they are to start looking for the man responsible for the attack at Mohandi's. You are to give them every assistance in that task."

"Yes, Comrade Colonel."

One would think that finding a single stranger in the world's largest city would be a chore, particularly in a place of such extremes as Calcutta. However, even with almost sixteen million people in Greater Calcutta, Dong knew that he wouldn't have to search the legendary slums to find an American or two. Even the poorest Chinese wouldn't stay in those areas, much less a fastidious Yankee. Since he knew that they had the woman with them, her local expertise would have guided them in their search for accommodations.

Dong's connections in Calcutta were extensive and weren't limited to his Dragon Egg teams. Money talked loudly in a nation as poor as India, and his connections in the Indian government would give him both immigration and airport arrival lists. His Indian police contacts were a source of information on foreign visitors staying in hotels, since all hotels were required to report the passport information of their guests to the police every day.

While that search was going on, Dong intended to have another unit start looking for Mohandi's receptionist, Rani Bargava. Although she was on his payroll, too, she was missing under suspicious circumstances and had just become expendable, as well.

Dong might think for a moment about eliminating a valued male operative, but no woman's life was worth any risk to his goals.

CHAPTER NINE

Calcutta

With India being the ground zero of the tea culture, Bolan and Katzenelenbogen were enjoying their early-morning instant coffee alone in their hotel room to let Jasmine Farjani sleep in. A puzzled look suddenly crossed Katz's face and he said, "You know, Striker, we completely overlooked something in that dustup we got into last night."

Bolan looked at him.

Katz pulled out the business card the Arab slave trader had given Farjani. "We went there to protect Jasmine from being kidnapped into a whorehouse, but we ended up in a firefight with the Dragon Egg guys again."

Since they didn't have a firm ID on the opposition yet, Katz had taken to calling them by their tattoos.

He leaned forward. "We got so wrapped up in that, neither one of us stopped to ask just how in the hell they knew she was going to be there."

Bolan smiled and lifted his coffee in salute. "I knew there was a reason I asked you to join me on this gig."

"Mohandi was going to sell her into a whorehouse," Katz continued, "so he sure as hell didn't call them. But someone connected with him did. Maybe a secretary?"

"Let's talk to Jasmine." Bolan glanced at his watch. "She should be up by now."

Going to the room next door, they found the woman dressed and enjoying her morning tea and biscuits. "Good morning," she said. "Care to join me?"

"We've got a problem," Katz stated, grabbing a chair, "and need your help again. Going over last night's activities, we came up with something that puzzles us."

Farjani had been hoping not to hear that. What had started out for her as an emotional reaction to seek revenge for her sister's death was turning out to be a quest. Even with Mohandi dead, the trail Belasko and Bronski were following hadn't ended, and she was starting to fear where it was going to lead her next.

"What's that?"

"Do you know how many people were working in Mohandi's operation?"

She thought for a moment. "All I remember seeing was just him and a receptionist."

"Do you know her?" Katz asked.

"Not very well," she replied. "Her name's Rani Bargava."

"Do you know where she lives?"

She frowned in concentration. "I think I can find the Bargava House. Her family is not as well off as mine, so she doesn't live close to my old neighborhood. But I think I can find it. The neighbors will know."

"Get your things," Bolan said. "We need to talk to her as soon as we can."

"But why?"

"We forgot to ask how the Chinese knew that you were going to be at Mohandi's last night."

Farjani hadn't thought of that, either.

THE SUBSECTION of Calcutta where Rani Bargava lived was a lower-middle-class neighborhood of well-kept, aging British-era apartment buildings built around central courtyards. Farjani had Bolan stop the car a couple of times to ask shopkeepers for directions.

"It should be right around the next corner to the left," she said when she came back the second time. "Number 2311."

Bolan had just made the turn when Farjani pointed. "That's her over there!" she said. "Those men have her!"

Neither of the Americans had ever seen Miss Bargava before, but it wasn't difficult to recognize when someone was being kidnapped in public. Midway down the block, three Oriental men in street clothes were hustling an Indian woman in a colorful sari down the street toward a Mercedes sedan parked with its back door open.

Bolan slid over to the curb, and Katz was out of the car before the wheels stopped turning.

"Hey!" he shouted. "Leave that woman alone!"

Rather than abort their kidnap attempt, two of the men pulled pistols to cover the withdrawal of the third, who held a knife to Bargava's throat.

Bolan drew the Desert Eagle as he ran and again went for the top-priority target, the man with the knife. The .44 slug tore out the side of the thug's throat, dropping him in a spray of blood. Suddenly released, the woman screamed and crumpled to the ground, paralyzed with fear.

Katz took out his first target with a burst to the chest before the Chinese could get a round off. The final gunman fired a single, hurriedly aimed shot at Katz before Bolan blew his brains out.

The people on the street had raced for cover at the first shot, leaving Bolan and Katz conspicuously standing alone. When they went to help the woman to her feet, she screamed and tried to pull away.

Farjani opened the rear door and yelled in Hindi. "Miss Bargava, over here! It's Jasmine Farjani. Come with us, Rani! Please!"

The woman was blood spattered and frightened out of her mind, but she followed the familiar female voice and started running for the car.

Bolan and Katz came in from behind her, scooped her up and shoved her into the back seat. Opening the front passenger door, the soldier slid across the seat and took off just as Katz got in behind him.

Bolan bootlegged his rental into a 180-degree turn and got back on the main street. "Which way to get out of here?" he asked Farjani.''

"Keep going straight.''

"We picked up a tail," Katz stated, looking over his shoulder.

The Executioner glanced into his side mirror and saw the black Mercedes slashing its way through the traffic behind them.

Seeing an alley, he turned into it. If he could make it to the next street over, he might be able to lose them. Bolan was ten yards into the alley when an oxcart pulled into the other end, blocking his exit.

"Into that door,'' Farjani shouted pointing toward what looked like a loading door opening into the alley. The vertical opening door was only partially up, but he thought he could squeeze under it. Hitting the lights so he could see into the darkened building, Bolan snap turned and skidded the Toyota sideways, clearing the far side of the door with inches to spare. The gas cans and tires stacked around the sides of the room inside told him that he was in a garage.

The Toyota was still rolling when Katz jumped out and pulled the door the rest of the way down.

"Stay here,'' Bolan told the women as he set the emergency brake and got out.

Joining Katz behind the door, he listened and looked through the crack at the side. When the Mercedes didn't pull into the alley, the two cautiously opened the door enough to slide under it. Making their way back to the street, they saw that the Mercedes was still caught in traffic, but a block farther on.

"Go get the car," Katz said. "I'll wait here."

Bolan opened the garage door, backed the Toyota into the alley and picked Katz up at the corner. On the street, he was able to work his smaller car through traffic and gained on his target.

"Mike!" Farjani almost yelled when she recognized the Mercedes in front of them. "What are you doing?"

"We're going to follow them now," Bolan answered. "If we're ever going to get to the bottom of this, we've got to know what we're dealing with here. So far, we've just been reacting to their moves. I want to go proactive."

"They aren't giving up," Katz said as they watched the big Mercedes move slowly and the two men inside scan the alleys as they passed.

Bolan tried to keep well back, but traffic was so thick that he had to make sure he didn't lose them. The Mercedes stopped abruptly, and the man in the passenger side got out to look over the roof into another alley. He was getting back in when he spotted the Toyota and shouted to the driver.

The sedan shot forward, clipping a small truck and upsetting a rickshaw as it made its escape.

"We can't catch them," Bolan said as he turned onto a street he recognized. "Time to go back and regroup."

BY THE TIME they returned to the hotel, Jasmine Farjani and Rani Bargava calmed down. The receptionist was crying quietly as Farjani washed the blood from the side of her face.

"What happened to you?" she asked in English.

Bargava choked back a sob. "They said I had betrayed them when they went to take you from the office."

"Who are they?" Bolan asked.

"Chinese smugglers," the woman replied. "Mohandi worked for them. But they also paid me to keep an eye on him because he was not honest."

She looked at Farjani. "When you returned to him, I was very surprised. I was glad to see that you had escaped, but I knew I had to let them know about you or they would hurt me and my sister."

"Why your sister?" Katz thought to ask.

"She works in a export shipping company, and she, too, passes on information to the Chinese. They pay well, and my family needs the money."

"What kind of information do they get from her?"

"They want to know about ships carrying certain materials. Lately my sister Hansa said that they are particularly interested in a shipment of tungsten being sent to Japan. I don't know what they do with the information, but I think they might use it to steal the cargo."

Since this operation was using slaves to aid and abet technology theft, it made sense that they would also use paid informers in nations where they couldn't place slaves.

Katz wasn't unhappy that they had saved Bargava, but they were starting to get too large a collection of hangers-on. It was time to move her on to safety.

"Miss Bargava," he said, "if what you say is true, I believe that your sister is in danger, as well as you. We can help get both of you to safety, but we need to know about this shipment the Chinese are so interested in."

"I don't know much about it," Bargava said. "But I can call Hansa. She will know."

WHEN JOHN KISSINGER stepped off the Air India 747 in Calcutta, he was wearing a tropical linen suit with his cowboy boots, a typical American. His paperwork from the Defense Department and the headquarters of the Indian army indicated that he was a representative of an American arms firm doing business with the Indian government. It was a risky cover, but it allowed his "wares" to get into the country quickly.

Yakov Katzenelenbogen was waiting in the passenger terminal to greet the armorer. "Where's the rest of your bags, Cowboy?" he asked.

Kissinger hoisted his single overnighter. "I didn't want anyone to think that I was staying too long."

"Where's the rest?"

"The cover-story stuff is in Indian customs, and Jack is bringing in what you guys need tonight."

Rather than discuss the details in public, Katz led him through the crowded terminal to his parked rental. Out on the highway, they wove their way through the traffic back into the city proper. Katz had transitioned well enough to the local conditions that he barely slowed, even for the oxcarts and rickshaws. Kissinger kept groping for a seat belt that wasn't there.

BOLAN ANSWERED Katz's knock and opened the door of their hotel room. Kissinger's eyes widened when he saw Jasmine Farjani.

"Jasmine," Katz said, "I'd like to introduce one of my friends, John Brown."

"Nice to meet you, ma'am," Kissinger said, extending his hand.

She took his hand and nodded. "Mr. Brown."

"Call me Cowboy, please." Kissinger looked lost in her deep green eyes.

Farjani laughed. "Like in one of your American movies, right?"

"That's it." Kissinger grinned as Katz elbowed him in the ribs.

"We've got work to do, Cowboy."

"Okay."

"Can I help?" Farjani asked.

"Not with this," Katz said. "But you might want

to help Miss Bargava and her sister find a place to stay.''

"They talked about flying out to New Delhi and staying with their cousin.''

"Good. And as soon as they're gone, we're going to need to find a new place to live, as well. We've been in this hotel for too long.''

"I know just the place,'' she said. "Quiet and out of the way.''

"Perfect.''

THE FAILURE of his team to snatch Rani Bargava sent Colonel Dong into a rage. Now that there was proof that the Soldier and at least one other man were still in Calcutta, he decided to go after them himself. His men were good, but none of them had the years of experience behind them that had made the colonel who he was.

A unique set of circumstances had brought Dong to be chosen to lead the Dragon Egg Project. For one, he was a half-breed. Or to be more precise, his maternal grandmother had been English. His British-educated grandfather had married her to gain a limited access to British society in Hong Kong. He needed that access because he was an agent for the new formed Communist Party working to undermine British rule. Dong's father had followed in the family's political profession, as had Dong himself.

Being a third-generation Communist Party member was all that had saved him from execution for his family "taint" when the Cultural Revolution swept China in the sixties. Even so, he'd had to work harder, and take more risks, than his comrades to survive the antiforeign paranoia of that era. He'd also changed his first name from George back to Gao. But when a more rational regime ruled again in Beijing, his international background became a plus. Like his father and grandfather before him, Dong had been educated in Great Britain and was chosen to work as an agent in the West. He'd been so good at his job that he'd been chosen to be China's point man for their technology-transfer operations.

The reason it was so crucial that the Soldier be captured or killed went beyond this mysterious commando having decimated two of Dong's Dragon Egg teams. He had another mission about to kick off that had an even higher priority, the hijacking of a Japanese bulk cargo ship full of high-grade tungsten ore. It was so critical that the colonel would have gladly sacrificed even more of his men to insure that the ore reached the mother country.

Getting a ride in the back seat of a Chinese air force J-8 supersonic interceptor, Dong flew from Hong Kong across China to the Indian border. There he boarded a helicopter, crossed the border and was picked up by an Indian-registered chopper that took him on to Calcutta. He was met on landing and quickly driven to the port area and a building marked Lee And Sons—Shipping Agents.

Entering through the side door, Dong assembled his people for a briefing.

"Why did you not capture the receptionist as I ordered?" Dong demanded of Wang, the leader of the second Dragon Egg team.

The Chinese operative paused only briefly; he knew better than to try to put Dong off. "She escaped from us, Comrade Colonel." He locked eyes with his commander. "Two armed men intervened as my men were taking her away."

"Did your men survive?"

"Only the driver and the security man in the car, Comrade."

"Do you have descriptions of our opposition?"

"Both were Westerners," Wang replied. Since he was still alive, he knew that the odds were good that he'd keep breathing for a while longer. "One was a tall black-haired man armed with a powerful handgun, and the other was an older man who used a submachine gun. They killed my men, took the woman and escaped in a rental car."

"You have traced the car," Dong stated rather than questioned.

"Yes, Comrade Colonel," Wang said. "It was rented by a native woman who paid cash for a week's rental. The contact address she gave turned out not to be valid."

Dong had expected that dead end, and the native woman had to be Jasmine Farjani. This was only more proof that he was up against professionals and that they were staying one step ahead of him so far. He hadn't gotten where he was, however, by letting anyone call the shots for him. He had to get this situation contained quickly.

"What have you found so far with the hotel canvass?"

Wang met Dong's eyes squarely. "Very little, Comrade. At first we were looking for a lone man and woman and investigated several such couples. Then, after the Bargava incident, we realized that we needed to look for two men and a woman. That is still under way."

"And the *Hanto Maru* operation?"

"We have better news on that, Comrade Colonel." Wang risked a slight smile. "Everything is in place and waiting for the ship's scheduled departure."

Dong didn't return the smile. He expected his operations to go as planned.

"Lead that operation yourself, Wang, and take as many men as you think you'll need."

"The crew is small and we expect complete surprise."

"Make sure you achieve it."

CHAPTER TEN

Stony Man Farm, Virginia

Aaron Kurtzman's Computer Room team was doing a little more support work than it usually did for one of Mack Bolan's private ventures, but they were enjoying it. Bolan had gotten into a situation this time that didn't lend itself to being solved by kicking in a door and delivering a few well-placed shots to the head. That, of course, would be the final solution. After all, it was the trademark of the way the man did business. But he had to get the right people in his sight picture for that to happen. And that's the goal Kurtzman's people were working toward.

Katzenelenbogen had forwarded the contents of the two computers he and Bolan had come across so far. The marvels of cyberspace made it relatively easy for that collection of binary code to be sent across a phone line. Sending it was one thing; hacking through whatever security systems were embedded in it was another matter. Not insurmountable by any means, but it was time-consuming.

Chu Wei's computer turned out to be protected by first-rate, U.S.-designed, commercial security systems and firewalls, and Hunt Wethers was teasing his way around the edges of them. Mohandi's computer had proved to be far easier to work with, as it wasn't secured at all. With it, though, the problem was partially that the contents were in Hindi and partially due to the personal shorthand notations the man used. The best codes, computer or otherwise, were always those that were understood by only one person.

Hunt Wethers's preliminary take from Wei's computer records revealed that he'd been a big player in the steal-the-technology game for quite some time. He hadn't yet discovered any bombshells like the Loral MRIV chips that had been freely given away with the blessing of the White House. But technology wasn't just the big pieces. For every major advance, there were the thousands of smaller parts that were needed to make the major application work properly. That was where Wei's operation had shone.

When building advanced weapons systems, off-the-shelf parts were rarely adequate for the job. Their heat, load and vibration tolerances could be perfectly fine for audiovisual, automotive or even commercial aviation applications, but they didn't cut it when they were used to build a ballistic missile or a supersonic jet fighter. For those uses, one needed to use Mil-Spec bolts, screws, switches, transistors, hinges, filters, lubricants, hoses, fittings, fasteners and a thousand other things.

For all these items, being Mil-Spec was the critical factor, and Mil-Spec hardware was supposed to be on the export-restricted list.

From what they were finding, though, not all Mil-Spec material was treated equally. Some of it was watched closely and safeguarded. Much more of it, however, was discarded every day and sold for pennies on the dollar in Defense Procurement Agency and NASA surplus sales. Not too surprisingly, it turned out that Wei's cover companies had been big buyers of the surplus material at those sales for several years.

"This's all stuff they shouldn't have gotten their hands on," Kurtzman growled as he scanned the printout Hunt Wethers had presented to him.

"If they didn't get it from us one way or the other," Wethers pointed out, "the French would openly sell it to them. Or the Russians. But I guess they'd rather have the stuff made in the good ole U.S. of A. The Russians are sloppy."

Kurtzman finished reading the printout and looked up. "Where's all the hot items, that classified stuff we discovered that was 'late' on delivery to the end user?"

Wethers shrugged. "We're still looking to make those matchups. There's a section on his hard drive that we're still working our way into."

"You should have started there first."

"We did, and this is the first of what we've recovered."

"How about Mohandi's stuff?" Kurtzman asked.

"We've got the Hindi translation program up and running, but so far we're just getting résumés, mostly from educated women. He's moved a lot of them recently."

"To where?"

Wethers grimaced. "That's where we're running into problems with a personal code of some kind. He's using initials instead of complete names."

"Any chance of breaking it?" Kurtzman asked.

"We'll keep trying, of course." Wethers shrugged. "But you know about trying to crack personal codes."

"Just keep on it."

Calcutta

WITH JASMINE FARJANI occupied calming Rani Bargava, Bolan, Katzenelenbogen and Kissinger went over the information Bargava's sister had provided them. Her handlers had been interested in every last detail she could uncover about a Japanese-registered bulk cargo carrier named the *Hanto Maru*. She had been able to provide her handlers with everything from the powerplant specifications to backgrounds on the crew and the cargo manifest, a load of tungsten ore.

"What I don't understand," Katzenelenbogen said, "is how in the hell do they thing they're going to pirate bulk ore and haul it off? It takes port facilities to be able to off-load that kind of stuff.''

"Steal the whole ship and take it to a Chinese port?'' Kissinger suggested.

"Isn't that a little obvious? I mean someone is bound to notice that a ship that big has gone missing, particularly the Japanese. They're fussy about losing things.''

"I'm not sure that the hijackers care who knows what they're doing after the fact,'' Bolan said. "So far, these guys have been pretty tightly focused on their mission to the exclusion of everything else.''

Katz grinned. "That's more than we can say about what we're doing. And, speaking of, what in the hell are we doing here, anyway?''

"I was kind of wondering that myself,'' Kissinger said.

"Well,'' Bolan replied, "this is obviously a work in progress. We keep reacting to what we stumble across and taking it from there. The real problem is that we're still chasing people we don't really know. We know they're Chinese and that they're in the high-tech theft and slave business, but we still can't put a name to who's in charge and who he's taking orders from.''

"You guys need to get serious with those people,'' Kissinger stated. "Really rattle their cage and see what falls out.''

Katz drank the last of his coffee. "He's right, you know, Striker. And since this ship is where we know they're going to be next, it's the right target for us. From what Hansa Bargava said, they went to a lot of work to set it up, which means they really need it. So, if we can figure out a way to keep that thing out of their hands, they may get angry enough to expose themselves.''

"Let's say we do stop that hijacking," Bolan said. "Where would they go for more tungsten? I agree that someone in China needs it badly, probably for their missile program, so where would they go to get more?''

"Damned if I know." Katz shrugged. "We'll have to ask the Bear. He can find it for us.''

"Because if we can short-stop this snatch, we can bet they'll go after another shipment and, if we know where they're going, we won't have to chase around after them. We'll swing around them and be there first.''

"What's the name of that ship," Kissinger asked. "The *Hanto Maru?*"

Katz checked his notes. "That's it and she sails tomorrow evening.''

"That doesn't leave us much time.''

"What's new?" Katz grinned. "We've been on the run since we got here.''

"What's new," Bolan said, "is that Jack's due in today and that'll give us a chopper.''

COLONEL DONG WATCHED from the Calcutta docks as the *Hanto Maru* cleared the harbor and headed down the Ganges out to the open sea. At least this part of his operation was going as planned. With the ore carrier finally going to sea, he would soon be able to return to his headquarters and not have to personally supervise this operation any longer. And with the losses the Dragon Egg Project had suffered lately, he had pressing work to do.

He had already decided not to try to restart Mohandi's slave-spy recruitment operation in Calcutta. India's Anglo-Indian population provided an endless source of perfect operatives for him, but he wanted to maintain a low profile for a while. He had a second such office in Singapore and would transfer everything there for the time being. Later, he might open another office in New Delhi or Bombay.

His most pressing problem right now was rebuilding his American operation. Reports from his remaining California operatives weren't good. The Yankee government had finally awakened to what they had been allowing to be sold, and major investigations were under way. He had no hope of rebuilding his pipeline anytime in the near future, but he would get started on it now anyway.

Being Chinese, Dong's operational planning was projected over future decades, not mere months. If it took him five years to find another American high-ranking government employee who was willing to betray his country for money, that was to be expected. In the meantime, he would shift over to buying the needed technical material from defunct Russian aerospace companies and agencies. Being Russian, the material would have to be carefully tested before being used, but that could be factored in.

Turning, the colonel walked back to the shipping agent's office to await the radio message that would tell him of the success of the *Hanto Maru* mission. The helicopter was already standing by to take him back to the Chinese border.

JACK GRIMALDI KEPT the running lights of his Bell 222 turned off as he flew a racetrack pattern in the night sky shadowing the *Hanto Maru* from three thousand feet. He'd rather have been behind the controls of something with a little more punch, specifically a well-armed gunship, but he was flying and that's what counted.

More to the point, he was going into harm's way and that's what really floated his boat.

"How's the fuel?" Mack Bolan asked from the copilot's seat.

Grimaldi glanced at his red lit instrument panel and saw that he was indicating eighteen hundred pounds. "We've got another hour and a half or so at this airspeed before we hit the point of no return on the main tanks. The reserve tank gives us a half-hour cushion."

Since the *Hanto Maru* was roughly making nineteen knots, that wasn't much travel time and she was still in the crowded part of the shipping lanes. Crowded, though, was comparative for ships. The closest ship was twenty-three miles away, and that was far enough for a pirate ship to come in unseen, capture her and escape again.

To the West, sea piracy was a thing of old Errol Flynn movies and TV shows. It brought up names like Blackbeard and Captain Kidd and visions of ships with billowing sails and muzzle-loading brass cannons on their decks. In Asia, though, piracy wasn't long-dead history. The South China Sea still included the most dangerous waters in the world, and they had been that way for a thousand years or more.

Usually, though, the South China Sea pirates were low-tech raiders in leaky old boats who preyed on the coastal traders, themselves sailing in leaky old boats. More recently, though, well-equipped, high-tech pirates in fast, tight hulls and armed with modern weapons were becoming more common.

"Heads up," Katzenelenbogen called up from the rear seat where he and Kissinger were also scanning the seas below. "I've got someone coming up from the northeast. She's fast, and she's running blacked out."

Since sailing in the shipping lanes at night without running lights wasn't legal, nor even intelligent, this was a candidate for their elusive commerce raider.

As Grimaldi flew in that direction, Bolan focused his night-vision glasses and spotted the ship's wake. "I've got her."

"She's on an interception course," Katz added, "and I'd say moving almost thirty knots. ETA maybe fifteen."

"That looks like our guy, all right," Bolan said. "Get our gear ready."

Bolan and Katz weren't on a humanitarian mission to prevent the *Hanto Maru* from being looted. As far as they were concerned, that was up to the Japanese captain and crew to look after. They would save the ship, but only to jab a stick in the eyes of the mysterious Chinese gang and keep the ore out of China. They also wanted to have a little chat with the captain or first officer of the pirate ship.

Bolan and Katz were both wearing mountain-climbing harnesses. They weren't STABO rigs, but they would do to get them down on a repelling rope and allow them to hook up again for a fast extract. Kissinger would handle the fire support and extraction chores.

Now that they had the target, Grimaldi pulled away to keep from being spotted. If the raider had aerial radar, they'd be screwed, but he didn't think they'd be expecting a threat from above. As they watched, the pirate came up behind the *Hanto Maru* and launched an inflatable boat. The little boat was soon alongside the bigger ship, and black-clad figures scrambled up grappling ropes. Two of them raced across the deck for the bridge while the others rigged a rope ladder over the ship's side.

BOLAN HAD GRIMALDI wait until the pirate was tied up alongside the cargo ship before giving the pilot the word, "Take us in."

Getting in was simply a matter of Grimaldi holding a high hover long enough for Bolan and Katz to do a fast rappel down the weighted lines to the raider's rear deck.

"We're down," Bolan sent over the com link.

"I'm clear," Grimaldi sent back.

From what they had seen, most of the pirate's crew was on the *Hanto Maru* so Bolan and Katz kept low as they headed up to the bridge on the seaward side. The two men in the wheelhouse were so confidently watching the Japanese ship that they weren't watching their backs.

Their rubber-soled boots quickly brought them within striking range, and Bolan smashed his clubbed fist against the side of the first mate's head. The man dropped.

The captain turned just in time to find Katz's prosthetic hook clamped around his neck. Wisely he didn't want his throat torn out, so he gave no trouble while Bolan secured his hands and ankles with riot restraints. The first mate was still out cold, so he was cooperative, as well. A finishing strip of duct tape went over their mouths.

Katz glanced over at the Japanese ship. "You know, if we've got a minute or two, I want to go below. I've got a couple of shaped charges in my pack, and we need to deprive these guys of this particular ship. With the Chinese now into high-seas piracy, we need to put a dent in their program."

"The *Hanto Maru* can wait," Bolan agreed.

The raiders' engine was turning over at an idle, and the noise level kept the man on engine watch from noticing that he had visitors. Since one of the black gang wasn't on their prisoner snatch list, Bolan simply shot the man in the head as he turned, something finally alerting him that he wasn't alone.

Katz quickly armed his two RDX minicharges and went to the rear of the compartment to find a place where they'd do the most good. They were small but powerful, and this ship didn't have a thick hull. He opted for placing them next to one of the ship's ribs to blow it out, as well as the hull plates.

"That should do it," he said. "They're below the waterline, so this tub's going to the bottom."

Back on deck, there was no sign of movement on the *Hanto Maru*. The grappling hook ladder the Chinese had used to storm the Japanese ship was still in place, so Katz kept watch until Bolan went up hand over hand.

Sliding silently over the ship's railing, he spotted a black-clad Chinese standing guard outside the hatch that led into the bridge with his back conveniently turned. From the prone position, Bolan lined him up in the sights of his Beretta, flicked the selector switch to semiauto and put a silence round into the sentry's head.

The guard's assault rifle clattered as he went down, but no one noticed.

Clicking his com link brought Katz up the ladder and the two went straight for the bridge. Opening the hatch revealed two crewmen tied up and lying on the deck. From the cut of one of the men's black jackets, Bolan took him to be an officer.

Signaling Katz to guard from the hatch, Bolan crossed to the officer, knelt and held a finger to his lips. The Japanese locked eyes with him and nodded as Bolan drew his knife. Swipes of the blade freed the man's hands and feet. He quickly freed the other man, as well.

"Who are you?" the Japanese captain asked quietly.

"That doesn't matter," Bolan replied. "How many pirates came aboard your ship?"

"Eight or ten," the man replied, rubbing his wrists. "I am not sure. After tying me up, they went below to my engine room and I think they want to take over my ship."

"That's their plan," Bolan confirmed. "And we're going to try to stop them."

The captain didn't ask why. He wasn't about to examine the motives of his saviors. This hijacking attempt alone was enough to end his maritime career, and he was glad to have any chance at all to get out of this alive.

"What can I do to help?"

"Where's the engine room and how many other men do you have on board?"

The captain quickly explained how to reach the engine room.

"You and your man there—" Bolan nodded to the

other crewman ''—lock yourselves in the bridge and don't come out until you hear our voices.''

''And,'' Katz added from the hatchway, ''please stay off the radio until we come back. They're probably monitoring your radio channels, and we don't want them to now that we're coming.''

''Hai!'' he replied and bowed from the waist.

CHAPTER ELEVEN

South China Sea

After making sure that the *Hanto Maru*'s captain had secured the bridge hatch behind them, Bolan and Katzenelenbogen went below to clean out the engine room. With both the bridge and the engine room back under control, the other raiders would be trapped.

As they made their way down the ladder to the lower decks in the stern of the ship aft of the cargo holds, the two men encountered no one. When Bolan reached the engine-room level, he spotted two bodies dressed in clean sailor whites crumpled at the foot of the ladder. Both looked to have been shot in the head. When he reached the deck, voices from the other end of the noisy room gave him the locations of their targets. Keeping to the bulkhead, he waited for Katz to join him.

A half-dozen raiders dressed in black were clustered around the engine-room control console. A Japanese crewman, obviously one of the engine-room crew, was tied to a chair and one of the raiders was shouting questions at him. The crewman glared defiance, and the raider slammed the butt of his pistol against the side of the men's head.

The raider was turning to slam the Japanese again when he spotted Bolan and Katz in their combat suits. Since they were wearing black, as well, he hesitated for a moment. That moment was long enough for him and his men to end up on the wrong side of a very one-sided gun battle.

Bolan had his Beretta 93-R snapping out 3-round bursts as quickly as he could acquire the targets. At his side, Katz's silenced mini-Uzi spit longer, but no less accurate, bursts. The raiders only got off a couple of panicked shots before going down in their blood.

The Japanese tied in the chair was bleeding from cuts on the side of his head and his lips. His eyes went wide when he saw Caucasian faces, but he understood that somehow he had been saved.

"Do you understand English?" Katz asked him as he cut the ropes holding him in place.

"A little." The man stood and bowed to his rescuers.

"Can you shoot a gun?" Bolan asked.

"*Hai.*" The Japanese bowed again. "I was in the self-defense navy."

Bolan picked up an AK from one of the bodies, cracked the bolt to make sure a round was in the chamber and the weapon was on safe. "Here."

WITH THE ENGINE-ROOM body count added to the sentry, Bolan figured that there could be another five or six Chinese aboard. With this being a bulk carrier, there were only so many places they could be, and the best bet was to look in the crew compartments.

With the *Hanto Maru* being a modern ship, the crew deck was small, half a dozen cabins with what looked like a day room at the end. The voices coming from the day room told them what was going on. Until the Japanese ship was under way again, the raiders were keeping the crew alive in case they needed to know something about sailing her.

Bolan and Katz kept to the bulkheads of the corridor between the cabins when one of the doors suddenly opened and a raider stepped out. Bolan snap shot a single silenced round into the man's head, but the thud of his body hitting the deck echoed loudly.

Katz rushed the open door to the day room, with Bolan on his heels. Four black-clad raiders were turning to bring their weapons to bear when Katz started firing.

He had the first target down and had the second in his sights when a burst of AK fire cut right past his head. A .44 Magnum slug from Bolan's Desert Eagle took the gunner out of play.

The big gun roared again in concert with the gruff Israeli's mini-Uzi, and the raiders were all down.

"There is one in our cabins," a Japanese crewman said in almost unaccented English. "The others are in my engine room."

"We got him on the way in," Katz replied.

"Are you the engineering officer?" Bolan asked.

"I am."

"Your engine room is clear, too, and your man down there is safe."

"Can I return to my duty station?" the officer asked.

Bolan shook his head. "Wait till you hear from the captain."

The officer bowed deeply. *"Hai."*

THE CAPTAIN of the *Hanto Maru* hardly waited for Bolan and Katzenelenbogen to step back onto the deck of the pirate ship before signaling his engine room to give him full-speed ahead. He had agreed to wait a few minutes before broadcasting his Mayday message, but he still wanted to get clear as fast as he could.

Bolan and Katz went to the raiders' bridge to collect their prisoners. The wrists of both men were bleeding, showing that they had tried to break the restraints. Better men than them had tried to overcome those deceptively weak looking plastic strips and failed. Getting both men to their feet, they led them out onto the ship's deck.

"We're ready for pickup," Bolan called over the com link to Jack Grimaldi in the chopper overhead. "Two prisoners."

"Roger," the pilot sent back. "Get the cargo out onto the rear deck."

"We're on the way."

Holding a hover at less than a hundred feet above the stern of the pirate ship, Grimaldi faced his chopper into the wind and fed in enough tail rotor pedal and cyclic stick pressure to keep from drifting off station.

"Ropes on the way," Kissinger called over the com link.

The first two ropes Kissinger lowered were intended to secure the prisoners and haul them up. The captain started to freak out when he saw what was coming, so Katz pinched down a bit on his neck again. Faced with a choice between being hauled up into the air on a rope and having his throat ripped out, the captain calmed himself immediately.

The first mate required the same treatment to get him to cooperate. But Kissinger soon had both of them hauled up and inside the chopper. The second set of ropes he sent down had climbing loops tied in them. Since he would be occupied keeping an eye on his two prisoners, Bolan and Katz would have to make their way back on board by themselves.

Bolan went up the rope hand over hand until he reached the chopper's skid. Standing on it, he unclipped his safety line and resnapped it on the inside of the door.

"Hang on, Katz," he sent over the com link.

Taking hold of Katz's line, Bolan pulled him up and helped him into the chopper.

"Okay," Bolan told Grimaldi as he slid into the copilot's seat. "Get us clear."

The Stony Man pilot fed in a little rudder pedal and turned the aircraft back toward land.

Katz waited until they were several hundred yards away before punching the button on the switch to the remote detonator. The pirate ship shuddered as the shaped charges cut through her hull below the waterline, and she started settling in the water immediately.

Kissinger was turning to buckle the first mate into the rear seat when the captain exploded into action. Kicking with his right leg, he connected with his officer's chest. The man tumbled out the chopper's open door, screaming as he fell to the waves two thousand feet below.

Shouldering a stunned Kissinger out of the way, the captain threw himself out the chopper's open door.

"Damn," Katz said. "There go our informants."

EARLY THE NEXT MORNING, Katzenelenbogen called the Farm to get Aaron Kurtzman working on the tungsten question.

"Tungsten's just become a red-hot commodity," Kurtzman said. "The word on that hijacking you foiled has gotten out, and the spot price doubled on the market this morning. No one seems to care, though, because if you're building rockets, you've got to have it. Chromium and manganese are substitutes for certain temperatures and pressures, but if you're going to go first class, you've simply got to have tungsten.''

"I know all that, Aaron," Katz said. "All I need to know is where it comes from and who might have some of it right now, a ship load to be exact, either in port awaiting loading or on the high seas.''

Katz could hear Kurtzman's fingers racing over his keyboard. "There's a bulk carrier half full of wolframite," he said. "That's what the ore's called, by the way, coming through the Suez en route for a port call in Alexandria. She's scheduled for a several-day layover there before going on through the Med and on up to Germany.''

"What's it called?''

"The MS *Horst Lyman* out of Hamburg.''

"Anything else, anywhere else?" Katz asked.

"Nope, that's it right now.''

"Looks like we'll be going to Alexandria, then," Katz said.

"You guys going into the exotic-metals market?''

"No. Just looking for assholes.''

Kurtzman laughed. "Good luck.''

"I, FOR ONE," Katz said as he pushed his lunch away, "am going to be very happy that we're taking this dog-and-pony show to the Middle East. The constant curry diet is starting to give me wind.''

"I like it," Jack Grimaldi said as he mopped the last of the curry sauce from his plate with his last piece of flat bread. "It's better than that rice flavored with goat fat you're gonna be eating in Egypt."

Katz ignored the pilot's inexpert culinary commentary. Grimaldi was known to eat damn near anything that didn't eat him first.

"The question we need to consider before we leave," he said, "is if we should cut Jasmine loose now. The Chinese nailed the guy responsible for her ordeal before we could, and she's still alive. This might be a good time to cut her exposure and let her go. I can ask Hal to put her into the program and get her set up somewhere in the States. With her talents, she'll be a real asset to someone."

"Let's ask her," Bolan agreed.

WHILE BOLAN and Katz had been working the *Hanto Maru* mission, Jasmine Farjani had been helping Rani and Hansa Bargava get out of Calcutta. After seeing them off at the airport, she had returned to her room to wait the return of the two secret agents who had come to her aid.

She was beginning to suspect that Belasko and Bronski were actually American CIA agents. Their access to information was too fast for them to be private citizens. So was their ability to call in other people to assist them. She knew that the CIA had a bad reputation in many countries, but she had seen nothing but honor in these men. She had been overjoyed when her two heroes returned the next morning and now waited to see what they were going to do next.

"How would you like to go back to America?" Katzenelenbogen asked her over breakfast. "We can set it up so you can stay there legally and work openly without fear."

The woman's heart leaped. The thought of having to stay in India had been tormenting her. With her relatives living in Calcutta, she could never stay. As she was unmarried, custom gave them power over anything she might try to do. Even though her first trip to America had been disastrous, it was the best place she knew to try to make a life for herself.

"When are we leaving?"

"We'll be sending you alone," Katz explained. "But someone will meet you in L.A. to take you through the formalities and get you set up."

Farjani looked from one man to the other. "You two are still going on with this, aren't you?"

"We are." Bolan nodded. "We still haven't been able to determine exactly who's behind all this. And until we do know, we have to keep on it."

She took a deep breath and made a flash decision. "As long as those men are selling women," she said, "I would like to continue to help you if there's anything I can do."

"It's pretty clear that the slavery thing is really a side issue with them," Katz explained. "The slaves are only useful for the work the Chinese can get out of them, not for the money. Men or women, the only thing that matters is that they can supply information they need. And it's a clever plan, no one has a reason to suspect that they're working for the Chinese government."

"We will do what we can to end their slaving, of course," Bolan said, "but the reason we have to keep after these men is that they're stealing equipment and materials to make sophisticated weapons that're dangerous to the rest of the world, not just to our country."

"I don't know anything about those kinds of things," she said. "But I know what it's like to be forced to work to keep my family from being harmed. Since the two seem to be connected, I think I can still help you. I don't know where you are going next, but I might speak the language there."

"We are going to Alexandria," Katz said in Arabic.

She smiled. "I've always wanted to see the fabled city of Iskandar," she replied in the same language.

Katz laughed. "You're on, my dear."

COLONEL GAO DONG knew better than to be grateful that his Beijing masters hadn't ordered his immediate execution for the loss of the tungsten shipment on the *Hanto Maru*. It wasn't an act of mercy, nor a reward for his years of faithful service to the Party. Those were Western concepts totally alien to the thinking of the leaders of the People's Republic of China. The only reason he was still breathing was that he was still useful to them. When that usefulness ended, so would his life. The lords of Beijing had long memories.

All this reprieve meant was that he had to secure another shipment of tungsten ore to replace the one that had gotten away from him. The ballistic missile program was at a standstill until more of the exotic metal could be secured. And to do that, he had to go to the Middle East, which presented another set of problems.

His Dragon Egg teams didn't have as high a presence in the Islamic nations as he would have liked. The problem wasn't for lack of trying, but rather cultural. Orientals were simply too rarely found in the xenophobic Arabic nations for them not to stand out and be constantly watched.

Fortunately for Dong, though, a ship bearing the ore the mother country needed was due to dock in Alexandria, which just happened to be the location of the only fully staffed office he had in the Arabic nations of the Mediterranean. True to her ancient heritage as the world's first truly international city, Alexandria still welcomed foreigners doing business, any foreigners. The Middle East in general had little that China needed except for oil, but the mother country was always looking to expand the markets for her export products.

Using common trade as a cover in Alexandria was perfect. Even more than Beirut, the port city was a true gateway to northern Europe. The Egyptian government's mostly pro-Western stance, at least for the moment, made it a safe harbor for Western cargo ships. They commonly stopped over before making the Suez passage into the Red Sea or on the way out.

Successfully hijacking a ship in the Mediterranean wouldn't be as easy as it was in the South China Sea. The ship could be taken over easily enough, but getting away was tough. For one thing, the shores of the sea were well patrolled by the navies and air forces of the nations that bordered it, and escaping their notice wouldn't be easy. Further, there were only two narrow passages, the Strait of Gibraltar and the Suez Canal, to get in and out of the mostly landlocked sea. A single patrol boat guarding each route would be sufficient.

To do the job Beijing required of him, Dong had come up with an audacious plan. He would hijack the cargo while the ship was still at the docks at Alexandria. That, too, carried risks, but they weren't as high as trying to run a stolen ship through the Strait of Gibraltar into the open Atlantic. To pull this off, though, he would need the help of his Islamic Brotherhood contacts in Egypt.

The radicals could be difficult to work with, but fortunately they were easily bought in the coin that China had in abundance—small arms, ammunition and explosives. With Russia no longer supplying and arming anti-Western terrorist groups, China had been happy to take over the business.

Unlike the Soviets had done, though, the Chinese didn't give weapons away like treats to children at a festival day. The military supplies the Islamic radicals sought were always available in China, but they had to be paid for. Often, the payment required was a terrorist incident to raise the tension in the region and draw the West's attention away from China and the Far East. At other times, though, simple information or assistance was enough. And this was going to be one of those times.

Dong already had a large shipment of 7.62 mm ammunition stockpiled in Egypt that should buy him all the manpower he needed. At the rate the Arabs used up AK ammo shooting holes in the empty sky at the slightest excuse, they went through it rather quickly. If he ever caught a solider of the Chinese People's Liberation Army wasting ammunition, Arab style, he would execute him on the spot, and then he would charge the man's family for the cost of the bullet. Nonetheless, the wasteful practice meant that he always had the means to secure cooperation from China's Islamic allies.

As all successful criminal gangs did, the Islamic Brotherhood had taken a page from the Yankee labor unions and had deeply infiltrated the port operations of Alexandria. Nothing moved in or out without their taking a small cut of it. That, of course, was in addition to the bribes to officials that were so much a part of Egyptian life. Those who objected to this surcharge on top of the customary bribery simply disappeared into the murky waters of the harbor.

What he was planning, though, would be a little

more complicated than stealing a couple of crates off the docks. A ship full of ore didn't lend itself to simply disappearing. The ore would have to be transferred while the ship was tied up to the dock. Fortunately, with the Brotherhood in control of the port police as well as the dock, it could be done.

To insure that it was handled properly, Dong would fly to Egypt himself with a second Dragon Egg team as reinforcements. This was the last chance he would have, and the operation couldn't be allowed to fail.

CHAPTER TWELVE

Beirut

Yakov Katzenelenbogen and Jasmine Farjani were enjoying Air India's first-class accommodations as the 747 from Calcutta banked on the downwind leg for a landing at Beirut International Airport. Farjani looked out the window as Katz quickly finished his meal. The curry in India had been getting him down, but Air India had a top-notch first-class galley.

In economy class, Bolan was putting away a mediocre lunch, but food was merely fuel to him. Kissinger was on his way back to the Farm, and Jack Grimaldi was on his way to Italy with a few tools of the trade to pick up a long-range helicopter. The plan was for Bolan to take a plane out of Beirut immediately for Alexandria to start keeping an eye on the world's only other tungsten shipment on the seas. Katz and Farjani would remain in Beirut to gather information by asking about acquiring ''stock'' for an imaginary cartel of European whorehouses. Playing a pimp was a new one for Katz, but he had no trouble getting into it. Having a stunning beauty at his side would only add to the cover.

As soon as the jumbo jet touched down and taxied to the terminal, Katz and Farjani left their seats without even looking back at Bolan in economy with the rest of the human cattle waiting their turn.

After clearing customs, Katz and Farjani took a cab to their destination on the other side of town. On the way, Katz used the time to reacquaint himself with the city. He was glad to see that Beirut looked to be well on its way to recovering from the disastrous twenty-year-long civil war. He could hardly tell where the old Green Line had been. New construction was going up everywhere, and the famed beaches were once more drawing well-heeled Europeans with a taste for wide-open fun and adventure.

The centerpiece of Beirut's revival, he knew, though, was once more their offshore banking. The city had been founded by the ancient world's most successful traders, the Phoenicians, and little had changed in several thousand years. The Swiss were noted for handling Europe's under-the-table banking chores, the Cayman Islands did it for Latin American and North American ill-gotten gains, and Singapore did it for the Pacific Rim. The banks of Beirut, though, were on their way back to becoming the Middle East's best place to store valuables, legal and illegal.

They didn't have vaults full of Nazi gold like the

Swiss did, but what was gold compared to petro-dollars? Many of their numbered petro-dollar accounts were the war chests of Islamic terrorist groups, drug smugglers and slavers. True to their ancient heritage, the Beirut bankers didn't care where the money came from as long as it came.

To make money by banking, though, meant having a healthy import-export economy to fuel it. Again, that was an age-old standby of Beirut. As a neutral ground between the West and the Middle East, the city was a perfect place to transship goods and materials between the two blocs. Cargo ships flying the flags from nations as far away as Brazil and Japan crowded Beirut's harbors side by side with European Union–flagged ships and the Mediterranean's own coastal tramp steamers.

With the Lebanese not too particular about what the West considered contraband, anything could be hidden in the cargo holds of those ships, and was. The West was awash in drugs and illegal immigrants, and much of that traffic originated in Beirut.

The address Katz was seeking turned out to be a modern office building in a newly revitalized part of town. The business card they'd recovered from the body of the Arab slave trader in Calcutta indicated that he'd operated an employment agency at the address.

The reception area was air-conditioned and furnished in European modern, as was the receptionist.

"Is Mr. Dalal Saoud in?" Katz asked the woman in Arabic.

"I'm sorry," she replied. "But he isn't available. He's out of the country on a recruiting trip."

And a trip from which he wouldn't be returning, Katz thought.

"Maybe Mr. Chamoun can help you?" the receptionist suggested.

"I have a delicate matter to discuss." Katz glanced over at Farjani. "And I was told to speak only with Mr. Saoud about it."

"And who recommended you?"

"A Mr. Mani Mohandi of Calcutta."

A look crossed the woman's face and she rose from behind her desk. "Just a moment, please. Have a seat."

A few minutes later, a younger version of the late Mr. Saoud came out of the back office. "Ah, Mr....?"

"Bronski," Katz said as he bowed slightly. "Lev Bronski."

"I am Fawzi Chamoun," the man said. "Are you a friend of Mani Mohandi?"

"We have done business," Katz replied.

"When was the last time you saw him?"

"I was in Calcutta on business two weeks ago, why?" Katz managed to look properly concerned. "Has something happened to him?"

"Oh, no," Chamoun said a little too quickly. "It's just that he's been out of contact for some reason."

How about because he was dead? Katz fought not to grin.

"Maybe you can help me instead." Katz sounded hopeful.

Chamoun glanced at Farjani.

"Oh...she's my business partner," Katz explained.

Even in modern Beirut, social niceties applied, so Chamoun had tea brought in. When everyone was served, he sat behind his desk. "How may I help you?"

"I manage gentlemen's clubs in several European cities," Katz explained. "These aren't common establishments catering to the working classes," he hurried to add, "but true palaces for the most discriminating clientele, if you understand."

"I don't remember having heard of you," Chamoun stated, politely calling him a liar." And I know that business."

"I'm not at all surprised." Katz didn't sound offended. "Most of these establishments have changed hands recently. A consortium in Moscow has taken them over, and the board of directors wants to upgrade the facilities with a new look. I was asked to accomplish that."

Even in Beirut, the activities of the Russian Mafia were known. Particularly their white slavery, since it had cut deeply into the business of the traditional Middle East flesh peddlers. If this was true, it could be a bonanza for men like him.

"I understood," Chamoun said, "that your Moscow associates usually preferred to work with Eastern Europeans.''

This guy was a suspicious bastard, but Katz couldn't fault him for it. He was in a dangerous business. ''That was once true,'' he said, ''but you know how it is when you're working with clients who excessively follow fashion. They get bored easily and desire new and different experiences. I was led to believe that you could help me accommodate them. And if at all possible, through Egypt or Morocco.''

He shrugged. ''But if not...''

Chamoun knew that it was time to fish or cut bait. ''You have references?''

''But of course.'' Katz pulled a note from his pocket with the name of a Beirut bank and a long number.

Chamoun didn't have to see more; he knew what the coded first four numbers meant. ''I am certain I can be of assistance. I just happen to know of a broker in Alexandria who has some stock I am confident will meet your requirements.''

Throughout this conversation, Farjani had kept her deep green eyes on Chamoun and her face calm. As Katz had explained, having her at his side was important to make his cover believable. Given her preferences, however, she would have slowly roasted this Lebanese slave trader over a roaring fire. After, of course, she had gouged out his eyes and castrated him with a dull knife. This ''stock'' he so casually mentioned were frightened young women like herself and her sister who were destined to become whores.

"Excellent." Katz beamed. "Can I place a deposit on the transaction with you now to hold them for my inspection?"

"Of course." Chamoun smiled.

WHEN KATZ HAD concluded his business, Farjani could barely contain herself. "That pig!" she spit in French as soon as they were back in their cab.

Katz put a cautionary hand on her shoulder and shook his head. In Beirut, you had to be careful what language you used, particularly French.

He had expected to have to spend a few days snooping around to find what he needed. But since he'd gotten a home run on his first swing, they had no reason to stay in Beirut and would take the next flight to Egypt. Bolan would need all the help he could get in Alexandria.

Egypt

GETTING OUT of his cab four blocks from Alexandria's docks, Bolan knew there was no way he could blend into the crowd. Even with as many Westerners as there were in the city, few of them looked like him to any degree. The combination of height, build and particularly the piercing blue eyes would have made him stand out even in Europe. It didn't, though, mark him as a target to be messed with. The street punks and petty criminals of Alexandria were known for their boldness, but they weren't stupid. One glance told them not to try their luck with him, and they gave him a wide berth.

He took his time like a tourist, mentally mapping his surroundings as he made his way down to the port. The heavy truck traffic hauling goods to and from the harbor added to the normally crowded traffic of the city's streets and alleys. He would have to come back at night to gauge it then, as well as locating a spot to park their car for a clean getaway. His recent experience in Calcutta had driven that point home.

The need for a getaway, though, was still problematical. Aaron Kurtzman had reported that the *Horst Lyman* was scheduled to remain in port for only a couple of days to rest her crew and take on additional cargo. And in that time, he had to find evidence that it actually was going to be hijacked. At this point in the game, the assumption that the Chinese would target it was just that, an assumption. His gut told him he was right, but he still had to prove it.

The harbor was crowded with dozens of ships of all sizes, from the gleaming floating palaces of cruise ships to sail-powered fishing dhows and everything in between. Looking as if he had nothing else to do, Bolan started checking them out without drawing undue attention to himself. The guidebook and camera around his neck helped.

A half hour later, he spotted the *Horst Lyman* tied up to a pier at the far eastern end of the harbor. The gleaming paint and unfaded red, yellow and black tri-color of the German Federal Republic flying from her stern announced her captain's pride in his vessel. The German merchant fleet was small, but it was modern and well-maintained. Kurtzman's report said that the master didn't have a German name, but all that meant was that he was a top-notch mariner. The German shipping companies hired only the very best captains.

A smaller, old tramp steamer was tied up on the other side of the pier from the German ship. It wasn't a complete rust bucket with her masts leaning and bilge pumps running full blast just to keep her afloat, but she wasn't a new ship. He couldn't make out the flag on her stern, but he knew it didn't matter what colors she was sailing under. If he was on the right trail, the steamer would be controlled by the same Chinese gang that had tried to hijack the Japanese bulk carrier in the South China Sea. Even if he was correct in his identification, the question was still how were they planning to pull this one off.

Trying for a high-seas heist in the Mediterranean simply wasn't going to cut it. He knew that and knew they did, as well. The people he was up against were bold and fearless, but they weren't reckless. The Chinese never were. As if on call, the answer to that question appeared to him when he saw a conveyor belt rig on wheels being pulled out onto one of the other docks.

As he watched, the conveyor belt was swung side-ways with one end going into the hold of a small

Middle Eastern freighter and the other end into an American-flagged bulk carrier. As soon as the conveyor was rigged, the contents of the smaller ship were soon on their way to the holds of the larger one.

With the small freighter moored alongside the *Horst Lyman,* all it would take would be to wheel one of those conveyor units in between the two ships and take the tungsten ore from the belly of the *Horst Lyman.* Of course, the German ship's crew would have to be dealt with, but he was sure that the Chinese, and their local allies, were up to taking care of that minor detail.

Now that he had an idea how this heist might take place, he left the harbor and caught a cab to the airport to link up with Katzenelenbogen and Farjani. Katz had just reported that he had come up with a contact name in Alexandria and that he and Jasmine were on their way to join him.

On the cab ride to meet them, Bolan went into planning mode. They had a lot of work ahead of them if they were going to prevent this hijacking, and Egypt wasn't the best place to be doing this kind of work. At least, though, Jack Grimaldi had secured an Italian-registered helicopter and was waiting on the west end of the Greek island of Crete, less than a hundred miles away. Stationing him in Egypt was a little too dicey for what he had in mind. Egyptian air-traffic control could get draconian and wasn't above ordering fighters to shoot down aircraft that didn't wait for flight clearance. Crete, though, was only a half hour's wave-hopping flight away.

And while that could be a long wait if the excrement was impacting the ventilation, it was better than having no air support to call upon at all.

KATZ WAS IMPRESSED when Bolan explained how he thought the Chinese were planning to loot the *Horst Lyman.* "If that's their plan," he said, "that's truly audacious."

"If I'm right about their getting the crew off the ship somehow, the Germans will return to an empty ship riding high in the water and not have a clue about where their cargo has disappeared to."

"How do you want to work it?"

"Rather than just stop the ore transfer," Bolan said, "I want to hold the Egyptians aiding the Chinese accountable, as well. The only way we're going to put an end to this is if everyone involved pays the price."

Bolan got a look in his eyes Katz knew well.

"I want the word to go out that doing business with the Chinese is bad for business, even fatal."

Katz smiled. "Sounds good to me."

OVER THE NEXT DAY and a half, Bolan and Katzenelenbogen took turns watching the *Horst Lyman* and gathering the gear they'd need if the Chinese made their move as expected.

Since sport diving in the ancient harbor was a major tourist pastime, securing Scuba gear for Katz was no problem. The Israeli made a couple of recon dives to acquaint himself with the dock area and found a way to get into the eastern end of the harbor without being seen.

Grimaldi tested the extraction route by making a low-level night flight to a deserted beach. The Farm had located a gap in the Egyptian air-defense radar network, but he wanted to test it himself. Tangling with Egyptian MiGs wasn't on his list of things to do. And since he was making the trip, he brought a few goodies Bolan had ordered.

WHILE THEY WERE watching and waiting for the Chinese to make their move, Katz recognised the address he'd been given in Beirut. The preliminary plan called for them to stop by on their way out of town. Grimaldi's pickup point was at the beach west of the city, and the slaver's address was right along the route out of town.

The target building looked as if it had been a hotel back in the twenties and thirties. During British rule back then, Egypt had attracted Europeans seeking a better climate for health reasons or who craved a walk on the wild side. Alexandria in particular had been the premier destination for the English expatriate literary and artistic crowd. A host of cultural luminaries had come to the city hoping to be inspired by the alien surroundings. Some had, but most hadn't.

The turmoil of Egypt's postwar Islamic revolution

effectively ended that kind of tourism, and Alexandria lost its expatriate European community. They were replaced, though, by modern tourism primarily practiced by Americans. Since Americans didn't like to stay in older accommodations, old hotels had been turned into local housing or put to other uses. This one had bars on the windows.

With this being a rough part of town, it wasn't surprising to see two men in security positions in front of the entrance to the building. Katz found a tea shop at the end of the block and spent a couple of hours reading Arabic newspapers, smoking a water pipe and watching the building. When he had seen what he had come for, he paid his bill and wandered on.

"Chamoun said that he had some twenty or thirty women in there," Katz reported to Bolan, "so I'm thinking that they're all up on the top floor. That way no one's going to hear them, and they're not going to try to jump out a window."

"Which puts their guards on the lower floors where we can take them out quickly."

"On the way out, like we talked about, though," Katz said. "We don't want to risk getting hung up in there before we do the harbor job."

Bolan glanced at the map. "That still works for me."

"What do we do about her?" Katz nodded toward the wall separating their room from Jasmine's.

"We'll leave her in the car with a com link. If we

get stuck, she can drive to the airport and get the first flight out to the States.''

"I'll have the Bear arrange to have a ticket waiting for her," Katz stated.

"And someone to meet her and bring her in.''

CHAPTER THIRTEEN

Captain Ian Williams, master of the MS *Horst Lyman*, didn't particularly like Alexandria. Most of the Arabic ports he called at were pestholes as far as he was concerned, and he rarely allowed his crew liberty in them. Alexandria was different, though. Every time he made the Suez passage from the south and had to dock in Egypt, he gave his men a couple of days in the city to wash the sand out of their guts. They loved the place, but he never went ashore here. The days were long past when he had been young enough to stomach goat meat or women who smelled of it. Even the air blowing from off the shore was enough to keep him in his cabin with the air-conditioning on full blast.

Fortunately he would be sailing on the evening's tide and could soon blow the stink off. Until then, he was working his way through the paperwork that came with being the ship's master. With the owners being bloody Germans, they were very fond of bloody paperwork. He was signing a manifest update when he heard a commotion on deck.

Going to his porthole, he saw a half-dozen uniformed Egyptians clamoring up his gangplank. He'd
had his final clearance inspection and didn't know
what in the hell was going on, but he intended to find
out. Shrugging into his tailored uniform jacket and
grabbing his cap, he stormed out onto the deck, his
face red with rage.

"What is the meaning of this, Officer?" he called
out to the man with the most clutter on his coat.

The police officer looked him up and down. "You
are Captain Ian Williams, master of this vessel?"

"I am, sir," Williams replied. "What is this
about?"

"You are under arrest."

"Under whose authority?" Williams was truly
shocked.

"My authority," the Egyptian said. "I am Alexandria Port Police Lieutenant Moamar Namadi, officer in charge of the antiterrorist unit."

"What in the hell are you talking about, man?"
Williams's face grew even redder.

"Some of your crewmen were found with explosives in their possession," Namadi replied, "and we
have information indicating that they intended to deliver them to radical groups."

"That's absurd!" Williams looked close to exploding. "I'm a merchantman's captain, not a bloody terrorist!"

"A captain is responsible for the conduct of his
crew," the Egyptian reminded him. "And you have

terrorists in your crew. That means you are a terrorist, as well.''

"If you have proof of any of this," Williams sputtered, "I demand to see it."

"That is for the courts to determine, Captain," Namadi replied. "You are to come with us."

"For God's sake," Williams pleaded. "At least allow me to contact my ship's owners. They have a shipping schedule to meet, and I have to tell them what has happened so they can fly in a replacement crew."

"We will be calling them ourselves," the Egyptian replied,, "to tell them that the *Horst Lyman* has been impounded pending the trial of her crew. We have severe punishment for those who promote terrorism in our country, Captain, and that includes impounding their property."

"Christ on his cross!" Williams roared. "I don't own this ship, and we're not bloody terrorists! I can vouch for every man on board. They've sailed with me for months."

"Take him away," the lieutenant said as he turned to his sergeant.

"You can't take me away from my ship!" Williams protested. "That's against international maritime law!"

"We have laws in Egypt, too," Namadi said, "and you are suspected of violating them."

Rather than be beaten into submission, Williams

gathered his dignity, squared his cap and allowed himself to be taken away.

AFTER POSTING TWO of his men at the gangplank, Lieutenant Namadi returned to his office in the port administration building. Waiting for him was a tall Chinese man in a Western-cut tropical suit.

"It's done," the cop said. "But I can only keep them in custody for two days at the most before someone will come looking for them."

"That will be more than enough time," Colonel Gao Dong replied. "We will start off-loading the cargo as soon as it gets dark tonight."

"As soon as I am paid," the Egyptian reminded him.

"Of course," Dong replied. "The shipment can be found in bonded warehouse 32 labeled as garden implements."

"And it is newly made?"

"Oh, yes," Dong said. "State Factory 65 supplies the People's Liberation Army itself. There will be no misfires in this ammunition."

The Egyptian smiled.

KATZ AND FARJANI WERE playing chess on the veranda of their hotel. She was a worthy opponent, and the challenge was a good way to pass the time. Katz hadn't yet filled her in on the part she was to play when, and if, the action went down. He had, however, arranged for her transportation back to the United

States if it came to that. One change was that Brognola had set it up for her to go the American Embassy and let them handle transporting her.

"Katz." Bolan's voice over the com link broke in on his concentration. He was pulling his watch from a position on the rock breakwater beyond the docks. "It's started. The German crew was just taken off by the port police."

"You were right," Katz replied. "And that means it's going down tonight. They won't be able to hold the crew very long, and doing the transfer during the day is a little too obvious even for them."

"That's what I'm thinking," Bolan replied. "I'm coming back and we'll get ready."

"It's tonight," Katz told his companion.

She didn't know whether to be happy about that or not. This was a strange business her two protectors were in. Bullets were flying or absolutely nothing was going on. She didn't know how they could be so patient.

"Now, my dear—" Katz leaned towards her "—we've made arrangements for you if things go wrong tonight."

UNLIKE THE CALCUTTA docks, the port of Alexandria was almost deserted now that the sun had gone down. A few longshoremen worked some of the cargo on the dock, but almost all of the ships were idle but for deck crew. Not so, though, the *Horst Lyman* and the steamer moored on the other side of the pier from it.

A dozen men were positioning one of the conveyor belt rigs into place between them.

Bolan went up the *Horst Lyman*'s bow mooring line hand over hand. When he reached the scupper, he eased himself over the side and lay flat on the deck. There was a little too much light on the docks for night-vision goggles to be effective, but it was still dark enough for his blacksuit and combat cosmetics to hide him in the shadows.

From what he could see, the crewmen transferring the ore were all locals, as were the security men. That didn't, though, make them noncombatants in the evening's activities. Anyone working for the Chinese was equally guilty and a legitimate target. For the message to be sent, they all had to die.

The only guard posted on the *Horst Lyman*'s deck was a man standing by the rumbling conveyor belt. He had a holstered sidearm along with what looked like a small two-way radio. Obviously his job was to keep an eye on the flow of the ore over the belt, because he wasn't watching anything else. Not watching his back was going to prove fatal.

Since the man stationed at the other end of the conveyor belt on the deck of the tramp steamer had his back turned, Bolan made his move. The noise of the belt covered any sound he might have made as he went in quickly, his Cold Steel Tanto fighting knife in his hand ready for a silent kill.

An iron hand clamped over the guard's mouth, and

the Tanto ripped into his kidney. Bolan wrenched the blade sideways, opening his lower back.

The man gasped in shock, but the hand gripping his mouth prevented any sound from escaping. The massive loss of blood sent him into almost instant unconsciousness. Bolan lowered him to the deck before rolling the body under the conveyor belt out of sight.

"I'm clear," Bolan spoke into his com link.

"So am I," Katz replied from the shore end of the dock where he was covering Bolan's back after having done his part for the evening.

"Wait there for me."

The man on the steamer turned back to the *Horst Lyman* to watch the conveyor belt, but didn't seem alarmed that his counterpart wasn't at his station. He probably figured that his partner was relieving himself.

Going back to the ship's bow, Bolan went down the mooring rope to the dock. Working his way midships, he crossed the dock in the shadow of the conveyor belt, went to the steamer's stern and up the mooring line again.

The noise of the conveyor belt was louder on the old ship as Bolan made his approach. A check of the wheelhouse showed that it was still empty. Over the rattle of the conveyor, he could feel a vibration that told him that there was engine-room activity. The crew would be preparing to bring her boilers on-line so she could make her escape.

Again he targeted the man by the belt. And again he made a silent kill with his knife.

After stowing that guard under the conveyor, as well, he headed down a hatchway looking for the engine room. Letting his ears guide him, he soon located it and wasn't surprised to see three Orientals working on the machinery.

Keeping to the shadows, he switched his 93-R to burst mode and waited until the three were in his target field at the same time. The three silenced triple taps came almost as fast as a full-auto burst, and the engine room was clear.

A quick trip past the machinery confirmed that the Chinese had been alone, and he headed for the cargo holds to finish the job. For the message to be sent, the bodies had to be found so there would be no question as to what had happened.

The cargo hold amidships was being filled first, and Bolan decided to start there. Since they'd been working with ships so much lately, he had a pretty good idea now how to find it.

The four men working the end of the conveyor belt were locals. Even so, Bolan gave them no quarter. Four more bursts put them down, and the incoming tungsten ore started to cover them.

Checking the other two cargo holds showed that he had swept the ship clean. "Coming your way," he said over the com link as soon as he was back on deck.

"You're clear," Katz sent back.

When Bolan rejoined his old friend, the Israeli had dropped his Scuba gear and was in his blacksuit ready for phase two of the evening's operation. A remote-control detonator was in his hand.

"Do it," Bolan said.

The flash of the limpet mines lit up the harbor as the side of the steamer blew out. Katz had placed his explosive toys so the damage they caused couldn't be missed. They wanted the Egyptian authorities to have to investigate this incident.

The two men slipped into the shadows between the warehouses to return to where they had left their ride. It had been a good night's work so far, but the night wasn't yet over.

THE TEA SHOP on the block across from the old hotel was closed and the street deserted, so Katz parked their rental around the corner. Leaving Jasmine Far-jani behind, they quickly went into action against their next target.

The two security men in front of the hotel didn't seem engrossed in their work. Both were talking and smoking, their weapons slung under their coats. They barely looked up when Katz walked up wearing the clothes of an Egyptian working man, his mini-Uzi tucked out of sight.

"What do you want, old man?" one of the guards growled.

"Is this the place?" Katz replied in Arabic.

"What place, old man?" the guard asked.

Katz grinned broadly. "I was told that this was the mother of all whorehouses. And I have come to see this marvel for myself."

"Where did you hear that?" the second guard asked.

"On the street." Katz spread his arms expressively. "Where else? Everyone knows that you have women in here. Many young, beautiful women."

The two guards exchanged glances as if they were trying to decide if they should awaken their boss. That lapse was all Bolan needed to make his move as he put silence 9 mm slugs in their heads.

After checking to make sure that the street was still empty, Bolan nodded toward the door.

Finding it locked, Katz knocked and they heard someone approach and unlock it from the inside.

When the man opened the door, Bolan put a silenced 9 mm slug between his eyes. Pushing his way past the body blocking the door, he found that all was still quiet inside.

When Katz joined him, they took the time to drag in the two bodies from the steps to join the gate-keeper.

The lobby was empty, but they found the first Egyptian sleeping on a cot in a side office behind the counter. Since they were on a rat hunt, Bolan put him into a deeper sleep with a single shot.

Katz paused to quickly cruise through the papers on the desk in the room. "They were getting ready to send these women to Sicily,'' he said as he read the cursive script.

''Where?''

''Palermo.''

''We'll stop there next.''

Stuffing his pockets with documents, Katz and Bolan left the office to finish the job.

They swept the rest of the first floor, finding two more sleeping guards and eliminating them before moving on. The second floor was empty, but they heard a man's voice on the third.

Covering each side of the stairwell, the two made their way silently up the stairs. The guard in front of a set of partially opened double doors was saying something to someone inside the room. He laughed and turned to sit back on his chair when he frowned at something he thought he saw. His AK was leaning against the wall and when he glanced at it, he collected a shot right above his ear.

Hearing his comrade's body fall, another guard stepped out into the corridor, buckling his pants. He looked down at the body and then up just in time to get shot in the head.

As when she had waited in the harbor, Farjani's instructions were to wait in the car for a call on the miniature radio. If things went bad, she was to run for the safety of the American Embassy. She doubted, though, that she'd have to flee like that. Whoever her protectors really were, they were good at what they did.

"Jasmine," Katz's voice said over her com link, "we need your help in here."

"I'm coming," she replied.

Farjani was getting used to the sight and smell of bodies by now. The first three were lying inside the front door, and others littered the lobby of the old hotel.

"Over here," Katz called out in Arabic from a side room that had once been a dining room.

Farjani saw twenty to thirty young women huddled in the room, some weeping, others staring in shock. She knew the feeling.

Katz came up beside her and whispered instructions in her ear. She nodded and went up to the group of women.

"You are free now," she said first in Arabic. "Go to the police and tell them what happened to you. They will help you go back where you belong."

When she repeated the instructions in French, a tear-streaked young blond woman asked, "Please! Do you speak English?"

"I do," Farjani said.

"I'm an American. You have to take me to the American Embassy. Please. My parents haven't heard from me in weeks."

"Give her the same instructions you gave the others," Katz quickly told Farjani in Arabic. "We have to keep going and can't take the time to help each individual.''

Farjani's heart went out to the woman, to all of the women, but she knew that Bronski was right. If they were to continue their crusade, they had to get out of Egypt as soon as they could.''

"I am sorry," she told the American woman. "We cannot help any more than we have done. Just go with the other women and you will be safe."

The woman fell to the floor and sobbed. A European woman, from her looks, kneeled beside her. "I will help her," she said in French-accented English.

"You have to help each other," Farjani said in several languages. "And you have to leave now."

After herding the women onto the street and pointing them in the direction of the closest police station, the three returned to their rental. Grimaldi was inbound, and they didn't want to keep him waiting.

Back in the car, Farjani allowed herself to shed a tear for those women, but at least they were free now and alive.

Katz patted her shoulder. "They'll be okay now," he said. "We will make sure that the police have to help them."

JACK GRIMALDI WAS waiting at the rendezvous spot on the beach, the rotors on his chopper whirling. Driving their rental down onto the beach, Bolan and Katz loaded their gear into the chopper.

"Hurry up, guys," Grimaldi called over his shoulder. "We gotta get out of here before the Egyptian navy shows up."

"That's the last of it," Bolan said as he tossed a bag in and climbed up into the copilot's seat.

"Where to?" the pilot asked.

"Northwest to Sicily."

"What's there?"

"The Italian Families are up to their old tricks again," Bolan said.

His question answered, Grimaldi pulled pitch and the chopper rose up into the air. Bolan's relationship with the Mafia, both American and European, was legendary. If he was after them again, someone was going to end up in the hurt locker, and it wouldn't be the Executioner.

CHAPTER FOURTEEN

Colonel Gao Dong stepped out of his car in front of the old hotel in west Alexandria. Several of his operatives were there with a dozen of Muhad Fuad's Islamic Brotherhood thugs. He still didn't understand what had caused Fuad to call him, but even a jumbled report of a raid on the hotel was enough for him to investigate.

Fuad saw him and hurried up, mopping sweat from his fat face. "It was Al Askari, I tell you," he said. "He came in the night, killed most of my guards and vanished."

"Show me."

The Egyptian took him inside the hotel lobby. The bloody drag marks from the two bodies right inside the door told him what had happened. Farther on, other bodies had been stacked against the wall, also revealing signs that they had been dragged there.

Dong was almost beginning to believe in the Egyptian's favorite bogeyman. It was obvious that someone had come in the night, killed these men and vanished. In itself, this was no great feat. Any halfway well-trained commando unit could have done the same. And that included his Dragon Egg teams. The only thing that impressed him was the apparent precision with which the operation had been carried out.

From what he was seeing, this Al Askari had apparently gotten into the hotel unseen and killed the guards one by one without an alarm being raised. There was no sign of a real battle having taken place here at all.

"The women?" Dong asked.

"They are gone." Fuad shrugged. "And only two of my men survived."

"You have survivors?"

"Yes. There are two men who lived through the battle and—"

"And they were so well-hidden that they didn't see anything, right?"

"They told me they fought," the Egyptian said, defending his men, one of whom was his favorite nephew. "But there was no stopping Al Askari. He came in like a whirlwind with a gun in each hand and killed everyone in sight. The bullets flew like rain, and no one could stand against him."

The Egyptian was apparently blind, as well as fat and stupid. The only bullet holes he saw anywhere were in the bodies of his Brotherhood thugs. A firefight of any intensity would have left holes in more than a handful of bodies. But he hadn't seen one single bullet hole out of place.

To his credit, Dong didn't draw his pistol and put a bullet in the Egyptian's head. It wasn't as much a matter of exercising restraint, though, as it was that this wasn't the time or the place to do so. As soon as he had put an end to this American commando, though, he would return to Alexandria specifically to kill Muhad Fuad. Until then, he could keep what was left of his miserable life.

The real loss, of course, were the women Fuad's men had supposedly been guarding. These hadn't been common whores, but talented, well-educated women from a dozen nations. Several of them had been prepared to be placed in the European offices of companies he was interested in looting. Others had been slated to become mistresses for prominent businessmen and politicians who lived double lives.

Hopefully most of them would be rounded up before they could find a place to hide, but this was a serious setback for Dong's operation.

"These women were scheduled to be sent to Sicily last week, right?"

Fuad nodded. "Yes, the usual connection."

"Why weren't they sent then?"

The Egyptian shrugged. "I had a call from Fawzi Chamoun in Beirut," he explained. "He said that he had a buyer coming in who would pay a premium if he could have first pick of the women I had available."

Dong's eyes narrowed. "Who was this buyer?"

The Arab shrugged. "He is connected with the

Russians, but I don't remember his name,'' he replied.
"I have it written down in my office. Chamoun said
that he had just come from India—Calcutta, I think.''

Dong kept his face straight. This blundering fool
had set him up to be raided by the American commando again. When he did get around to coming back
and killing him, it was going to be a slow death.

It was more than apparent now that he was in a
fight to the death. And he couldn't say that right now
he was winning. It was a feeling he didn't like.

DONG WAS TURNING to go when one of his men approached him waving a cell phone. "Comrade Colonel!''

"What is it?" he snapped.

"Trouble on the dock, Comrade.'' The man stiffened to attention. "Our ship has been sunk.''

Dong didn't believe what he was hearing. "What
do you mean it sunk?''

"A mine blew a hole in its side, Comrade, and it
sank in the harbor.''

"What about the ore?''

"Most of it is still on the German ship.''

Where it would remain, Dong realized. Even with
the bribes he had paid and the assistance of the Brotherhood, the Egyptian government would be forced to
investigate now. Since a European vessel had been
involved, they would have no choice but to look into
the incident or risk losing revenue-producing shipping

traffic. And when they got involved, he and his men would have to be gone from Egypt.

Dong also knew that he needed to be gone from here quickly if he wished to continue to breathe air. He had failed for the last time, and the lords of Beijing would send the Tiger Squad after him. Before he died at their hands, though, he intended to find the man or men who had done this to him and kill him first. And to do that, he had to take the time to fully analyze what had brought him to this place.

This mysterious American commando had entered his affairs when he had stumbled onto the Farjani woman being disciplined in California. From there he had gone on to raid the *Singapore Queen,* possibly to free the other slaves in her hold. Somehow, he had made a connection to Wei's operation and had shut that down, too. From there, he had appeared in Calcutta with the woman and sent her to Mohandi's office in an obvious attempt to trap him into betraying himself. Had not Bargava tipped the Dragon Egg team to Farjani's presence, the Yankee would have kidnapped Mohandi.

The theme that kept running through this entire sequence of events appeared to be slavery, though, not the technology thefts made possible by it. Even though the Soldier had just struck at the ore transfer here and made it impossible, he had still taken the time to wipe out the slavers in Alexandria. It all kept coming back to the slaves.

He couldn't understand the man's obsession with female slaves. But then who could understand the mind of a Yankee? In his mind, they rarely did what a rational man would do. But that didn't mean that their motives and future actions couldn't be discerned.

If he was going to live long enough to carry out his own irrational quest, though, he had to leave here and go into hiding immediately. And what better place to go than to his contacts in Sicily? If he was correct about what the Yankee was doing, the man would follow the slave trade and that would lead him directly to the Italian Mafia and the French Union Corse. Fortunately both organizations owed Dong heavily, so he would call in the debt. It was good to have people indebted to him at a time like this.

He knew that his fall from grace with Beijing had tainted the men of his Dragon Egg teams, as well, and they would also have to flee before the Tiger Squad arrived. He would invite a few of his Alexandria staff to join him, but the rest of them would have to make their own accommodations with the circumstances they were now in.

Some of his men might want to try to reconcile themselves with Beijing and take their chances. The more experienced operatives would know better and opt for disappearing into the West. If they could get to America, he had Tong contacts who would be glad to accept them. The Tongs were always looking for a few good men.

Stony Man Farm, Virginia

EVEN THOUGH Bolan and Katz weren't on a White House–sanctioned mission, Hal Brognola couldn't keep himself from checking in on their progress every chance he got. With things pretty quiet in his corner of the Justice Department for the moment, he was flying down from D.C. every other day on any excuse he could come up with.

"Well, I'll be damned," Barbara Price said when she saw him walk out of the elevator into the Annex. "It's Hal Brognola, leader of the free world's most potent clandestine-operations force. What brings you all he way down here from our nation's capital, Mr. Brognola? Do you have a new mission for us from the President? Is the peace and security of our fair nation threatened once again? Or is the fate of one of our many freedom-loving, democratic allies around the world on the line this time?"

Brognola should have known that he couldn't sneak into the Annex without her knowing about it.

"Actually I'm just strap hanging today. You know, playing tourist."

"A tourist with a morbid curiosity?"

"I just wanted to know how they're doing," he said. "The contents of that warehouse they turned over in California is causing a real shit storm in the Defense Procurement Agency. A couple of GS-14s are answering questions to a grand jury about fixing auctions of Mil-Spec surplus in return for kickbacks. When the court's done with them, they're both going to jail for a long time. So, since this has kind of turned into a national-security thing, I thought I'd just—''

''Bull. But pretty good bull, I have to admit. And since you really are the boss around here, or at least that's what it says on our executive order, I guess you can stop by any time you want.''

She winked. ''You wanna cup of coffee?''

''Sure,'' he replied as his hand went for the ever present roll of antacid tabs in his jacket pocket.

''The pot's over there,'' she said and walked off.

Aaron Kurtzman was holding his sides to keep from laughing as he watched Price's little performance.

''What the hell's wrong with her today?'' Brognola asked.

Kurtzman shrugged. ''Not enough to do around here. I think the downtime is getting to her.''

''Christ, I'd better create a crisis to give her something to do.''

''Actually we have a minicrisis going, but Striker and Katz seem to be handling it. There's a ship sitting on the bottom of the Alexandria harbor and twenty or thirty ex-slaves, women all, including at least one American, in Egyptian custody awaiting UN extradition.''

''How the hell did the UN get involved?''

''I have a feeling that someone placed a call to the Anti-Slavery Committee.''

''I take it that he got clear of the area first?'' Brognola asked.

"He did," Kurtzman confirmed. "And he just arrived in Sicily, where he plans to make a call on his old friends, the Mafia."

"I'd better call the Italian minister of justice and give him a heads-up."

"I'd hold off for a bit," Kurtzman cautioned. "We don't want Striker to get involved with the carabinieri. You know how he feels about having to shoot at the good guys."

"Good point."

Sicily

DON GIOVANNI MORO WAS from an ancient Sicilian family. How ancient he had no idea, but he was confident that the blood of the Carthaginians ran in his veins. He was sure, though, that the Moros had been one of the founding Families of what the world now knew as the Mafia. And unlike some of the other founding Families, the Moros were still on their traditional lands doing business as of old. For Sicily, that made them almost royalty.

The Families of Sicily hadn't all abandoned the island to relocate to the United States in the twenties and thirties. Some of the island's crime lords hadn't wanted to leave their ancient lands to carve out new empires in the New World. Those who remained in Sicily just continued doing what they had done for centuries. In many ways, the old-line Sicilian families weren't as blatant about their business as the American Mafia Dons, but they still ran criminal organizations.

Many of the Mafia operations on the island were the old standbys of Sicily—smuggling, drugs and control of commodities. Gambling wasn't the big deal for them that it was for the American Families because the Europeans didn't have laws prohibiting it. Prostitution wasn't a big moneymaker for them, either, for the same reason. Criminal gangs have always profited greatly from anti-sin laws. People always wanted to engage in some kind of activity that other people didn't approve of. The list was long, and the list of laws attempting to prohibit them was even longer. To make laws against those kinds of things, though, simply enriched criminal organizations that were more than ready to support those "sinful" activities.

With the EU now deeply involved in evening out European trade barriers, though, even the old standbys weren't bringing the Mafia Families the income they needed to support their lifestyle. With tariffs and barriers falling in the name of European free trade, smuggling tax-free cigarettes, for instance, was hardly worth the effort anymore. Even the drug trade had been largely usurped by the new Eastern European gangs. To reduce the gap in their profit-and-loss statements, the old Families had gotten back into one of their oldest pastimes, slavery.

Centuries ago, the Sicilian Families had been the middlemen for the white slave trade. The slaves, mostly young women and strong men, had been rounded up by Arabs and sold to the Sicilians, who then moved them on to Europe. When the European nations outlawed open slavery in the 1800s, the Sicilians kept their hand in the trade by stocking European bordellos with Middle Eastern women and supplying European women to the Turks and Arabs. Even that cozy arrangement came to an end after World War I and the fall of the Ottoman Empire, and the Families gave it up.

The socioeconomic realities of the twenty-first century, however, had given new life to the slave trade, and the Sicilian Families once more saw a chance to make a profit from it. In this newest incarnation, though, the trade had changed somewhat. Along with the traditional hookers from the Third World who were lured by the boatload with the promises of well-paying jobs in Europe, the Families had joined with the Red Chinese in their technology-related spy program.

While this might have been one of the world's most extreme examples of culture diversity, the Chinese were easy to work with. Their word was good, they paid well and they paid on time. Don Giovanni Moro had done well for the Family from his dealings with Colonel Gao Dong, very well in fact. And that was why the phone call he had just received from Muhad Fuad was so troubling. This disaster in Alexandria couldn't have come at a worse time.

He'd taken earnest money payments on most of the

consignment he'd been expecting from Alexandria. The girls' transport had already been delayed because of some stupid Egyptian, and now they were all gone. Not only would he have to give back the money he'd been paid up front, but it was also a black mark against his Family. The word of a Moro had been good for centuries.

"I don't believe a single word of what that Egyptian bastard said," Moro spit. "But the Chinese has never lied to me yet. He is on the way here to discuss this with us, but the one thing he said in his message bothers me."

"What is that, Uncle?" Moro's nephew Alfredo, his second in command and heir apparent, asked from the comfort of the Don's guest chair.

The Don leaned across his desk. "He said that the man the Arabs call Al Askari was behind that hit."

As a boy, Alfredo had been raised on legends of shadow warriors who had stuck at the Families' business. This Al Askari the Arabs talked about was just their version of these stories. Nonetheless, a prudent man was a cautious man when it came to threats.

"Speaking of Arabs—" the Don jerked his thumb toward the faint sounds of a party going on in another part of the house "—how much longer is that going to go on?"

Alfredo shrugged. "You know what they're like, Uncle. They like to relax."

"Only when they are with infidels like us," Moro snorted. "They get drunk like that in their own countries and they'd be shot. And when you think about it, what do they have against alcohol? Wine is one of God's greatest blessings. That's why it is part of the sacraments.''

Now that Don Giovanni was an old man, he talked about God often, but Alfredo let him ramble on without commenting. It wouldn't be long before he was the head of the Family, and he would also expect such respect. While he was listening, though, he was planning what needed to be done in case the Family's security was actually being threatened.

CHAPTER FIFTEEN

The Mediterranean sky was lightening when Jack Grimaldi finally arrived back at the drop-off point with their new rental, a Chevy Blazer.

"Sorry I'm late, guys," he said as he stepped out. "I got hung up at the airfield."

"What happened?" Katzenelenbogen asked.

"Those bastards in customs weren't buying my story," the pilot grumbled. "They didn't like my American accent and figured that I was running drugs from Crete. They searched the bird twice from top to bottom, dogs and all, before they'd turn me loose."

"The Egyptians would have given you a body-cavity search, as well." Katz chuckled.

Grimaldi grimaced. "Italians aren't into that."

"Don't try that with the carabinieri," Katz cautioned. "They'll turn you inside out if they think you're packing something."

"No, thanks."

"It's too close to daylight to do anything now," Bolan said. "We're going to have to hole up for the day."

"Maybe that's best." Katz looked at the sky. "We need the time to make a decent recon and see what we're really up against here."

Bolan's inclination was always to take the war to the enemy on swift wings, the swifter the better, to keep the bastards off balance. They'd been running and gunning for several days now, but so far the gods of war had been riding flank security for them. They were fickle bastards, though, and maybe they'd been pushing their luck. Even though they knew exactly whom they were going up against this time, and where they were located, it wouldn't hurt to take the time to do a good recon and thorough mission prep.

"There's a little hotel on the outskirts of town," Grimaldi said, yawning. "Maybe we could crash there and get some decent sleep."

"Please," Jasmine Farjani said.

"Why not?" Katz agreed.

LATER THAT AFTERNOON, Bolan and Grimaldi took the Blazer for a close-in recon of the evening's target. The pilot had suggested using their chopper for a fly-over, but Bolan nixed that idea.

"If we go in close enough to do any good," he said, "we'll spook those guys. I don't think there're all that many choppers around here except for police aircraft, and we don't want them to think that the carabinieri are after them again."

"Okay." Grimaldi shrugged. "I was just trying not

to have to climb that damn hill in the sun. This place is hotter than Egypt.''

Bolan smiled. ''Tell you what, Jack. You drive me in and I'll do all the footwork.''

''Deal.'' Grimaldi grinned.

Following the map, the pair used the Blazer's V-8 and four-wheel-drive to make it up what looked like a goat path running up to a ridgeline. Stopping below the crest of the hill, the two continued on foot to the top.

''Nice place they've got down there,'' Grimaldi said as he studied the villa through his field glasses. ''Out of the way, not too many avenues of approach and all of them easily guarded.''

''That's why they put it there,'' Bolan said as he looked for a covered route down the front side of the hill. ''Wait for me in the truck and if I run into trouble, come down like Custer and pick me up on the fly.''

''Got you covered,'' Grimaldi replied.

BOLAN TOOK his time working his way down the ridgeline, keeping to the scattered boulders and ground cover. The valley surrounding the compound was mostly covered with an olive grove. The picturesque ancient trees made for good postcard photos, but the Moros had apparently forgotten that they also provided cover for would-be intruders, as well as for his early-warning sentries.

Stopping before he reached the plain, Bolan found good cover and took out his field glasses. They didn't show him any real surprises at the compound. Its heart was a large, rambling stone villa in the center of a working farm with the various outbuildings needed to support the agricultural side of the family business. Too bad that the rest of the family's activities couldn't have been that bucolic.

From the number of expensive cars parked in front of the main house, the Don looked to be holding some kind of meeting. The black Mercedes four-doors were a dead giveaway. Bolan had always enjoyed crashing Mafia meetings, so that wasn't a problem for him.

The old men guarding the villa grounds didn't look as if they had their hearts in their work. They were probably on duty more because of time-honored Sicilian traditions than for security concerns. The modern Families no longer engaged in multigenerational warfare against one another. It simply wasn't a good business practice. Instead, any disputes that arose were settled in a council of Family leaders. Personal vendettas still existed, but even they were discouraged. Killing people got the police involved, and no one wanted that.

He took no photos and made no notes of the villa's defenses in case they were stopped on the way back to the hotel, but he didn't need to. He had already chosen the avenue of approach he would use and had one in mind for Katz to use, as well.

WHILE BOLAN and Grimaldi were making their recon, Katzenelenbogen sent Jasmine Farjani to take care of a few minor mission-prep chores. With her Italian, she was able to make purchases in town without arousing suspicion. She naturally aroused interest, but only because of her stunning looks, not because she looked out of place.

While the woman was gone, Katz contacted the Farm to see what they had been able to come up with on the Moro Family operations. Within seconds, the portable fax started spitting out hard copy. Kurtzman and his team had been busy, and he saw several Justice Department letterhead items, as well. It was nice to have that kind of backup.

He started reading immediately.

THE MOON WAS DOWN when Bolan began his approach that night through the olive grove. It wouldn't appear in the sky until 4:18 a.m., and by that time, they'd better have this thing wrapped up and be moving on to the mainland. Grimaldi had dropped off Katzenelenbogen at his infiltration point on the other side of the valley before driving the Blazer back up onto the ridgeline to wait.

As Bolan had noted from the recon, the olive trees worked well as a covered avenue of approach, and his NVGs made it the proverbial walk in the park. He had covered three-quarters of the distance when he spotted his first security man sitting under an ancient tree with his back to the trunk. He looked to be asleep with what appeared to be a double-barreled shotgun laid across his lap.

The shotgun wasn't quite a modern security force weapon, but it was a traditional Sicilian accessory. About all it would be good for was early warning for the guards closer to the house. Since early warning was exactly what Bolan couldn't afford to have happen, he moved in to reduce the threat.

Taking his time, he worked his way up behind the tree. When he was close enough to see that this guard was just a teenager, he decided to give the young man a chance to turn his life around. The fact that the kid was sleeping made it easy to give him a break.

A well-tempered blow behind the ear put the young man out cold. Next, a pair of plastic restraints went around his wrists and another on his ankles, with a strip of tape across his mouth to complete the save. Bolan really didn't have much hope that this kid would get smart enough to get out of the Family business. His genetics and culture were working against that happening, but he had to give him a chance to give up the "life."

After laying the kid in a comfortable position, Bolan continued his infiltration. The open ground between the olive trees and the front of the main house was still littered with sedans, so the conference, or whatever it was, was still on. Bolan was glad that he hadn't missed it.

The next guard the Executioner encountered didn't get the break he'd given the first. This guy was in his thirties with a Beretta Model 12 submachine gun cradled in his arms, and that made him fair game. He wasn't sleeping, but he might as well have been. He was leaning back against a waist-high stone wall, smoking and listening to the party noises coming from one wing of the villa. Even Mafia hardmen needed to relax at the end of a long day plotting their next criminal activity.

Bolan quietly moved into a clear firing position, his silenced Beretta 93-R in hand. He stroked the trigger, the silenced pistol chugging out a single round. The man went down without a sound, a 9 mm slug in his brain.

Bolan was reaching to click his com link to signal Katzenelenbogen and Grimaldi that he was inside the security ring when he spotted a flash of shiny movement high on the wall of the main house.

As he went facedown in the dirt to avoid the security camera, he knew he'd been sucked in like a newbie. The traditional old-boy guards during the daytime had been on duty to lure potential intruders into a false sense of security about the villa's defenses. Video cameras weren't a traditional Sicilian architectural feature.

When the camera tracked away again, he crawled over to the body of the guard he'd just put down. Along with the Model 12, he had a two-way radio on his belt and a set of NVGs around his neck. That gear told Bolan that someone in there was watching the grounds closely, and that threw their prepared mission profile out the window. They would have to go free style from now on.

After rolling the body of the dead guard closer to the base of the wall to get him out of range of the camera, he keyed his com link.

"They've got video cameras covering the grounds," he whispered to Katz. "Keep an eye out for them mounted high on the walls."

"Damn," Katz muttered. "That's going to make this dicey, Striker."

"What's new?" Grimaldi broke in. "You want me to join you down there?"

"No," Bolan sent back. "We'll keep to the plan as much as we can, but be ready to make a save."

ALFREDO MORO WAS a traditional Sicilian, but he wasn't a rustic by an means. He was a true child of the electronic age and wasn't at all fearful of modern gadgets. While he had a full complement of electronic toys, his favorites were the things he could use in his business. In his line of work, he well understood the need for security cameras and monitors.

He had only started wiring the compound, though. His uncle had been a hard sell on replacing the old Family retainers with never-blinking electronic eyes. The compromise he'd finally been able to reach with the old Don was that the cameras would only be a backup, and the guards could continue to patrol as they had done for generations. He would have been happier with more cameras and fewer men; he was tired of finding them asleep. But Giovanni had been insistent, and for a couple more years at least, he was still the Moro Family Don.

The men Alfredo had picked to monitor the cameras were young enough not to be afraid of digital readouts and monitors. Like most Western Europeans, their personal lives included DVDs, computers and cell phones. He trusted them to use the security system properly, but he still made a point to wake at least once during the night to check on the security-room guys on duty. He told himself that was what his hero and role model would have done.

Alfredo's favorite American movie of all time wasn't the *Godfather* series, although he did like them; it was *Patton*. When the general had driven the hated Germans from Sicily, men of the Moro Family had fought at the side of the Americans as Partisans. He regretted that he hadn't been born then and had listened avidly to the tales of those glorious days. He had also read everything he could find on the famous American general and liked to think that Patton would have approved of how he conducted his operations. Whenever he was faced with a problem, he just asked himself what Patton would have done and then did just that.

"Anything going on tonight?" he asked Guido, the man on duty.

"No, Alfredo," the man said as he looked up from the screen. "Everything's quiet."

The younger Moro studied the bank of monitors on

the wall. The video coverage of the grounds wasn't as good as he would have liked, and he was waiting for a shipment of infrared sensors he had ordered to come in to fill the gaps. But with the gear he had added to the eyes of the Family retainers, he was confident that he could spot any enemy before they got too close.

"Make sure to wake me if you see anything," he said. "The Chinese are coming in tomorrow for the meeting."

"Will do."

Moro left his command post and went to the guest wing of the villa. The Arabs were still awake and it was good business to stop in and have a quick drink with them. It would be only a quick one, though. He didn't want to have to deal with that damn Chinese with a hangover. Giovanni liked Dong, but he wasn't fond of the sneaky bastard. He could never tell what he was thinking.

NOW THAT HE KNEW the true extent of the villa's defenses, Bolan took extra care. With the video surveillance, sooner or later someone was bound to notice that the foot patrols were being thinned out. It was going to push his time frame, but he had no choice but to do it that way. Assaulting the house while he still had enemies on the prowl was a recipe for certain disaster.

Keeping one eye out for cameras, he made a counterclockwise tour of the outer grounds, his silenced 93-R in his hand. Katz moved in, as well. Between the two of them, they took out the eight-man security team without a hitch.

Once the last guard was down, it was time to do the break-and-enter before the guy behind the monitor noticed that his men were AWOL. With all of the activities that seemed to be going on in the west wing, Bolan decided to start there. Taking out whoever was in there should cut down the odds against them tremendously.

"Go with flash-bangs," he said to Katz, who had slipped in beside him.

"Good idea."

Snatching a flash-bang from his harness, Bolan thumbed the fuse. "On my count...three...two... one!"

He side-armed the stun grenade through the window and heard it crash inside right before it detonated. An instant later, he was through the blown-out window, the guns in his hands blazing fire.

ALFREDO MORO HAD just gone to bed when the grenades went off. Springing to his feet, he got back into his pants and ran into the hallway barefoot and shirtless.

"What is going on?" he asked the man on duty in the security room.

"I don't know." The man switched from one video camera to the next without seeing anything out of the ordinary.

"Where is Don Giovanni?"

"His bedroom?" the man replied. "I have not seen him since he went to bed."

Moro snatched a two-way radio and a Beretta Model 12 submachine gun from a rack on the wall. "I'm going to the guest wing."

"Wait until the men come, Alfredo," the security man implored.

That might have been the safest thing to do, but Alfredo Moro knew that his hero wouldn't have waited. Patton had never waited for reinforcements, and he had always admired his officers who led from the front. He had also buried a lot of them for that very reason.

Even knowing that, Alfredo Moro rolled the dice. If he foiled an attack on the Family, his name would be remembered for generations.

"Just tell them where I have gone," he said as he raced off.

CHAPTER SIXTEEN

Alfredo Moro wasn't the only man in the Moro compound who was rudely awakened by the flash-bang detonations. A few of the men in the party room of the villa's west wing had drunk themselves into a stupor, while others were dozing in the discreet cubicles with one of the working girls the Moros had provided for their guests. Some of the guests, though, were still sober enough to know when they were being attacked.

Even though these men were honored guests of the Moros, they were well-armed guests. When their eyes cleared from the flash of the grenades, they scrambled toward their weapons, but they weren't quite quick enough.

Bolan had come through the window with both hands full of tooled steel spitting flame. Close-range snap shooting at half-drunken men wasn't a test of his markmanship skills by any means, but it did keep him occupied for a few moments.

A Slavic-looking man who had rolled off his chair

and was digging for the iron in his shoulder holster was number one. Two was a Moro man reaching for a shotgun leaning against the wall. And that was just as Bolan made his entry. The third was a snap shot as he spun away to the left.

Katz had come through the adjoining window and was performing the other half of this well-practiced battle ballet of theirs. He landed in a combat crouch and was putting down a base of fire in 3-round bursts from his Uzi, getting hits each time. Seeing Bolan roll away, he hosed down the gunman tracking the Executioner before moving on himself.

Bolan scratched Katz's back in return when a naked man jumped out from one of the cubicles behind him with a gun in his hand. A well-placed .44 Magnum slug slammed him back into the cubicle.

After the opening round, things quickly got hectic. Even the most drunken man could be brought around by enough gunfire going off around him. Screaming women added to the confusion, but at least they'd had the good sense to take immediate cover facedown on the floor.

Most of the previously comatose partyers made the mistake of reacting instead of selecting the only intelligent option left open to them, surrendering.

Even so, Bolan had his hands full for a long moment. A hasty shot aimed through blurry eyes sang past his head from behind. Since he was placing a controlled 3-round burst into a guy's chest at that moment, he had no choice but to let Katz pull off the save. The stutter of the Uzi told him he was clear.

The last guy standing had grabbed a Czech-made Skorpion subgun. But he didn't have time to fold out the buttstock. A final .44 round punched his ticket, and all was quiet.

BY THE TIME Alfredo Moro reached the corridor leading to the west wing, he was no longer alone. A trio of half-dressed Family retainers had joined him. The young heir was crazy, but Don Giovanni would slowly roast them over an open fire if they allowed him to get hurt.

Had the Moro gunmen arrived just a few moments earlier, they might have had a better chance of survival. As it was, they raced up to the door of the party room a second after Bolan's last shot, and their pounding feet sounded loud in the sudden silence.

Bolan dropped the half-empty mag in his Desert Eagle and refreshed it before putting three shots through the closed door at chest level. A fourth shot into the door lock sprang it open enough for Katz to dump half a mag of 9 mm rounds in a single burst. Much of that stitched Alfredo Moro across the belly.

The young Moro had a look of complete disbelief on his face but a firm grip on his Model 12 when Bolan punched his lights out.

From there, it took only a few minutes to clean out the rest of the house.

In the process, they came across an old man in

pajamas lying dead in a hallway of the main house, his hand clutching his left arm. They ignored him and moved on.

FROM A HILLTOP position overlooking the Moro compound, Jack Grimaldi watched and listened over the com link as the battle played out below them. The pilot would have rather been down in the dirt with Katz and Bolan, but he was the cavalry. If the assault turned to crud, the Blazer was their escape vehicle.

Beside him, Jasmine Farjani also listened over her com link. Unlike just a few days earlier, she was now able to listen to the fighting without being frightened. She had come a long way from the naive young woman who had sailed off to a new job in America not so long ago. She knew that she'd never be as brave as Belasko and his comrades, but she'd never go back to what she'd been before. Wherever she ended up, though, from now on she was going to control her own destiny and never again be a pawn for anyone, male or female.

"Jack," Katz's voice said over the com link, "we're clear down here. Come on in from the back."

"On the way."

The pilot reached down to give Jasmine a hand getting up. "Let's go."

KATZ VECTORED Grimaldi down to the rear of the villa and met him when he pulled up.

"Clean sweep?" the pilot asked when he saw that he had almost run over a corpse.

"Looks that way," Katz said. "Unfortunately I don't think there's anyone left to talk to."

"Bummer."

Katz nodded toward Farjani in the cab of the Blazer. "I think we'd better leave her in the truck while we do the sweep. It's pretty messy in there."

"I can take it," she replied as she stepped out.

"Are you sure?"

She locked eyes with him. "I'm sure."

Katz shrugged. "Okay."

THE WEST WING of the villa was an abattoir. Almost twenty bodies lay scattered in the party room alone. A half-dozen women huddled in a corner. None of them appeared to be hurt, but they were blood spattered and scared out of their minds.

"Tell them that we're not going to hurt them," Katz told Farjani. "As soon as we're done here, we'll let them go. Caution them to forget us, though. Tell them that if they talk about us to anyone in any way, we will return."

Farjani knew that the men wouldn't hurt these women, but she made the threat anyway. The whores all vowed on the Holy Mother that they would say nothing.

Bolan and Katz didn't have to check passports in the party room to know that most of the casualties weren't Sicilians. There weren't too many harsh-faced, tall Slavic blondes on the island. Most of the foreigners, though, were Middle Eastern. Katz spotted a couple of men who were obviously Turks or Greeks, but most of them appeared to be Arabs. They did, though, take their IDs to run them past the Farm.

In their search, they found a Arab who had taken a blow to the head, from the looks of it by an exploding flash-bang fuse. He was still out, but appeared to be otherwise unhurt. Before he could regain consciousness, Katz bound the man's hands behind his back with a plastic riot restraint. Another one secured his ankles. The captive was then sat in a chair, and Katz slapped him awake.

The man's eyes fluttered open and he looked around in shock. "Who are you?" he asked in Arabic.

"Who are *you?*" Katz replied.

"I am Musa Ghenzarli," the Arab replied. "What do you want with me?"

"We are looking for a group of kidnapped women," Katz answered.

The Arab looked around at the carnage again in disbelief. "This was all about women?"

"It was."

The Arab frowned. "But they're just women, and they're not even women of our people. We sold them to the Italians, and they moved them on."

"Where did they go?"

"I do not know." The Arab shrugged as best he could with his hands tied behind his back. "They are not any of my business now."

Farjani had been following the conversation and turned to Bolan. "Sir, may I borrow your blade?" she asked loudly in Arabic.

Bolan glanced at Katz. "She wants your knife," the Israeli translated.

Bolan drew his Tanto, handed it to her hilt first and was surprised to see her take it properly. Most women held a knife with the blade extending down from the bottom of their hand, but she had grasped it blade up.

Leaning down over the Arab, she slid the blade under his belt and sliced through it as if it were paper. Another swipe went through the belt band of his trousers into the upper leg, cutting the cloth without touching his skin.

The Arab was shocked speechless.

Looking up at Katz, Farjani asked in Arabic. "I heard some pigs out there, didn't I?"

Going along with her game, Katz nodded and said, "There's a large pen of them by the barn, big female pigs."

"Good." She smiled. "Because I am going to feed this scrawny pig's withered manhood to his pig sisters."

The Arab yelped and tried to stand, but found the point of the Tanto pricking his neck.

"Please," Farjani said, smiling, her green eyes locked on his, "thrust your neck onto the knife so I do not have to soil my hand with your pig blood."

"In God's holy name," the man pleaded to Katz,

"get this witch away from me, she's a demon. You're a man of the book, don't let me die this way."

Katz kept the smile from his face. "She's concerned about a cousin of hers who is missing. She thinks the girl was taken to be a whore, and she wants to get her back."

Bolan's Arabic was limited, so he left the ball in Katz and Jasmine's court. Anyone who thought that women were the weaker of the sexes had never seen them in action, and Jasmine Farjani wasn't the first fierce woman he'd seen. He had to admit, though, that he was surprised at the transformation. But discovering the women imprisoned in Alexandria had tripped something off deep inside her.

So long as it was useful, he'd keep a close eye on it and let her run with it.

The Arab started to speak rapidly in Arabic, and Bolan's comprehension completely dropped off.

"They're in a hideout somewhere," Katz said, translating, "but he's not sure where. If they're still in Italy, the Mafia has them, but they were determined to be sold to the Union Corse in France."

The Union Corse was the French version of the old Italian Mob Families. They, too, had been in the crime business for generations, but unlike the Italians, they hadn't immigrated in droves to the New World. For a time, they had been the major heroin connection in America, but now they were into anything that could make them a criminal dollar. With white slavery being a booming business right now, it wasn't surprising that they would have a hand in it.

"Where in Italy and France?"

"Naples and Marseilles."

Since they were so close, Bolan thought, it made sense for them to stop by Naples next.

"Get everything he knows about Naples," Bolan said.

After interrogating the man for another five minutes, Katz turned to Bolan. "What do you want to do with him?" he asked in English.

"The pigs." Farjani snapped her head toward the door leading to the barn outside. "I'm going to cut him so he bleeds and feed him to the pigs."

"Please, not that," the Arab suddenly said in accented English.

"And why not?" Farjani answered in the same language as calmly as if he had refused a second cup of tea. "You're a pig and not fit for anything else."

"In Allah's name—" tears came to the man's eyes as he turned to Katz "—give me a clean death."

Katz paused long enough to raise the guy's blood pressure another point or two. "Tell us what you know of the Chinese involvement in this slave traffic," he said in Arabic, "and you might live to see the dawn."

Again he simultaneously translated as their captive spoke in rapid-fire Arabic. "He says that he has never met the Chinese slave traders himself. He only knows what the others have said about them. He thinks that their leader name's Dong or something like that. He says they pay well for educated young women who speak Western languages."

"That fits the profile," Bolan said. "Does he know who this Dong works for?"

"He says that it's widely known that he's an officer of the Chinese secret service."

Bolan didn't have to say what that meant. The sound in his mind was of that last vital piece clicking into place like the slamming of a vault door. They'd known that the Chinese were involved, and things like the special-ops hardware had pointed to a Beijing-sanctioned operation, but this clinched it.

And it all fit. He had known that whoever was backing the Dragon Egg hardmen had money. It took big bucks to field an operation of that scope. Knowing that they were official answered the question of who was picking up their tab. It also told him why they had been so bold and persistent even when they'd been getting their butts kicked. When Beijing paid people to do something, they expected to get their money's worth.

It also meant that they needed to be on the move again, quickly.

Now that the questioning seemed to be over, Farjani asked again, "Can I kill him now?"

Bolan took her arm and led her out into the hallway. "You don't really want to do that, Jasmine," he told her. "I know you think you want to kill him. But, believe me, if you do, you'll regret it."

"But what can I do?" She looked up at him, her eyes tearing. "I'm not really much use to you and Lev in putting an end to this terrible thing, and I'm not helping all the young girls like my sister."

Bolan held her gaze. "You're helping us more than you know, Jasmine. You handled that Arab beautifully in there. We'd have never been able to get him to break as easily as you did. You scared him much more than we could have."

"Really?"

"Really. And because you got to him, he gave us the critical piece of information that we've been missing."

"What are you going to do with him?" she asked.

"Jack's going to take him across to Italy and put him on a plane back to where he came from."

"That doesn't seem like much punishment."

"It will be when he goes back to his organization," Bolan promised her. "They'll kill him for you."

"Just as long as he dies."

"I think we can count on that."

THEIR BUSINESS with the Moros concluded, Bolan and the others went into their planned egress mode with a minimum of fuss. After dropping off Jack Grimaldi at his chopper, they drove to the rendezvous point they had used previously to wait for him to join them with the chopper. Once Grimaldi touched down, they loaded their gear and their captive on the chopper for transport to the Italian mainland.

As soon as his rotor beat faded into the night sky, they drove the Blazer to Messina and took the early-morning ferry to the mainland. After arriving at Salerno, Bolan called a halt and they checked into a small hotel. Not only did they need the rest, he wanted to contact the Farm.

So far, they'd pretty much been running free form, shooting at what ever popped up and moving on to the next target. Now that they had a firm handle on who was pulling the strings, Bolan wanted to pause and regroup. Doing what came naturally had always been a good formula for him, but planning and intelligence gathering had their benefits, as well. Between Katz's tactical mind and Kurtzman's cyber crew, he didn't figure to be out of action for long.

CHAPTER SEVENTEEN

Palermo, Sicily

Gao Dong and the three experienced Dragon Egg operatives he had picked from the survivors of the Alexandria debacle landed at the airport in Palermo with valid passports identifying them as Taiwanese businessmen. The Moro Family was well-known for the variety of its commercial activities, and businessmen wanting to see Giovanni Moro weren't uncommon. A helpful customs officer quickly cleared them and directed Dong to the car-rental agency.

When Dong approached the Moro compound down the dirt road through the olive grove, he saw that the place was crawling with police in full riot gear. When an ambulance pulled out, he turned off the road to let it pass. Another one soon followed behind it.

Not wanting to draw attention to himself by running away, Dong decided to go on in. Whatever had happened here, he needed to know about it. He'd been depending on Don Moro to give him the cover he needed while he tried to locate the Yankee who was tormenting him.

He had no sooner stopped the car when a police officer walked up to the open driver's-side window. "Passport," the officer demanded in Italian.

Dong smiled what he hoped looked like a nervous smile. "I am very sorry," he said in English. "But I do not speak good Italian."

The cop called out and another officer walked up. "Show me your passport," he asked in English.

"I am here to see Giovanni Moro," Dong said as he handed it over.

"You are too late." The cop smiled, but it wasn't friendly. "He is dead along with most of his family."

"What a terrible accident," Dong replied.

"Accident?" The cop laughed. "This was no accident. Someone broke in last night and killed every last one of the Moro bastards and their friends."

Dong really looked shocked. "Who would do such a terrible thing?"

"Who cares." The cop shrugged. "We will find them, and when I do, I am going to give them a gold medal and a handshake. The Moros were not nice people." The cop turned serious. "What is, I mean, what was your business with the Moro Family?"

"Light bulbs," Dong answered without missing a beat. "My company in Taiwan makes light bulbs, and Giovanni Moro was looking for a new supplier."

Since Moro had a legitimate electrical-supply operation, the cop bought the cover story. "He's really

going to need a few light bulbs where he's going."
He laughed.

"Please?" Dong frowned. "I do not understand."

"He's going to the darkest pits of Hell. Not much
light down there."

Dong had no answer to that. Christian mythology
held no interest for him.

"And," the cop continued, "since the man you
came to see is no more, I suggest that you leave before we run you in for questioning."

"Since I have no more business here, sir," Dong
said, "I will call on my other customers."

"That is a good idea," the cop said as he handed
Dong his passport. "A very good idea."

As Dong carefully turned his car, he saw the cop
take down the rental plate number. They would have
to switch to their alternative passports before they
boarded the next plane. The question was where he
would go next.

He wasn't too surprised at the attack. It had only
proved the vulnerability he had spotted in all of the
Italians' operations. He understood the value of family, but to trust poorly trained men to guard you simply because they were family wasn't wise. The Union
Corse was also organized along family lines, but its
leaders weren't willing to put up with incompetence
and weren't above killing their own to improve the
breed. He would go to them next rather than risk himself any further in Italy.

Naples

WHEN THE TRIO checked into its bay-front hotel in Naples, Katz felt as if he were on a never-ending tour of the world's greatest port cities.

Naples had once been Nea Polis, a Greek port founded back when Rome had just been a village of mud huts. Since then, it had changed hands so many times that even the city's official historian had a difficult time trying to keep track of the comings and goings of everyone from Vikings through the Moors to the French. At all times, though, it had been an important port city.

Visiting NATO warships, oil tankers, bulk carriers and countless smaller cargo freighters all called at Naples. Since much of the Sicilian Mafia's dealings involved sea transport, it had always been important to them, as well. Many of the safehouses they had established long ago to store smuggled cigarettes now held heroin, hash and cocaine. Others had been recently refurbished to house slaves in transit. As they always said in business school, all that counted was location, location, location, and Naples had it in spades.

The problem Katz was going to have planning their excursions here was that while their Arab informer had given them the general location of these places, he hadn't been to the sites himself and couldn't provide the kind of details they needed. With Naples being a Mafia company town, it wasn't going to be easy for him and Bolan to recon freely without being spotted by someone's unfriendly eyes.

THE FIRST THING Bolan did after they were checked in to their hotel was to contact the Farm. He had reported right after the Moro takedown, and it was time to see if Kurtzman had worked his magic again.

"I was just about to call you," Kurtzman told him. "Hunt came up with something that might clue us to the guy you're after. He hacked into a Beijing state security site and came across something they're calling the Special Economic Project."

"That sounds promising."

"It does," Kurtzman agreed. "It appears that they've formalized their technology-raiding operations and they're being run out of this office. Anyway, it turns out that their operative heading it is named Dong, Gao Dong, educated in England, where he was known as George. We pulled up an old university photo of him, but that's about all. The Chinese are even worse about photos of their spies than Galen was."

The legendary German spy master, Galen, was known for only one photo ever having been taken of him and even that was before he had taken over the Abwehr.

"What's really interesting, though, is that this guy runs what are called Dragon Egg teams."

"Bingo," Bolan said. "The tattoos."

"Yeah." Kurtzman laughed. "Some guys have to

mark themselves so they can remember who in the hell they are when they wake up drunk. Think of all the guys with *'Semper Fi'* on their arms.

"Anyway, the best part is that it appears that Dong isn't in very good odor in the Forbidden City right now. We found a 'kill on sight' order on him and all of his people."

"That tells me that we've been pretty successful."

"Looks that way," Kurtzman agreed. "The bad thing is that, not surprisingly, Dong's evaporated. The last report of him is from Alexandria."

"Do you have a feeling for how many men we're dealing with here?" Bolan asked.

"Not really." Kurtzman admitted. "But with a price on his head, he can't have all that many friends. That kind of thing's contagious, you know."

Bolan chuckled. "If that's the case, he's going to need to find a place to hide, and I think he's likely to try to disappear here in Europe. Since he appears to have contacts in the Euro mobs, I'm sure they'd welcome him."

"That's likely. What do you need from us to sort this out?"

"First off," Bolan replied, "I need everything you have on Naples's resident bad boys. Particularly anyone who's allied with the late Moro Family. You might ask Hal to hit up his buddies in the carabinieri on that one, as well. And if this Naples thing falls into place, we'll be moving on to Marseilles next, so that means we'll need anything you have on the Union Corse."

"You've just given a new definition to the term 'data dump.' And the Union's going to be a little more difficult," he warned up front. "The gendarmes have been hitting them pretty hard lately, so they've been laying pretty low.

"In fact—" he paused to call up a new menu "—if I remember correctly, they just popped a bunch of them for running a slave operation, as well."

"That would fit in with what we got from the Moro raid informant," Bolan replied.

"Yeah…here it is," Kurtzman cut back in. "The headline reads 'Union Corse Warehouse Raided, Over Twenty Illegal Immigrants Found.'"

"What's the date on that?"

"Last week."

"Send me hard copy on that one for sure."

"Will do," Kurtzman replied. "You might want to tell Katz to stock up on printer paper, as we'll have a lot of stuff coming to you."

"Just keep it coming."

"And," Kurtzman said, "now that Hunt's deep in Beijing's cyber knickers, I'll keep him rooting around and see what else we can come up with on this Dong guy."

"Good. We're going to have to take care of him for this to be over."

BOLAN AND KATZ SPENT the afternoon going over the background Aaron Kurtzman sent on the Sicilian and

Italian Mob Families. Hal Brognola had even included some classified Justice Department intelligence reports that hadn't yet been entered into the Farm's data banks. By nightfall, they were locked and loaded to take their act on the road to see if they could rattle the cages of a local organization known as the Tamboli Family.

This was a mainland branch of the Moros whose job was to serve as their middlemen and run the cargo-shipment operations. No matter what the Moro cargo—heroin, weapons or women—the Tamboli Family was involved with its movement. With the Moro compound out of business, the old Don, his successor and the Family leaders all dead, the Tambolis stood to inherit one of the largest Mafia operations on the continent. Bolan's mission, as he saw it, was to make sure that they didn't.

To do that, though, was going to take a bold plan. Fortunately Katz had a patent on that kind of operation. It shouldn't take him long to put something together that would bring down the House of Tamboli.

KURTZMAN'S DATA showed that, like the American Mafia Families, the Tambolis had legitimate front operations. In their case, a couple of tourist hotels and nice restaurants gave them all the front they needed to cover their other operations. Along with the tips to the more upscale establishment of the Tamboli empire, Katz had been given the address of a strip club reputed to be a family hangout.

With those addresses to work with, Katz and Bolan sat down with a map. "How do you want to do this?" Katz asked.

"Let's start off with a bang," Bolan suggested. "I don't want to spend too much time with this. The Moro job will have these guys a bit jumpy anyway, so we're not going to be able to sneak up on them. I think if we slam them hard, like we did in Alexandria, the Chinese will pull out rather than get caught up in it. I don't think that Dong's going to want to go to the wall here in Naples."

"You're thinking that he'll move on to his Union contacts, then?"

"That's what I'm hoping. So far we've chased him from L.A. to Sicily, and he hasn't been able to stop us yet. By this time, he'll have found out about the Moro takedown and won't be comfortable about trusting the Tambolis."

"But the Corsicans are a different bunch," Katz finished for him. "They're hard-core and eat Italian Mafia punks for lunch."

"That's what I hope he's thinking."

"And if he isn't?"

Bolan shrugged. "I'll worry about that after we thin out these scumbags."

CHAPTER EIGHTEEN

When Bolan, Katzenelenbogen and Farjani hit the streets of Naples that evening, they were locked and loaded. They had no expectations that they would be able to put the Tamboli Family out of business in one night as they had done to the Moros. That had been a fluke. But they would hurt them and hopefully free some girls. If nothing else, they would cause enough damage that the Italian authorities would have to become interested in what was going on.

Katz was staying with the bordello-manager cover story he'd used in Beirut. There was a risk in using it again if Chamoun had mentioned his name to the slavers in Alexandria and they had passed it on, but the risk was small and they didn't have the time to work up another angle. By striking fast, they'd be out of town before anyone had the time to do much background on them.

Bolan wasn't bothering with a cover because once they cornered the opposition, he was simply going to kill them. He could smell the enemy in Naples, and the stench told him to be more than alert. He was in one of the home cities of his oldest enemies, and he wasn't unknown to them. Not that they would recognize him on sight, but the legends of the Executioner were as well-known to them as they were to their stateside cousins. But while they might not recognize *him.* he knew exactly whom he was going after.

STOP NUMBER ONE on the target list was the nicest of the three restaurants the Tamboli Family operated, an upscale place habituated by the local Italian elite. Bolan and Katz didn't think that they would encounter any of the Family's gunmen on duty there, but it would be a great opening diversion for act two.

As he had expected, the rear door was unguarded and opened wide to cool off the kitchen. Inside, the staff was busy preparing the sauces, soups and pastries for the evening's customers. Everyone was so busy, in fact, that a blacksuited Bolan was able to enter unnoticed. Walking up behind a man in a big cook's hat, he tapped him on the shoulder.

The man turned, finding the barrel of a Beretta aimed at his head and Bolan holding a finger to his lips. The cook wasn't a stupid man, and froze. When Bolan pointed at the door, the cook nodded in relief. A single unsilenced shot into the ceiling got everyone's attention.

"Out! Out! Out!" Bolan motioned toward the door.

Most of the kitchen staff knew who was signing their paychecks and knew better than to get involved in a Mafia turf war. At the first sign of a gun, they split.

Now that he had the kitchen to himself, Bolan decided that the big tiled oven against the wall would be a great place to start. It was big enough to contain the blast, yet still would cause enough debris to completely trash the kitchen. He pulled the fuse lighter on the small satchel charge and tossed it into the hot oven with the pastries.

Exiting quickly, he closed the door behind him and sprinted down the alley. He had gone only a few steps before the kitchen went up with a bang.

KATZ WAS TWO BLOCKS away behind the wheel of their rental car when the restaurant blew up. "You're up next," he told Farjani.

She smiled as she punched in the number of the news desk at the local TV station on her cell phone. "I am the spokesperson for the Decency Brigade of Naples," she said in her best Italian. "I have an important announcement to make. Are you taping this call?"

"Yes, I am," the TV man answered. "Go ahead."

She read from the paper she and Katz had prepared:

"There has just been an explosion at La Traviata restaurant. Everyone knows that establishment is owned by criminals of the Tamboli Mafia Family, but they ignore it and do nothing about it. We of the Decency Brigade are tired of taking our families, our innocent children, into places that are owned by gangsters and pretending that they are not. What kind of message is that sending to our children? To save our families from this pollution, we are dedicated to ridding our city of these criminals. If the police and the courts cannot do it, we most assuredly will. Long live decency!''

She clicked off and turned to Katz. "How'd I do?"

"Great." He grinned. "You've got a great career ahead of you in broadcast news. You're sure to be picked up to be the next Connie Chung."

Farjani frowned. "Who's she?"

Katz laughed.

"Coming up on your six," Bolan's voice came in over the com link.

"Welcome aboard." Katz hit the starter of the Lancia as Bolan slipped into the back seat.

THE NEXT STOP on Bolan's target list wasn't caught napping. While cell phones worked well for them in their operations, they worked equally well for the opposition. The manager of the restaurant had placed a panicked call to the Tambolis before the dust had even settled.

The two gunmen standing outside the lighted back door were visibly nervous. Both openly packed silenced Beretta subguns, the weapon of choice in that part of Italy. One of them, though, had his piece slung over his shoulder so he could fan the air with his hand Italian style while he shouted over his cell phone.

With only one gunner ready for action, Bolan targeted him first with his own silenced Beretta product, the selector switch flicked to burst mode. One barely audible 9 mm pop, no problem.

The guy on the cell phone turned at the sound of his partner's body hitting the cobblestones. For a frozen instant, he couldn't decide if he should keep on using his off hand as a speaking aid or go for his gun.

While he was making up his mind, Bolan killed him.

Figuring that there would be more gunmen inside, the Executioner unclipped a pair of flash-bang grenades from his assault harness. Rather than storming inside and trying to sort out the Mafia gunman from the cooks and dishwashers, he decided to let them come out into the lighted alley where it wouldn't be so difficult.

Opening the door a crack, he thumbed the fuses on the grenades and side-armed them in, one to the left, one to the right. He closed the door and stepped back.

The twin detonations reverberated like the crack of doom and were followed by panicked shouting. The door slammed open, and men in cook whites splattered with tomato sauce charged out in blind, screaming panic. One of the bombs had to have ended up in a simmering sauce pot.

Bolan gave the cooks a pass. He wasn't after guys working for a paycheck. They might want to carefully consider who was signing those paychecks next time they went for a job interview, though. Working for scumbags carried on-the-job risks that usually weren't covered by worker's compensation.

He was beginning to think that the two gunmen out back had been the extent of the security when three more thugs stormed out, their unsilenced subguns blazing. Their blind fire sent the fleeing kitchen staff face first on the cobblestones.

To keep the fleeing cooks from becoming collateral-damage statistics, Bolan took the gunmen under fire. The first one went down to a 3-round burst without a clue.

The other two were so wired on adrenaline that they didn't seek cover, but spun and emptied their magazines in Bolan's direction. This time he sought the cobblestones as the fire flashed over him. But prone or standing didn't make any difference to him. Two quick 3-round bursts sent the gunmen to join their late comrades.

Getting to his feet, Bolan exited the alley. Phase one was complete and the night was still young. Now it was time for Katz and Jasmine to go into their routine while he stood guard on their backs.

BOLAN HAD HIT the Tamboli restaurants early for two reasons. Since Italians ate late by American standards, fewer people would be in them that early, which would limit possible innocent casualties. Second it would get everyone's attention focused early. With the "Decency Brigade's" TV announcement already going out over the airwaves, hopefully both the Mafia and the cops would be looking in the wrong place.

Katz pulled the Lancia to the curb in front of their hotel, where he and Farjani got out. "See you later," he said as Bolan slid into the driver's seat.

Bolan shot him a thumbs-up as he drove away.

"Shall we go, my dear?" Katz took the woman's arm to escort her to the waiting limousine.

JASMINE FARJANI stepped out of the back of the limo in front of the Kit Kat Klub and held the door open. Katz emerged, an opera cape thrown over the shoulders of his Armani suit, and strode for the club's entrance. His eyes flicked up to the gaudy, flashing neon sign depicting a nude woman in high heels waving a martini glass in one hand and a cigarette holder in the other. Neither the sign nor the club's name was very original, but what could you expect from the Italian Mob?

Farjani reached the club's door before he did and had it open before he even needed to break stride. "Thank you, my dear," he said in French as he stepped inside.

She went up to the bouncer and announced him as Lev Bronski, an associate of Giovanni Moro.

That got the appropriate response.

The club's manager anxiously raced out to greet a friend of the recently deceased Mafia Don.

"Have you heard?" the manager asked in Italian.

Farjani translated into French, and Katz replied in the same language. "Heard what?"

"Don Giovanni! He is dead! And all his family!"

"*Mort?*" Katz allowed himself to know that much Italian.

"*¡Sí!*" the manager launched into a rapid-fire delivery of the news accompanied with much waving hands. Farjani didn't miss a beat as she gave a running translation.

"What a tragedy." Katz looked properly shocked. "I must admit that I am surprised. I had thought that the days of vendetta were long past."

He put his arm around the man's shoulder. "That does present me with a problem, though," he said. "Maybe we can talk about it inside?"

"*¡Sí!*" the manager led him in.

For all the Vegas-style flash outside, the Kit Kat Klub was just another strip joint. An elegant strip joint to be sure, but it had the same tired ambience of all such establishments with one addition. The added attraction was that there were several well-armed men scattered around the room. They weren't packing openly, but the posture and the loose cut of their jackets was all Katz needed to see.

"A table at the stage?" the manager asked.

"Somewhere we can talk, please."

"Of course."

The manager showed Katz and Farjani to a table along one side wall. As soon as they were seated, the manager snapped his fingers and the waiter hurried to bring a bottle of champagne. After the champagne was poured, the manager asked, "Is there anything else I can do to assist you?"

"There is." Katz handed over his card. "Please have a seat."

"Thank you." The manager sat. "What can I do for you?"

Katz leaned close. "I was expecting to go on to Sicily tomorrow to inspect a shipment from Alexandria for my organization in Moscow."

He glanced toward the stage to indicate what kind of goods he was interested in.

"From what you have told me tonight," he continued, "the purchases I intended to make will not be available there, and that creates a problem for me. I oversee a group of gentlemen's clubs—" he gestured broadly to take in the strip joint "—not unlike your own establishment here. And my principals want to freshen up their stock. I'm sure you understand that wealthy customers become sated with the same tired old goods."

"I understand perfectly." The manager brightened immediately. This man was speaking his language. "It so happens that I can put you in touch with the man who worked with Don Giovanni in this trade. I can assure you that he will be able to fulfill your requirements with fully trained staff."

"Excellent!" Katz beamed.

"I will make a phone call." The manager excused himself.

ALL THE TIME SHE WAS translating from French to Italian and back, Farjani kept her eyes on the girls on the stage. One of them had the unmistakable combination of features and coloration that could only be Arabic. There was another one who wouldn't have looked out of place on the streets of her own hometown of Calcutta, and there were some Slavic faces, as well. Unless she was dead wrong, these girls were more slaves who had come through the Alexandria pipeline.

She also knew that dancing nude on a stage wasn't the worst these women were having to endure. These men wouldn't be satisfied with that; the women were too beautiful. She had escaped being forced into prostitution, and had a vast amount of empathy for what these women were going through. She could take heart, though, because she was fully confident that Belasko and Bronski wouldn't leave them in slavery very much longer.

"I'm in place," she heard Belasko's voice say over the tiny earpiece she was wearing.

"Come on in," Bronski replied softly. "The water's fine. Just give me a heads-up when you're ready to hit the main room."

BOLAN KNEW that going in through the back door of the club wasn't going to be easy. Gangster hangouts were never left unguarded, and this one was no exception. Two men stood guard with the subguns he had come to expect. These two, though, looked to be alert and the setup didn't lend itself to the long-range silenced head shot.

For this excursion, he had changed back into civilian clothing, shirt and pants with a sailor's long coat that could hide a multitude of things and let him get in closer. Affecting a drunken stagger, he approached the two gunmen. The unlit cigarette in the corner of his mouth gave him a reason to talk to them.

The gunmen were accustomed to seeing drunken sailors wandering the back alleys of Naples. The town was the favorite port of call in the Mediterranean, and sailors were famous for getting a load on when they reached dry land.

"Light?" Bolan pantomimed flicking a lighter as he walked up. "Light?"

One of the gunmen chuckled in Italian. "Drunken bastard," he said, but pulled out a plastic disposable lighter from his pocket.

"Thanks," Bolan slurred as he fired up. "Ya wanna cigarette?"

"Okay." The man with the lighter laughed. "Marlboro?"

"Yeah, Marlboro." Bolan grinned slack-faced.

Bolan stumbled up to him, his hand digging in his coat pocket. When it came out, though, he wasn't holding a Marlboro, but his Tanto knife. The chisel-pointed blade slammed into the side of the man's neck, severing his windpipe, carotid and jugular.

Since Bolan was bigger than the Italian, the other gunman didn't see the attack. When he glanced over, all he saw was the drunk turned toward him now and his hand in motion. He died before he could bring his subgun into action.

After taking out the security light and rolling the bodies out of the way, Bolan tried the rear door of the club. As he had hoped, it wasn't locked. He shrugged out of his sailor's coat and readied his weapons.

"I've got the back door," he whispered over the com link.

"Bring it on," Katz replied.

THE ITALIAN WALKING past the back door when Bolan opened it barely looked up. The manager had sent him to bring out Marina, the Russian with the big breasts and the little black who danced with her—Salt and Pepper, as they were called—for his special guest. Plus no one came in by the back door unless he had a good reason to do so.

He did look up, however, when the man blocked his path. He automatically raised the riding crop in his hand, but didn't strike. Facing the sound suppressor on the muzzle of Bolan's 93-R froze him in place. The finger on Bolan's lips told him not to cry out for help because it would come too late.

Bolan slammed the pistol against the side of the

man's head, and he crumpled to the carpet. A strip of tape over his mouth and two plastic restraints secured him.

Deciding to explore the back rooms first, Bolan continued on the way the Italian had been headed.

CHAPTER NINETEEN

A door fitted with a locking bar stood at the end of the club's hallway, but the lock was unsecured. Figuring this to be the place he was looking for, Bolan went in. It was a double-sized combination dressing room and sparse lounge for almost two dozen women. They appeared to be from almost every major ethnic group on the planet, and the only thing they shared was their advanced state of undress. Most of them wore only a G-string.

No one looked up as he entered, so Bolan said, "Excuse me, ladies. Does anyone here speak English?"

Everyone in the room turned fear-filled eyes to face him and the gun in his hand, but there was no panic.

"I do," a Slavic-looking, long-haired blonde hesitantly said.

"Me, too," someone added.

"Okay," Bolan said. "There's going to be some shooting in the club in a little while. Please tell the other girls to get dressed and take cover on the floor in here. When the shooting's over, run out the back door and get out on the street. When the police come, they will help you.''

"The guards?'' the blonde asked quietly, fear showing in her eyes.

"*Fini.* No one will stop you.''

"The girls who are dancing on the stage now?'' a dark-haired girl asked. "Will you help them, too? One of them is my sister.''

"I'll see that they stay safe, too,'' he promised.

"How about the girls who aren't here tonight?'' the blonde asked. "We have friends being held by these bastards.''

"Where are they?''

"The Tamboli Family has a big villa on the hill at Via Legioni. There's a modern building inside the walls that they use for—what is the word?—a dormitory.''

"That's the word,'' Bolan replied. "We'll go there after we're done here.''

"Please don't forget them.'' The blonde teared up. "They rape us and make us do things so we will have to be whores for them.''

"I won't leave them there,'' Bolan vowed.

KATZ HAD BRIEFED Bolan on the positions of the six gunmen he had positively identified, as well as two other possibles. His money was on there being more than just those, but they had to start somewhere.

"Not yet,'' he said. "But give me six-zero to clear

the glassware from the table. I don't want to get chopped up by broken champagne flutes.''

''Six-zero it is.''

''He's on the way, my dear.'' Katz leaned toward his companion. ''You might want to take cover under the table.''

''No way,'' she said, her right hand in her purse gripping a pistol. ''This time, I will not hide.''

BOLAN'S ENTRY into the club's main room went unnoticed. The gyrating dancers were stripped down to their bare skin, and all male eyes were on the stage. To open the play, he walked up behind the nearest of the targets Katz had ID'd. The man was sweating as he stared unblinkingly and didn't even notice when Bolan brushed against the shoulder rig showing through his thin jacket.

He was packing, so Bolan put the muzzle of his unsilenced Beretta into his beefy side and pulled the trigger. Since this was a contact shot, the blast gasses that would have let everyone know that he was in play was soaked up by the man's body cavity, effectively silencing the weapon. Crude and messy, but effective.

Holding the guy by the collar, Bolan eased his body back against the wall, quickly fixed the sound suppressor to his 93-R and brought out his .44.

Time to go to work.

He targeted the two gunmen farthest away. One got

a 9 mm slug and other went down to the authoritative roar of the Desert Eagle.

That put his cards on the table, and almost all eyes were now on him. So far, he'd halved the known opposition, but he wasn't keeping score. The jokers in the deck had yet to be played. One of those wild cards popped up just as he finished doing preselected target number four and was on his way to lining up on number five.

Katz trumped that joker with a short Uzi burst, followed by another when the man behind the bar reached down and came back up with something shiny in his hand. It might have been a martini mixer or an ice-cream scoop, but this was no time to get loosey goosey with target selection. If it looked like a duck, it got quacked.

With a few drinks under their belts and the security guys' attention split being between two shooters, it impeded their target-selection process. With indecision being the mother of disaster, Bolan went on the move to further disrupt the process.

One Tamboli thug lined up on him, but a customer jumped up in front of him and blocked his shot. By the time the gunman was clear, Bolan was off to his side, drawing a bead on him. The thug tried for a save, but a round from the .44 knocked him off his feet before he could finish his turn.

The legitimate customers had been much slower to react than the gunmen, but that was to be expected. They had come to the Kit Kat Klub to relax, if getting all steamed up over wiggling naked women could be called relaxing. They hadn't come expecting to get tangled up in a gun battle. It took them a while, but once they got their minds switched over from mating mode to survival, they panicked.

With the target field corrupted, Bolan and Katz took that extra split second each time to confirm their aim before triggering. There was a risk in doing it that way, but they didn't want anyone killed by accident.

Farjani was stunned at the speed with which the hit was going down; it wasn't at all like the gunfights in action movies. A camera wasn't focusing on either the shooter or the target in turn so she could figure out what was happening. It was like being inside of a whirlwind crashing through a crowded insane asylum.

She had her little pistol out and was trying to watch Katz's back when a man moved toward Katz's blind side with a gun in his hand. As she'd been taught, she held the Beretta in both hands, aimed it at the center of his body with both eyes open and pulled the trigger three times.

She was surprised at how little noise the pistol made and even more surprised when the gunman got a puzzled look in his face and fell down. That hadn't been difficult at all. She turned back to back with Katz and sought another target.

By this time, the club was almost cleared. Anyone still on his feet wanted nothing to do with them.

"Okay," Bolan sent over the com link, "fall back to the door behind me."

Sending Farjani first, Katz covered her as she crossed the room before joining the Executioner. "Straight through to the alley," Bolan said.

Outside, the last of the girls were just clearing the alley. Bolan led his team the other way to the side street where he'd stashed their Lancia. They drove off to the wail of approaching sirens.

"They're playing our song again." Katz looked out the rear window.

"Just as long as it stays back there."

THE DORMITORY, as the girl at the club had called it, was as she had described. It was in the middle of a spacious walled villa compound that looked to be at least a couple of hundred years old. But since nearly everything in Naples dated to well before the American Revolution, that alone didn't make it stand out. The commanding position it occupied on the small hill did. The original owners had obviously not wanted to be bothered by the notorious antics of the Naples street mobs. The same went for the current occupants, and they didn't want anyone looking too closely at them, either.

According to their informant, not only was this place the stopover holding area for the women, but it was also where they were trained for their new "jobs." That this training was conducted by the Tamboli Family thugs and their invited guests was a valuable perk that went with being associated with the Tambolis. Buying loyalty with sexual favors was an old story.

From the sounds reaching the street from the walled villa, a party was going on inside. Apparently the word of their attacks on the restaurant and the Kit Kat Klub hadn't reached here yet. Or, even better, it had and was being ignored. Bolan liked dealing with people who felt secure behind walls. They didn't think in terms of walls as creating holding pens as much as they provided protection.

This compound was better equipped, security systems wise, than the Moros' bucolic country estate had been. That, though, was to be expected. This was modern Italy, not a rural backwater like Sicily. The cameras and sensors appeared, however, to be hard-wired, and that wasn't state-of-the-art.

A careful recon of the villa's perimeter revealed that as Bolan had hoped, the security system looked to be wired into a separate circuit. The downside of that was that unlike in the United States, electrical wiring in Europe was rarely strung on poles, and that was the case here. Instead, the power wires came out of their subterranean conduits on the outside of the wall, and closer inspection showed that one of the wires looked to be newer than the others.

Figuring it to be the hook-up to the surveillance system, he'd cut it and see what happened.

While Bolan prepared to cut the wire, Farjani

turned to Katz. "I'm going in there with you, Lev," she told him straight out.

"It'd be best if you didn't," he replied. "This isn't going to be a walk-through like the club. It's going to be as bad as the Moro job."

"But," she countered, "There are girls in there, and they'll need someone to tell them what to do. Plus, I can shoot now, too. You saw that in the club."

Katz folded his cards on this hand. The woman was becoming a handful.

"Okay, but don't complain to me if you get yourself killed in there," he growled.

"But I have you and Mike to protect me." She smiled.

"We're going to be a little busy."

Bolan made the cut, and the little red telltale on the camera went dark, but the main house was still lit. Just as he'd hoped.

"We're in," Bolan announced. "Let's do it."

Since someone would most certainly be watching the video monitors, they needed to get inside before someone came to see why the cameras had suddenly gone dark. Bolan went over the wall first. "We're clear," he sent over the com link.

Katz gave Farjani a leg up and then followed himself.

If the Tambolis followed the Moro pattern, most of their manpower would be concentrated in the dormitory, taking part in the party-training session. That concentrated them nicely for what Bolan had in mind, but it also exposed the women.

"Let's clean out the big house first," Bolan suggested. "That way, we won't get flanked by reinforcements like we did last time."

"Good point," Katz said.

Bolan led them across the manicured lawn, with Katz covering his back. Farjani followed behind, her Beretta in her hand.

CLEANING OUT the big house was like a rat hunt. In this case, though, the rats were big, dumb and not at all worried about someone coming after them, which made it a whole lot easier. To start off, Farjani went to the back door and knocked politely.

The door was jerked upon by a man wearing an undershirt and dirty pants. "What you want?" he growled.

Farjani pointed back toward the party. "They want you in there."

"Who wants me?"

"I don't know his name." She turned and looked toward the building. "He's over by the door."

When the man stepped out to get a better look, Bolan shot him in the head.

After stashing the body out of sight, the three entered and found themselves in the kitchen area. It was unoccupied, so Bolan turned to Jasmine.

"Stay here and watch this door from inside," he

said. "If anyone comes, fire to give us an early warning."

The woman nodded and took up her position.

The two men split up. For such a large house, not many people were in it. Bolan came across three guys drinking and playing cards and put them down with three double taps. The last guy did manage to get to his feet, but his piece was on a table on the other side of the room, and he didn't reach it in time.

Katz found a couple of bedrooms that were occupied. In one of them, a young woman was sharing the bed with an older man. Since the man was Italian and the girl appeared to be Middle Eastern, Katz didn't take her to be his wife and let her sleep it off. The guy got his ticket punched.

Bolan found the master bedroom and the apparent lord of the manor asleep in silk pajamas. With the press of time, he didn't bother to wake him and pass pleasantries. A silenced 9 mm round to the head hardly even mussed the covers.

"I'm clear on the top floor," he sent to Katz.

"We're done here except for one room," Katz sent back. "And I want you to see this. First floor, right off the kitchen."

"On the way."

In the room off the kitchen, the guy who was supposed to be watching the security camera monitors, wasn't. From the scenes on the two monitors that were still lit up, he'd been watching the activities in the party room before he passed out. The empty bottle of grappa beside the overflowing ashtray accounted for his snores.

Snoring usually wasn't a capital offense, but Bolan put a bullet in his head anyway. Being drunk on duty was.

Having the cameras in the party room still hot was a bonus. It gave them a chance to study the layout inside before they hit it. Unlike at the Moro party, the ratio of women to men looked to be about three to one—eight thugs and about two dozen women. That made their job much easier in one sense. But with so many noncombatants, they'd really have to get firm IDs before pulling the trigger.

"How do you want to do it?" Katz asked.

"We'll both go in the front door," Bolan said, studying the monitors. "It looks like the only quick entrance."

"And the only exit," Katz commented.

"Let's do it."

Again Bolan had Farjani watch the door when they went inside. He didn't want to have to watch her back, as well as Katz's.

Being safe within the walls of the family compound, none of the Tambolis or their guests expected to see trouble come through the door. The only guy who even bothered to look over and see who was joining the party didn't recognize the threat. Before he could, Bolan put him down with a sound-suppressed shot that couldn't be heard over the music.

The girl he was with, though, saw his brains blow

out the back of his head and she screamed loud
enough to be heard. But screams weren't out of the
ordinary at a Tamboli party, and that was too bad for
the Tambolis.

Bolan and Katz both got one more man apiece before the survivors realized that they were in trouble.
With alcohol-and-sex-dulled reaction times, two more
thugs went down before the first shot was fired at
them.

That gave Bolan clearance to bring out the heavy
artillery, and the Desert Eagle roared. The .44's first
victim was the Tamboli shooter, and the heavy slug
tore through his chest and spine, folding him in two.

That sent a jolt of pure adrenaline shooting through
the bloodstreams of the remaining thugs, and things
got interesting for the next sixty seconds.

A flurry of gunfire exploded from subguns and pistols as the gunmen fought like cornered rats. The gunfire, though, wasn't as loud as the shrieks and screams
of the terrified women. When the last gunman went
down, the women were still screaming.

As HAD BEEN the case in the aftermath of the Moros'
party, some of the women were blood splattered, but
none seemed to have been shot. The crying, screaming and shouting was starting to ratchet down to simple sobbing and wailing.

"Here's what you came for." Katz went to the
door and motioned Farjani to come inside. "Tell them
that they're free and can go home."

"Attention!" the woman shouted in Italian and followed it with English, French and Arabic.

Quite a few heads turned her way.

"If you will be quiet." She switched back to English, the only true international language. "I can tell you what is happening. We came to free you and you won't be hurt."

"Who are you?" a woman asked in accented English. "The police?"

"No," Farjani replied. "We are part of a United Nations antislavery task force."

Katz had come up with that idea at the last minute, and she loved it.

"Oh, thank God," a woman said in French as she fell to her knees. From the bruises on her faced, she'd not had an easy time during her incarceration here.

"Is anyone wounded?" Farjani had to shout over the babble that instantly broke out. "If you are, we have medical aid on the way. The rest of you can leave anytime you want, or you can stay here until the police arrive. They will help you."

Permission to leave almost caused a stampede for the door. None of the women even considered sticking around. A few did pause long enough to put on more clothes. Most ran seminaked into the grounds.

When the last woman was gone, the trio followed them out, but turned away from the path leading to the main gate. That area was going to be the center of attention for some time to come, and they didn't need any of it.

CHAPTER TWENTY

Naples

Bolan, Yakov Katzenelenbogen and Jasmine Farjani pulled back into the open area of the grounds to wait for their extraction. Jack Grimaldi had been in the air, on station for a quick snatch, since their evening's adventure had begun. It was time to give him something useful to do.

"We can use a ride," Bolan called the pilot. "There's a cleared space north of the main house you can put down on with no sweat. We're waiting there."

"Roger," Grimaldi came back. "ETA eight mikes."

"Turn up the wick and get here as fast as you can," Bolan advised. "We made a lot of noise up here."

"Roger, I'm clocking 110 percent right now."

"Don't blow your transfer case," Bolan cautioned. "I don't want to have to walk off this hill. The traffic around here's going to get pretty crowded shortly."

"Give me some strobe," Jack radioed a few minutes later. "I'm on approach."

Bolan unclipped the ministrobe from his harness and, holding it skyward, clicked it on. With the collar slid up around the lens, the flashing light wasn't noticeable from the ground.

"I've got your strobe," Grimaldi called. "Flare out in one mike."

Blacked out, the chopper flared out over the clearing and settled down on the grass. "Get your ass on board!" Grimaldi yelled. "The cops are coming."

The pickup went quickly and Grimaldi switched on his running lights as soon as he lifted off and had a little altitude over the city. Below, the flashing lights of emergency vehicles were racing up the hill to the villa. The headlights on the lead cars were starting to pick up the gaggle of barely clothed women running for freedom. They screeched to a halt and Grimaldi saw cops get out to assess what in the hell was going on.

"That'll slow them down for a while." Katz laughed. "I hope they brought their translation team with them."

Grimaldi kept his chopper low as he flew north over the city. As before, he had arranged for a vehicle to be waiting for them at an isolated place well outside of Naples. Again Striker would leave their gear with him to fly into France.

Trying to run this gig in a half-dozen countries was making the transport of their weapons and equipment

more difficult than it really needed to be. But the
French were a little touchy about guns and bombs
coming in lately. Getting popped at a border crossing
with a trunk full of hardware wasn't going to cut it.
Neither was getting booked into a French jail on international terrorism charges.

Stony Man Farm, Virginia

WHEN BARBARA PRICE did her walk through the Annex early that morning, she found Aaron Kurtzman
dozing in his chair at his workstation. From the
amount of trash littered around him, he'd pulled another all-nighter again. That wasn't as difficult for
him as it would have been for a man who had not
suffered a back wound that had paralyzed him from
the waist down. His butt never got tired.

He was tough; there was no doubt about that.
Nonetheless, tough or not, he didn't take care of himself as well as he should. It was time for the Bear to
go back to his den for at least eight hours. After, of
course, he stopped off in the shower first. Hunt and
Akira could keep track of things until he surfaced
again.

"Aaron?" She laid her hand on his shoulder.

"Man." He woke instantly and rubbed his eyes.
"I'm beat. Striker and Katz took Naples apart last
night, and I've been sweeping up after them."

"What happened?"

Kurtzman gave her a quick rundown on the Naples

escapade. "And," he concluded with a grin, "they got away clean again."

"What's the local reaction?"

"The same as before in Sicily." He shrugged. "A nasty gang war breaking out. Nothing yet about the girls they released. But, I got the UN involved so they won't just disappear again. Apparently some of the women they freed in Alexandria vanished off the streets before they could make it safely to their embassies."

Considering the Islamic Brotherhood's involvement in the slave trade, that wasn't too surprising. Alexandria was a Brotherhood town.

"Where're they going next?"

"They're going on to Marseilles," he replied with a yawn. "Should be there tomorrow local morning time. They're still chasing the Chinese connection."

"Do you have any more on that Dong Guy?"

"According to the carabinieri—" he perked up and reached for his keyboard "—your Taiwanese businessmen visited the Moro compound the morning the police were carting the bodies out. The cops got the tag number off the car, but it was a rental. Running the name on the rental form didn't turn up diddly of course."

"If that's all that's going on," she said as she took the handles of his wheelchair to pull it away from his workstation, "you're going to bed for a while."

For once, he didn't argue. Calling ahead for one of the blacksuits to meet her, she wheeled his chair to-

ward the elevator to the tram. Kurtzman was asleep
again before she reached it.

Marseilles

MORE THAN EVER BEFORE, Gao Dong, former colonel
of the Chinese People's Republic's Security Services,
was a man with a mission. This time, though, it was
a personal mission instead of one for the mother
country. His usefulness to China had ended, which
meant that his life was over; he was a dead man walking, as the Yankees liked to put it. He knew the men
of the Tiger Squads, and there was no place on earth
short of the North Pole where he could hide from
Beijing's assassination teams. As sure as the sun rose
and set, sooner or later they would track him down
and kill him.

Dying was not his main concern, though. Every
man born was slated to die. Dying with his personal
honor, his face, intact, though, was vital. He would
not go into the World of Spirits with this weight of
failure on his shoulders. He would die, but he would
die proudly and only after he had brought retribution
to the man who had brought him to this state. The
spirits of his ancestors demanded at least that much
from him.

Most people who had the misfortune to find themselves on one of Beijing's "shoot on sight" lists
saved themselves much misery and simply put a
round in their mouths. When a man found himself

with no options left, it was by far the less painful avenue to take.

Dong, however, had lived in the shadow world of Chinese clandestine operations long enough that he was not without his resources. Part of the success he had enjoyed as an operative for the People's Republic was that he had brought a lot to the table with him that the lords of Beijing didn't know about. The personal connections that his father and grandfather had made years ago were still in place, and he had called on them more than once in his career. Never, though, had he needed them more than he did now. And making contact with them had never been so easy.

What he was learning from them was troubling, though. It turned out that the man the Arabs were so frightened of was apparently well worth fearing. The problem, though, was that no one knew who he was or if the exploits of more than one man had been credit to this Al Askari of the Arabs. Nonetheless, Dong's Tong and Triad contacts, his Taiwanese sources, the Japanese Yakuza bosses and the Latin American cartel people all were reporting the same kind of stories about this man that the Arabs had told.

After sorting through the reports, Dong had formed his own picture of this one man, an American who, alone and unafraid, fought to protect the interests of his country. When not doing that, he eliminated drug traffickers and other merchants of human misery.

It was the stuff of mythology—all cultures had such heroes, particularly the Americans and their cowboy heroes of the Old West. Nonetheless, Dong had long ago learned that there was truth in all myths.

Dong had earlier speculated that the Soldier had found him through his investigation of the slavery component of the Dragon Egg Project. That guess had not yet been confirmed by other sources, but he still felt that it was true. Other recent stories told of similar actions. For a professional warrior, this man had a surprising concern for the noncombatants he encountered on his missions. To Dong's mind, that was a decided weakness in a warrior. But perhaps it was a weakness he could exploit.

The Soldier's strengths, as he felt he knew them now, could also be turned against him. Sun Tzu had written extensively of how strengths, as well as weaknesses, could be turned against an enemy. And there was no doubt that this man was the greatest opponent he had ever faced.

Taking his vengeance, though, was not going to be easy to set up and execute. Part of the problem was that he was still not certain if he faced more than one man.

One of the Moro family retainers had escaped destruction at the family compound because he had spent the night in the local village with his mistress. When he had talked to a friend in the local police unit later, he had learned that the carabinieri were convinced that more than one man had assaulted the house. Exactly how many, they weren't certain. But ammunition cases from more than one unaccounted-for weapon had been recovered at the scene of the massacre.

One ammunition type had been distinctively American—.44 Magnum automatic handgun cartridges. The other cartridge cases that couldn't be traced were standard 9 mm that bore no head stamps, a giveaway of a clandestine operation. The American military was famous for having their strike forces use such unmarked ammunition. That indicated that he had at least one battle companion.

Dong also felt that the Farjani women was probably still involved. Exactly why he felt that, he couldn't really say, but he felt she was driving the operation. He now knew that her younger sister had been eliminated in the cleanup of the *Singapore Queen* in California, and that could be her motive. A desire for revenge wasn't exclusively a masculine trait. It could burn just as strongly in a woman who felt that she had been wronged.

In her thirst for vengeance, an inexperienced woman, as this Farjani appeared to be, was often blinded to caution and made mistakes. If he could trap her into doing something reckless, he might be able to draw the Soldier in to rescue her. One way or the other, though, he needed to separate Al Askari from the others who might be helping him so he could track him down and kill him personally.

Baiting such a trap could be expensive in terms of manpower, but he had never been concerned about that expense. The men he had brought with him were among his oldest and most trusted subordinates. And while they were almost like family to him, there was a crucial difference. When Dong stood before the spirits of his ancestors, he intended to have his face intact. And to accomplish that, he would sacrifice anyone not of his bloodline.

Along with his own men, he would need to bring in outsiders to create such a target-rich environment that a man like Al Askari would not be able to resist. One thing he had learned was that the Soldier didn't seem to fear overwhelming odds. Fortunately he had a ready source for the men he would need to expend—the gunmen of the Union Corse. His business relationship with their leader, Napoleon Garza, was strong and profitable enough that he should have no problem recruiting his full-fledged assistance.

He was approaching the outskirts of Marseilles and would know shortly where he would go from here.

BOLAN DIDN'T WANT to put in an all-night drive, so they stopped right before the border to sleep. Before he turned in, though, he placed a secure cell phone call to the Farm.

Akira Tokaido recognized Bolan's number on the caller ID and answered.

"Where's the Bear?" Bolan asked.

Tokaido chuckled. "Barbara highjacked him and sent him off to bed. He'd been following you guys all night and was nodding off in his chair."

"Give me Hunt, then."

"You guys've had a profitable evening," Hunt Wethers chucked. "A couple more nights like that and the Naples Mob would have to import some of the American families just to stay in the game."

"God knows we tried," Bolan said. "But they were just collateral damage. We still haven't caught up with the Chinese."

"They were right on your heels in Sicily," Wethers said. "Five of them showed up at El Rancho Moro the morning after your visit."

"Damn, we should have hung around," Bolan said. "This would be over by now."

"The Bear was working up the data you wanted on the Union Corse in Marseilles, so you'll have that going in."

"Good, send it."

EVEN BY THE STANDARDS of twenty-first-century Euro mobsters, the Union Corse were brutal thugs. Originally they had been no more than pirates based out of the rocky coves of Corsica. Like Sicily, this Mediterranean island had changed hands often over the centuries, but right now it was French. All this really meant though, was that the French had the responsibility to try to keep track of them. No one had ever been able to shut them down.

Like the Sicilians, the Corsicans had a long history of buying and selling human flesh. Now that the market was high again in that commodity, they had dived right back into it. Mostly they shopped common whores to stock bordellos. But when Gao Dong had approached them to get their help with placing his Dragon Egg operatives in France and Spain, they had gladly taken his money. They never minded someone showing them a new enterprise.

Other than piracy, slaving and associated criminal activities, the island was mostly known for having been the birthplace of the first great despot of the modern age, Napoléon Bonaparte. As Corsica's favorite native son, some said the only one of note at all, many Corsican men bore his name. So it was with Napoleon Garza, the current Godfather of the Union.

Garza even liked to think that he resembled the one time scourge of Europe. And if things kept going his way, he might soon become almost as powerful. His relationship with the Chinese had opened Garza's eyes to a new twist to one of the age-old Corsican pastimes, commerce raiding.

The twenty-first century was shaping up to be as threatening to the established order of the world as the start of the twentieth had been, and chaos always favored the bold. The so-called Third World nations were no longer willing to sit with their begging bowls in hand patiently waiting for the great nations to drop a few techno scraps in their laps. They wanted the benefits of the modern age and they wanted them now. As in right now and at as little cost to them as possible.

The cold war had flooded the Third World nations with more modern weapons than many of them had trained men to use. But modern technology was not limited to weaponry. There was a wealth of new things that could make the lives of the Third World elite healthier, happier and more secure.

In particular, the technology that would insure that the elites of these nations would always remain the elite was in great demand. After all, there was no point in being a member of the elite if you had to fear being overthrown by filthy peasants all the time. Techno-toys worked well to keep the lower classes in their proper places, the mud. At one time, guns had served that purpose, but every stinking, mud-splattered peasant had an AK these days.

Feeding export-restricted high-tech toys to strong-arm regimes in Africa and the Middle East had now become a major sideline for Garza's Union Corse. Tying it into his slaving operations made it even more lucrative for him. The Third World elite got their techno-toys, and he got exotic, young women. And the exchange rate was quite favorable to him. Women weren't all that valuable in most of the world.

So when Dong said that someone was coming to put him out of business, Garza took him at his word. The single agent the Chinese operative said was being sent against him was not entirely unknown to him. This man had crossed swords with the Union before and the Corsicans had not won those encounters.

But to a Corsican, revenge was not the only dish best eaten cold. A war was also something that a good leader needed to pick the right time for.

And this was the time Garza would go to the wall to protect his turf. If this shadow warrior wanted to declare war on the Union, he would find a battle waiting for him and his comrades. Let them come and see that Napoleon Garza was more than able to protect what he had worked so long to put together.

Even before Dong arrived to give him the details, Garza started marshaling his forces.

CHAPTER TWENTY-ONE

Marseilles

Ex-Colonel Gao Dong wasn't at all angered when he was stopped by a full squad of armed guards at the main gate to the Union Corse leader's villa. At least someone was taking his warning about the American commando seriously. He, his men and their car were professionally searched before being allowed entry.

At the main house, he was met by more armed guards, and two of them ushered him into Napoleon Garza's office.

"Colonel Dong." Garza rose and walked from behind his desk. "I'm so glad you made it. We have a lot to talk about."

Garza nodded at the guards who had positioned themselves on each side of the office. "As you can see, I have already taken steps to counter this American you spoke of."

"So I have seen," Dong replied. "And that is good. Have you heard the news from Naples this morning?"

"News?" Garza frowned. "No."

"This Yankee almost wiped out the Tamboli Family last night. He raided several of their business establishments and then hit their main compound. Dozens are dead, and even worse, all of the women they were training were released and have been taken into custody by the authorities."

"That is not good news. That will put your project back several months and will cost me money, as well."

"That it will," Dong replied. He didn't bother to give Garza the other half of the bad news. The Corsican didn't need to know that he and his men were under a Beijing death sentence. He trusted the man, but Beijing could make it very profitable for the man who turned him in.

"What actions do you think we should take?"

Dong liked hearing the "we" in Garza's thinking. It meant that this effort might have a better outcome than he had thought.

"For one thing, I don't think that we'll need to do much except be very prepared and very alert. I guarantee you that the Yankee will be coming here soon."

"But why does he want to come after me?" Garza frowned. "That's what I do not understand."

"He is following the woman I spoke of."

"That is the stupidest thing I have ever heard of," Garza snorted. "If this man is who you say he is, and I do not doubt you, why is he doing something foolish like this? What is the big deal? Most women are born to be whores.''

"I could not agree with you more." Dong bowed slightly. "But this woman is burning with a desire for revenge. Her sister became a problem to her handler and had to be killed. I think she is sleeping with the American and has her claws in his manhood. It's the only thing I can think of that makes any sense to me."

Dong didn't think anything of the kind, but it was a convenient explanation that Garza would take at face value. Like the Italians, Corsican men showed open contempt for women but secretly feared their power. Garza would buy that motive and that's all Dong wanted from him.

"If he's coming here," Garza boasted, "I am ready for him. I have two dozen of my best men stationed here right now, and teams have been posted at each of my other facilities."

"They must also be your best night fighters," Dong said. "And well-equipped to fight in the dark. So far, the Soldier has struck only at night."

Garza chuckled. "My men fight well enough at night. After all, my business is mostly conducted after dark. And—" he walked over to an arms rack in the office and grabbed a pair of night-vision goggles "—I have only the latest in night-fighting equipment. I get it directly from the Russian Spetsnaz. They sell it cheaply enough for drugs."

Dong smiled inwardly. The once great Russian Bear's most feared fighting forces had been reduced to being drug dealers and, as he knew, drug users. It was only another indication that the West was doomed.

"That is all good," Dong said, "but we need a plan, as well as the fighting men to carry it out. This Yankee is different than the other men you have gone up against before. He is a fighting machine and, along with the woman, there may be another commando with him this time."

"Three people. What kind of threat is that?"

"These three people shut down one of my operations in Alexandria," Dong reminded him, "went on to Sicily to wipe out the Moros and then to Naples to destroy the Tambolis. I don't count the woman for much, but the two Yankees are not to be sneered at.

"What do you suspect?" Garza asked. Unlike many crime bosses, the Union Corse leader wasn't so egotistical that he didn't recognize when he could use expert advice. He was good at what he did—that was evident—but so was the Chinese and they fought different battles.

Dong leaned forward. "I want to set a trap for him. And if it is at all possible, I want to try to capture him. It will be well worth your while if I can have him alive."

Garza didn't need to know what Dong wanted to do with this man, only what it would bring him. "How much is this 'worth my while'?"

When Dong mentioned a figure, in gold, Garza smiled. "There is a way to do that," he said. "I have used this method before when I have wanted to have face-to-face talks with some of my competitors. It has never failed me.''

''What is that?''

Garza leaned forward. ''It is the picture of simplicity. First we find them.''

BOLAN, Katzenelenbogen and Jasmine Farjani drove up into a hilly region inside the French border to meet up with Jack Grimaldi and make the arms and equipment transfer. Once in the agreed location, they made a quick call and the chopper landed a few minutes later.

''Get a move on,'' the pilot shouted from the cockpit as he tossed a suitcase onto the ground. ''I'm under French air-traffic control and can only be off the radar for a couple of minutes before they think I'm running drugs.''

''Tell them that you had to set down to take a leak,'' Katz suggested.

''Everyone tries that one,'' Grimaldi replied. ''I try that one and they'll put my ass under a microscope.''

''That's it,'' Bolan said as he pulled out the last bag. ''Take off.''

''I'll meet you in Marseilles,'' Grimaldi sent over the com link as he pulled pitch to lift off again.

After loading their gear in the car, the trio went back down to the main highway along the coast to Toulon, the next major city in the region.

''I think we should stop in Toulon,'' Katz said as

he looked up from the road map. "It's about thirty mile from Marseilles. We need a little time to do our map recon and check in with the Farm before we get too committed. It shouldn't take more than a couple of hours."

"Sounds good to me," Bolan replied.

AARON KURTZMAN'S Computer Room crew had to have been working overtime because the data dump they sent to Toulon was extensive. Both Interpol and French sources on the Union Corse had been scrutinized and the important material compiled. CIA and NRO files had been gone over, and for what it was worth, the Organized Crime Division of Brognola's Justice Department had also made a contribution. In their hotel room, Bolan and Katz each took half of the stack and started reading through it.

Like many European mobsters, Napoleon Garza was also a prosperous legitimate businessman. He owned shipping agencies, dockside warehouses, repair yards and other businesses that supported the shipping industry. He was also into land transportation and light manufacturing. It was quite an empire for a man who was basically a drug dealer, pimp and slave trader.

"We've got a lot of ground to cover here," Bolan said as he read through the list of Garza's holdings. "But Dong's going to be there somewhere."

"When we get there," Katz suggested, "why don't Jasmine and I get into our tourist outfits, hang a camera or two around our necks, rent a car and go for a drive? You know, take in the scenes, hit the high spots and maybe get some picturesque shots.''

''While you're doing that,'' Bolan said, ''I'll get Jack to make a couple of flyovers of Garza's major sites and take a few pictures myself.''

GAO DONG DIDN'T HAVE any solid proof that the Soldier was going to hit the Garza operation in search of him, but his gut instincts, as well as his training, told him that the American would continue his quest. The Soldier had chased him from Asia, through the Middle East to Europe, and there was no reason for him to stop now. The American's aim was obviously to kill him, as well as to shut down the Dragon Egg Project.

One thing Dong had going for him in Marseilles that he'd not had in Alexandria was the raw manpower that Garza would be able to bring to bear on the operation. The Union Corse ruled this town, and the entirety of that power was even now being brought to bear.

Dong had a photo of the Farjani woman, and copies were being sent to everyone who did business in any way with the Union or who owed Garza in any way. Everyone from cabdrivers to flower-stand girls, hotel clerks, pimps and even a few cops were on the lookout for that woman in the company of an American. The reward that was being offered for information on the pair was large enough that the calls had started coming into Garza's operations center almost immediately.

When the tag number of the car they had rented came in, Dong knew he had them. Leave it to an American to want to drive instead of using public transport. He quickly had Garza provide the rental's make, color and plate number to his informants and upped the reward for the first sighting of the car.

KATZ AND FARJANI WERE making the rounds of Marseilles with a guidebook in hand like any tourists. Regardless of the port city's age, it wasn't that much of a tourist draw.

To make it look good, they hit all the touristy places first, the town square, the cathedral, the old town hall, the gardens. From there, they widened their scope and started taking in the bridges, certain selected grand homes and villas and manufacturing facilities. Anyone following them would see that they were interested in more than just Union Corse operations.

"The next stop on our tour is right around the corner," Katz said as he pulled over to the curb and parked by a corner newsstand.

They got out, guidebook in hand, and turned off the main street into an alley leading down to an abandoned industrial area. The only thing interesting about it at all was that all the buildings were owned by Garza.

Farjani was so busy listening to Katz that she didn't

overhear the whispered conversation in French the newsstand owner was having over the phone. Nor did she see the smile on his face when he hung up.

She and Katz were only a hundred yards into the alley when it was suddenly full of gunmen cutting them off, and he heard a car drive in from behind him.

"Run!" Katz pushed her behind him. "Get out of here!"

"But…" She rummaged in her purse for her pistol.

"Run, dammit! I'll cover you!"

Farjani obeyed by running for the side alley while Katz laid down a base of fire with his mini-Uzi to cover her. He scrabbled against the curb, seeking what little cover there was, and keyed his com-link.

"We've been ambushed," he said as he ripped off another burst. "We're down in the—"

He felt a blow to his chest and glanced down to see a feathered dart embedded between his ribs.

Then everything went black, and he pitched forward onto his face.

WITH ONE OF HIS ENEMIES down, Dong called back his men who had started after the woman. He had his prize, and she could live a little longer. After all, he still needed her to take word of this back to those the Soldier worked for. He wanted the Yankees to know that he had taken down their legendary champion as if he were a novice. Garza's plan to use a tranquilizer dart gun like those zookeepers used had worked as well as he had said it would.

Walking over, Dong looked down at the American commando as his men rolled him over onto his back. This couldn't be the fearless warrior who had terrified so many for so long. Something just wasn't right. While this man was fit, he was too old. Also his physical description, even allowing for Arabic and Latin hysteria, didn't match with the Soldier at all.

"Comrade Colonel," one of his men searching the American said. "Your Yankee has an artificial arm."

That clinched it for Dong. No man with only one arm could be the legendary commando.

"Strip him," he commanded, "and remove it."

"Yes, Comrade Colonel."

Without the prothesis, this Yankee looked even less of a legend. Since he had been with the Farjani woman, though, he had to be a comrade of the Soldier. And if that was the case, it could be even better than having the man himself. If this game had to go on, he had just been given a better pawn than the woman would ever have been.

The Soldier was known for his loyalty, both to his country and to the men who fought beside him. With this man being older, he might be the Soldier's warrior mentor. If that was the case, the commando would be duty bound to attempt to free him. This was going to work better than if he had planned it to happen this way.

"Put him in the car," he commanded. "And give the arm to me."

The man handed the prothesis to Dong. The colonel took out his pen and quickly wrote the Chinese characters for Dragon Egg on the prosthesis. Walking over to the curb, Dong laid the arm in the gutter before walking back to his car and driving away.

Garza had been right; it had been easy. Now that the trap was baited, he would wait.

ONCE FARJANI WAS in the clear, she took a cab back to their hotel to wait in Belasko's room for his return. He and the pilot were doing aerial reconnaissance, but she thought she had heard Katz calling them over the com link.

She didn't have long to wait before she heard a knock on her door.

"Were's Lev?" Bolan asked as he entered with Grimaldi right behind him.

"We were ambushed." She shuddered. "And he was either killed or taken captive. I don't really know which, but I think he was still alive when they took him away."

"Was it the Chinese?"

"There were several Orientals, and they might have been Chinese. The others were locals."

"Where did this happen?"

"I'll show you."

WHEN THE WOMAN GUIDED Bolan and Grimaldi to the street where Katz had parked their rental, they found that the car had been already driven away.

"Someone's cleaning up after themselves," Grimaldi commented.

"The Union's not a nickel-and-dime outfit," Bolan replied. "They're pros."

He turned in the passenger seat. "Is that the alley you went down?" he asked Farjani.

When she nodded, Bolan had Grimaldi stop the car and he got out. "Cover me."

Grimaldi stayed behind the wheel of their rental with the engine running and a Beretta subgun on the passenger seat while Bolan entered the alley.

There were almost no signs that any kind of gun battle had taken place here, not a single empty cartridge case, and the only bullet marks on the stones were farther down. He was almost starting to doubt that this was the right place when he spotted an artificial arm lying in the gutter and rushed over.

There was no blood on the cobblestones anywhere near where Katz's arm lay. Reaching down, he picked up the prothesis and immediately saw the two inked Chinese characters. Though he couldn't read them, he knew that they were a message from Gao Dong. They were also a challenge to him, and that challenge would be met.

He turned back to the car and signaled Grimaldi to pick him up.

THE NEWSSTAND MAN on the corner carefully noted the car that drove down the alley and decided to call it into the Garza number because the woman in the photo was a passenger. They had paid him well for the first report—and he expected to be paid again. He wanted to send his wife on a long vacation to visit her sister so he could visit the truck-driving neighbor's wife while he was on the road.

"It looks like they took the bait," Dong told Garza. "We have a report that the woman took two men back to the alley where we got our prisoner."

"Two men?" Garza asked. "You said that he might have one man with him, not two."

"One man or two." Dong shrugged. "What does it matter? You have more than enough manpower to take down two men, don't you think?"

Garza couldn't admit to not being able to kill two men whoever they were. But this operation kept changing every time it was discussed with the Chinese.

"I will send more men to the factory," he said.

"That should do it," Dong agreed. "Now we have to let the Soldier know where his friend is being held."

CHAPTER TWENTY-TWO

Stony Man Farm, Virginia

Barbara Price was in her small office in the old farmhouse, working her way through her daily pile of routine paperwork. The glories of running the world's most successful clandestine-operations organization didn't come without the mundane accoutrements of reality. She was on the next-to-last page in the pile when her secure line rang.

"Price," she answered abruptly.

"I need a secure patch through to Hal," Bolan's voice came over her speakerphone, "and I want you to listen in on this, too."

"Conference call?"

"More or less," he replied. "Feel free to break in if you have something to add."

"I'm on it." Price dialed Hal Brognola's secure line number in the Justice Department.

Bolan sounded calm, but there was a tone to his voice, though, that told her that she really didn't want to hear what he was going to say. But the government paid her the big bucks to take the shit with the shinola, and she knew which one was coming down the pike this time.

"Hal, Striker's on the line."

"Where are you, Striker?" Brognola asked.

"Marseilles," he replied. "I have to report that Katz is either dead or captured."

"Damn," Brognola said softly. "What happened?"

Bolan quickly ran through the lead-up to the recon and the ambush that had been sprung on Katz and Farjani.

"You and Jack get the hell out of there right now," Brognola said. "And I'll get the French on it immediately."

"No."

Brognola and Price both knew what it meant when the man of few words went into single-syllable responses. His mind was made up and that was that. Counting the grains of sand on a beach was easier than changing Bolan's mind when he had decided to do something.

"Okay." Brognola knew enough to back off. The terms of the agreement between him and Bolan required that he not push when he wasn't working directly for the Farm. "What do you want to do? Do you want me to launch Phoenix?"

"It's okay to alert them," Bolan said, "but don't send them in yet."

"Dammit, man, don't you need some help?"

"Not yet," the Executioner said calmly. "What I need now is information. The game has changed."

"What are you talking about?"

"Dong's making this personal."

"What do you mean?"

"He had a chance to take out Jasmine, as well, but he didn't. He also left Katz's prosthesis behind as proof that he has him. He's daring me to try to get him back. And I will."

"WHAT DO YOU THINK?" Brognola asked Price when Bolan clicked off the line.

She paused before answering. "I'll be damned if I know, Hal. I really don't."

"I don't either." The confusion was plain in his voice. "And if there's anyone in the world who should know what's going on in that man's mind, I should."

Hal Brognola and Mac Bolan went back all the way to the days when he had been a young Fed and Bolan had been traveling through America eliminating the Mafia one nest at a time. They had been on opposite sides of the law back then. But Brognola was also the man who had later hatched the plan to create Stony Man Farm and who had convinced Bolan to come in from the cold, as it was termed back then.

He was proud to be counted in the very exclusive circle of men who could call the Executioner friend, and he knew that the friendship was reciprocated.

But Katz was also one of that very small number of friends. And a friend in need always had Bolan's fullest support. There was no way that he wouldn't make the attempt to recover him dead or alive.

"I'm coming down," he told her.

"Are you going to give the Man a heads-up?"

As a courtesy, Brognola sometimes privately briefed the President on the side missions Bolan had undertaken. It kept him from being asked embarrassing questions in the National Security briefings.

"Not right as yet," he said. "There's time to that later if I have to."

Neither one of them voiced the circumstances that would make that announcement necessary. They weren't willing going to go there just yet.

"I'll let Buck know that you're coming in," she said.

"I'll be down as soon as I can get to Andrews."

"I'll call your chopper if I hear anything."

"Do that."

As soon as Brognola hung up, she dialed Buck Greene, the Farm's chief blacksuit.

Marseilles

BOLAN HAD BEEN alone when he'd called the Farm, having sent Jack Grimaldi to Jasmine Farjani's room to keep her company. When he hung up, he phoned them and the pilot answered. "Jack, come over here for a moment. Alone."

"On the way."

"What are we getting from the Farm?" Grimaldi asked when he walked in.

"Nothing," Bolan said. "When we do this, we're doing it alone, just like the good old days. I don't want anyone else to be exposed if we go down."

Grimaldi didn't believe what he was hearing. They'd only been able to do the takedowns against overwhelming odds in Italy and Egypt because they'd had the element of surprise. Here, the enemy knew that they were coming. "But, Sarge—"

"I don't want to get anyone else involved," Bolan stated flatly. "This is personal now, and it's going to go down too hard.

"Remember," he said, softening his tone, "we're in France and the last thing we want to do is anything that would reveal the Stony Man teams on an un-authorized mission. The French would cause us far too much trouble. We've had to play it real tight before in Western Europe, and we're just going to have to do it that way again."

"Okay." The pilot shrugged. He and Bolan went back a long way, and if this was going to be the place where it all came to an end, that was fine with him. Life had been good to him since he and Bolan had first crossed paths, and he owed the big guy more than one life anyway.

Plus, Katz had always been good to him, and if there was even the slightest chance that he was still alive, it would be well worth the risk to try to get him back.

"Okay." The pilot sat back, his mind clear. "How do you want to work this?"

"First off, I'm going to need a diversion, something spectacular to draw as many of them off as we can. That's your main mission. If I can get through while you're drawing their attention, and if he's still alive somewhere…"

Bolan paused. "Hell, even if he isn't, I want to get the body out. After I find him, I want you to make the pickup, STABO style. A hot snatch."

"How about you?" Grimaldi asked even though he knew the answer he was going to get.

"I'll stay on the ground," Bolan said, "to cover your extraction."

Having more than a few hot LZ extractions on his pilot's résumé, Grimaldi knew that the critical point of one of those was always keeping the bastards off base while he built up enough airspeed to get the hell out. If Bolan was going to handle those chores this time, his chance of living through it was zilch, zip, nada.

He'd hoped he'd never have to look back over his shoulder on lift off and see a lone man on the ground giving his life so that another might have a chance.

"That sucks, Sarge."

"You're right. It does. Now let's start putting this thing together. And one of the first things I have to do is to get Jasmine back to the States where she belongs. I should have done that a long time ago.''

"She's not going to like that," Grimaldi replied. "Katz was doing his fatherly thing with her again."

Bolan smiled. "Some father, take his daughter to firefights instead of the park, but I know what you mean. Nonetheless, I don't want her in the line of fire this time. Someone has to survive this thing."

"You've got a point there."

"And while I'm doing that—" Bolan reached for a pad and a pen "—I need you to see if you can pick up a few things for us in town."

JASMINE FARJANI WAS still stunned at the loss of the man she knew as Lev Bronski. Throughout this entire episode, he had done the most to protect her. She had been scared out of her wits on several occasions, but he'd always made the most frightening things seem like some kind of lark and made her feel safe. She felt that she owed the man for his kindness if nothing else, but didn't know what was going to happen next. She was sure that Belasko and Grimaldi would do something. She just didn't know what it would be.

When she heard a knock on her door, she hurried to open it and found the man she knew as Mike Belasko standing there. "We need to talk," he said.

"Please come in. Have you learned anything about Lev?"

"No."

"Can I get you something from the minibar?" she offered.

"No, thank you."

She had been working with this man for quite some time now, but she had no clue as to what he was thinking. It would have something to do, she was certain, with Lev's loss and getting him back.

"What are we going to do next?"

He leveled his eyes at her. "I want you to get your things packed up as soon as you can."

"Where are we going?"

"You're going back to the States...alone."

"But I don't understand," Farjani said, fighting back tears. "I've been with you and Lev all the way from California, and you even said that I was valuable to your operation. Why do I have to go away now?"

"The situation's changed," Bolan told her as gently as he could. "It's far too dangerous for you to be here now. Dong knows that we're after him, and the advantage has gone to him now."

"But what about Lev?"

"We're working on getting him back right as we speak," he said. "Jack and I have worked up a plan."

He didn't want to burden her with the knowledge that he and Katz were probably not going to come out of this one in good shape even if they managed to stay alive. So far, she had toughened up enough to handle enemy casualties. But he didn't want to have to involve her in his or Katz's death. Plus, if she were captured, her death wouldn't go easy for her. Dong would see to that.

She knew Belasko well enough to know that the look on his face was telling her that she had no option but to do exactly as he wanted.

"I will pack," she said.

"Can I help?"

"No, I can get it."

THE DRIVE to the airport was strained and silent. There was so much she wanted to say, but didn't know how. After finding a place in the parking lot, Bolan carried her one small bag to the ticket counter at the small airport.

"I'm sorry that we had to meet in these circumstances," he said as he paid for the ticket he had called ahead for and handed it to her. "And when we're done here, I'll look you up in the States. You'll be met by my people in Atlanta and settled down wherever you want. We owe you that much."

"It is I who owe you and Lev," she said. "You two put yourselves in danger for me more than once. I have never known men like you, and I owe my life to you."

Bolan smiled. "You have fully repaid any debt you think you have by risking yourself in this operation. That's how the system works."

"It's not enough." She lowered her eyes.

"I'll see you to the plane."

With nothing else to be said, she followed him to

the gate where the other passengers waited for the plane to Paris.

FARJANI WAITED at the gate until Belasko left the small terminal and she saw him drive off before making her move. Her experiences with Belasko, Bronski and the pilot had given her a completely new way of thinking. If they thought that she was going to run away now that the man behind her sister's death had finally been run to ground, they didn't know her. Regardless of the increased danger Belasko had pointed out, she still had a personal mission to accomplish.

Going back to the ticket counter, she had her bag brought back from the luggage cart, canceled her reservation and cashed in the ticket. Going outside, she hailed a waiting cab and had it take her back into Marseilles. Finding a small pension on the outskirts of town, she had the driver stop there. It would make a base camp for what she had in mind.

After checking into her room, she went back down to the desk and had the clerk call a cab for her. Since she had so little with her, she would need to stock up on a few items. Belasko had retrieved the pistol she had been given, so that was her first necessity.

Her thinking had changed so much in these past few days. She wanted a weapon first instead of clothes.

WHILE BOLAN WAS sending Jasmine Farjani back to the States, Jack Grimaldi was working his way through their shopping list. Since Bolan didn't want to get the Farm involved, even with making a resupply run, they were going to have to put their mission requirements together through local sources, and it wasn't going to be easy.

The south of France, particularly the sun-drenched Riviera, wasn't a hotbed of sport mountaineering. There were the Pyrenees, true, but they weren't close by and mostly in Spain on top of that. However, on his second try, Grimaldi was able to find an outfitter who had a pair of climbing rigs, some 'beeners and climbing rope in stock. For pulling off the gig Bolan had in mind, they were essential.

The shop also had a stock of one-liter propane camping-stove fuel tanks and Grimaldi bought a dozen. Pound for pound, they would make better bombs than C-4, and he added a dozen of them to his pile. The ignition systems were going to have to be jury-rigged, so he picked up a dozen roadside scratch flares to go with them.

From there, he went looking for a longer list of items that were non essential but nice to have. It was also nice to have a charge card on a major European bank with no credit limit. It was too bad that he wasn't in the States; he could have had a field day with that piece of plastic. Europe, though, just didn't have many outlets for the things they needed most. Hand grenades and ammunition weren't going to be easily found anywhere in the EU.

CHAPTER TWENTY-THREE

Jasmine Farjani had also gone shopping to pick out a couple of outfits for her mission. One was in basic black, combat black. A trendy boutique catering to the rave crowd had provided a set of black military fatigues complete with cargo pockets on the pants and a matching pistol belt. A pair of black running shoes and a camouflage head scarf completed the very chick outfit.

There were still a few more critical accessories for that outfit she needed to acquire, but to get them, she first had to buy her second outfit.

To find out what she needed to make her look authentic, she went to one of the busiest main highways leading into town and watched the working girls work the truck drivers. In a few minutes, she knew what she wanted and hailed a cab to take her back into town.

When she walked out of the second boutique, she had what could only be called a working girl's uniform in her bag—hot pants and a skimpy halter top. She had passed on the six-inch heels, though and opted for something she could run in—low platform heeled boots.

Stopping in the ladies' room of a subway station, she changed into her hooker outfit and took a train to the dock area. Since Marseilles was another major port, the sailors' hangouts would be centered in that area, as would the petty criminals who made their living preying on them. Such men ought to be able to tell her how to get the last few things she needed.

It took a while, and several gropes, before she had the address of a man who might be able to help her buy a gun. The address proved to be one of those shops where sailors pawned their belongings for enough money to get drunk, but never bought them back. She didn't see any weapons on display, but since they were illegal to own in France without a police permit, she hadn't expected to.

The ferret-faced man in the shop couldn't keep his eyes off her breasts as she looked around, but she didn't mind. That was why she'd bought the outfit. If she could keep this moron entertained, he'd be easier to work with.

"Can I help you, lady?" the man asked.

"I want to buy a pistol," she said, the man's eyes fixed on her chest.

"Why does a good-looking girl like you need a gun?" he asked. "You can get hurt with one of those things if you don't know what you're doing."

She took a deep breath and leaned over the counter. "A girl like me needs to be able to protect herself, you know? And—'' she paused ''—I'm sure that you can show me how to use it properly.''

Ferret-face gulped. ''What kind of gun did you have in mind?'' he asked her breasts.

''A Beretta,'' she said, remembering the make of the pistol Katz had given her.

''I have a Beretta 92,'' he said.

''Let's see it.''

''Come into the back of my shop. I have a firing range in the basement.''

Farjani allowed herself to be led through the junk and down the stairs to the soundproofed basement. Ferret-face went into a vault and came out with the pistol. She remembered seeing a similar weapon being carried by the pilot, and if it was good enough for him, it would work for her.

''I need two magazines,'' she said.

''Show me how to load it,'' she demanded when he came back with a second magazine.

The man quickly loaded a magazine and handed it to her along with the pistol.

''You can save half the price if you want.'' Ferret-face almost panted, his bulging eyes locked on her breasts.

She snapped the magazine into the butt of the pistol, racked the slide back to chamber a round and smiled. ''I don't think so,'' she said as she lined up the sights on the target at the far end of the room and fired.

When a hole appeared in the center body mass, she

half turned to face the proprietor, the pistol ready in her hand. "Not today."

The man blanched even paler and looked away for a brief moment.

"How much is it?"

The Beretta 92 with two magazines and a box of fifty 9 mm shells was very expensive, but she had expected that it would be. Rather than even try to pay for an illegal weapon with the credit card Lev had given her, she had made a major cash withdrawal from a bank machine and planned to pay for it with cash.

"Give me a large knife to go with it," she said.

He shrugged and brushed past too close to her to fetch it. She didn't even ask him about a holster; he'd want to show her how to wear it. The pockets on the black military jacket were big enough to carry the gun and extra ammunition.

"If there is ever anything else you need..." the proprietor said as he pocketed the cash.

"I'll remember you," she replied. "You can be sure of that."

As soon as she left the shop, she went into the women's rest room of the closest subway station and changed out of her hooker uniform into her black outfit. After loading both magazines, she transferred the pistol and extra magazine to her right jacket pocket and put the loose ammunition to the left.

The only thing that made her plan even plausible wasn't the pistol she had managed to acquire; it was the com link she had in her purse. When Belasko had taken her pistol back, he'd apparently forgotten that she'd been given one of the team's small radios with the built-in battery charger. With it in her ear, she'd be able to eavesdrop on everything Belasko and Grimaldi said.

Plugging the small earpiece into her ear, she walked out looking for all the world like just one more rock-and-roll girl out looking for fun as she listened to her radio.

YAKOV KATZENELENBOGEN awoke on a narrow bed in a small cell with a splitting headache and a nasty taste in his mouth. Whatever he'd been hit with was a killer. His head was throbbing, and he was sweating as if he had malaria. He reached up to brush the matted hair off his face and realized that his prosthetic arm was gone along with his clothing.

"That rotten son of a bitch!"

Where most people saw a one-armed man as being disabled, as long as he had his prosthesis, Katz had proved time and again that he was as good as any two-armed man and better than most. With just the stub of the arm, though, he was at a bit of a disadvantage.

Looking around his cell showed him that he was going to be there for a while, at least until his captors let him out. Even with both arms, this didn't look like a place he could get out of easily. He had forgotten to put a small shaped charge in his pocket.

Since he wasn't going anywhere, he decided to lie

back down and get as much rest as he could. Something told him he'd be needing his strength before too long.

KATZ DOZED OFF and awakened to the clang of his cell door opening. When he saw that the men who had come for him were Chinese, he knew what had gone down. He and Striker had been sucked into a trap. His escorts led him out to an interrogation room, tied him in a chair and took up positions against the wall by the door.

A few seconds later, a tall Chinese walked in. "I am Gao Dong," he said, "colonel of the security forces of the People's Republic of China."

"Good for you," Katz said. There was no use in his playing nice with this bozo.

"Your papers say that you are Lev Bronski," Dong said, "but that is the name of a Russian Jew. Why are you working with the Americans?"

"They pay well."

Dong took another tack. "Your partner," he asked. "The one they call the Soldier, what do you think he's going to do now that I have captured you?"

Katz was torn between telling this asshole nothing or letting him know that Striker was going to track him to the ends of the Earth and tear his head off.

"You think too much, Mr. Bronski," the Chinese said. "You don't know whether to tell me the truth or what you think will put me off guard so as to aid your rescuer."

Dong smiled. "Let me tell you what I think your brave comrade is going to do. From everything I have been able to learn about him, and I have been able to learn much, he is a man who feels his missions deeply. He has an almost godlike sense of responsibility and feels that he must act to right wrongs as he sees them.''

Katz was surprised at Dong's insights into a man that few knew well. Either his sources were more than top notch, or he was a hell of a lot smarter than he had sounded so far. If the latter was true, Katz was in big trouble.

''You know,'' Dong said, ''when I was a child in Hong Kong, I used to enjoy going to the movie houses on Sunday to watch American movies. My favorites were the classic Westerns where the lone hero rides into a hostile town to take his vengeance for a wrong done. In every film, somehow, some way, the hero fights against overwhelming odds to ultimately win. I'm sure you know the plot. It's the archetypical American fairy tale, and I know it well.

Dong smiled in remembrance. ''You can't imagine how much those movies meant to the son of a man who was working as a menial for the British authorities who were occupying that part of the motherland. Only later did I learn that my father was actually one of those lone heroes fighting to free the workers from the evils of capitalism. He didn't live long enough to see his dreams brought to life—'' Dong leaned closer ''—but I followed in his path, and I did.''

Katz had heard this Communist bullshit all of his life, and it didn't make any more sense to him now than it had done the first time he'd heard it. You'd think that they'd get a new song and dance.

"I'm sure that the oppressed proletariat of Hong Kong are real happy now that the Brits have bugged out and turned it over to a real oppressive regime."

"Not all of them," Dong freely admitted. "But their children will be. We will see to that."

Katz shook his head.

Dong smiled. "I think the Soldier will not be able to keep himself from trying to rescue you. Even knowing that I will be waiting for him and will kill him, he will come. He is a hero, and he cannot do anything else."

Katz had no doubt that Bolan would do exactly that, but the knowledge brought him no relief. Being the bait in the trap to kill Striker wasn't going to be his finest moment. His first thought was to try to kill himself to nullify Dong's plan. But even if he was able to do it, there was no way that Bolan could know it. This trap was intended as much for him as it was for Bolan and Grimaldi.

"I guess what I don't understand," Katz said, "is why you're going to all this effort for one man. It's true that we stumbled onto your slave-spy operation and put a pretty good dent in it, to say nothing of eliminating a few of your Dragon Egg thugs in the process. But isn't this excessive? I mean, didn't Sun Tzu tell you that you should never allow the enemy's actions deflect you from your purpose?"

Dong bowed slightly. "Master Tzu did voice a cau-

tion on that matter. However, the war god's one true
son had never contemplated a man in my position.''

''How is that possible?''

''I find myself in the position of one of the doomed
outlaws in your Western movies. I am under a sentence of death, and I do not intend to die alone. I will
take the Soldier with me. You, though, will live and
be sent to my superiors in Beijing to apologize for
my failures. I am certain that they will enjoy talking
to you.''

Now Katz understood what he and Bolan were up
against. The Chinese didn't have a kamikaze tradition
like the Japanese, but the same cultural desire to go
to death surrounded by the bodies of your enemies
applied. Dong had screwed up big time, and the only
way he could save face was to go out in a blaze of
glory. It was the plot of too many movies, but Dong
was acting as if he had invented it himself.

''You realize,'' he said, ''that the American authorities are completely aware of your economic-
espionage program now, and they'll be alert to it.''

Dong laughed. ''So what? You can print the details
of my operation in every newspaper in the country
and it will not make any difference. Do not forget
that all of you Yankees are motivated by pure greed.
When one of your Presidents will sell us classified
missile guidance secrets·in return for a few million
dollars in campaign contributions, you have no secrets
worth fighting for.

''And what a politician on the take will not sell us,
any of your greedy businessmen will. Your people are

hopelessly corrupt and rotten to the core. In their greed and lust for power, they are selling out their own people.''

Katz knew the truth of that, but scumbag politicians and businessmen weren't the heart of America. Foreigners always took the wrong lessons from the assholes who always seemed to represent the United States instead of learning what the real Americans were like.

"So, let's say your plan works," Katz said. "You kill my partner, and I take a tour of the Great Wall before you kill me. Then what?''

"Then what?'' Dong asked. "Then in a few years the mother country takes her rightful place in the world. The People's Army moves to eliminate the last remnants of greed and capitalism, and the workers—''

"Bullshit!'' Katz exploded. "That's pure bullshit and you know it. All you're talking about is a handful of twisted, bitter old men who can't get it up lording it over the rest of the world. Didn't you guys get enough of that shit when old Green Teeth was still alive?''

Dong completely lost it. "I will not let you talk about the Great Leader Mao in those disrespectful terms,'' he hissed.

"Why not?'' Katz shrugged. "Everyone knows your Great Leader never brushed his teeth. How very civilized, how very Mandarin.''

Katz knew that he was digging his own grave by

goading Dong. But if it could put him off his stride, it might give Striker a break.

"And how about the Great Cultural Revolution?" He laughed. "What a wonderful success that was. You guys were great a thousand years ago, but you haven't been competitive since you weren't able to figure out how to do something useful with the gunpowder you invented. I mean, the great Chinese accomplishment of history was learning how to carry two buckets of shit with one stick and picking up one grain of rice with two. Nothing that makes modern China powerful originated there. When was the last time you guys invented any—?"

Dong's fist exploded, smashing into Katz's face, and he felt the skin over his eyebrow split open as his head snapped back.

A second and third blow struck him, and he leaned into it as much as he could. Fortunately Dong hadn't paid enough attention to his martial-arts classes.

Dong realized that he had lost control and pulled back. These were the same racist insults and slanders that Dong had endured during his years at Oxford. The Chinese were a great people and the world would learn to fear them as they paid back the West for all of the years that they had been so ruthlessly exploited.

Blood was flowing into Katz's eye from the cuts on his eyebrow and face, but he was overjoyed to see Dong's eyes bulging with rage. This was one guy who wasn't too tightly wrapped, and he was glad to see it. He'd feared that Dong was going to be one of those cold, calculating bastards who were so hard to get to.

By growing up in Hong Kong, he had to have missed a few classes in proper Chinese thinking.

"You are going to take a long time dying," Dong stated.

"No big deal." Katz smiled and shrugged. "Everyone dies sooner or later."

"We will see about that," Dong said as he turned to the guards. "Put this man back in his cell."

Katz allowed himself to be untied and dragged back to his cell.

KATZ GOT the blood stopped and would have given anything for a couple of aspirin to fight his headache. He knew that he'd come real close to being beaten to death back there, but he'd found Dong's buttons. He might have pushed them a little hard, but he'd won that round. Hopefully he'd get another chance to tweak the bastard again. The more he could get Dong fired up, the easier it'd be for Striker to make his play.

And thinking of that, he decided to try to get some clothing. He'd never liked fighting in his boxers.

Going over to the cell door, he started kicking it. "Hey," he yelled. "I'm freezing my ass off in here. How about giving me some clothes?"

CHAPTER TWENTY-FOUR

Marseilles

Bolan's belief that Dong was targeting him personally was reinforced when the hotel desk clerk transferred a phone call to his room. A French-accented male voice simply gave him an address and hung up.

"We've been made," he told Jack Grimaldi, "and our target's changed."

"What do you mean?"

They had originally planned to hit Napoleon Garza's villa. That's where they figured Katz would be if Garza were calling the shots. But the address Bolan had been given was an abandoned factory complex.

"The caller gave me the address of that abandoned factory you and I reconned close to where they ambushed Katz and Jasmine. Dong's playing games and wants to suck us into another trap."

"Nice of him to let us know where they're holding him, though."

"That's what I'm worried about," Bolan said. "Katz might or might not actually be there. He could be leading us into a kill zone."

"But we're going there anyway, right?"

"What choice do we have?" Bolan said. "Get your gear—we're pulling out."

JASMINE FARJANI watched as Belasko and the pilot left their hotel. Having watched how Belasko had spotted the car that had tailed them in Calcutta, she tried not to make the same mistakes that driver had done. She already knew where the pilot had parked his helicopter and when she saw that was the direction they were heading, she stopped following them and turned her car around.

This was where it was going to get real tricky. Following a chopper with a car wasn't easy. In fact, it was impossible. So rather than even try, she quickly drove to the ridgeline northeast of the city to see if she could spot the chopper when it took off and determine where it was going. Her bet was that they were going for Garza's villa, but with those two guys, things were never obvious. Nor were they with the elusive Dong, damn his eyes.

The chopper lifted off and flew in the direction of the part of town she and Katz had been walking when they were ambushed. That abandoned factory! They had to be holding him there. Napoleon Garza must not have wanted to get his house shot up and had more than likely stashed Bronski somewhere less vulnerable to damage. Even Mob bosses hated cleaning up after an attack.

Pulling back onto the road, she raced down into the city, the car's tires squealing in the turns. There was no way that she could beat the chopper, but she didn't intend to be too far behind it.

WHAT FARJANI COULDN'T see from her vantage point was that Grimaldi had flown off alone. Bolan had waited a couple of minutes before getting back in their car and driving to the target area. Parking two blocks away from the factory, he got out and started his infiltration. This part of town wasn't well illuminated—who wanted to waste electricity on derelict buildings?—so he led with his NVGs.

With Dong having a military background, there was a chance that he had posted sentries outside the factory walls, so he was careful as he went in. The new-generation night-vision goggles he wore gave him a clear, if glowing green, view into even the deepest shadows as he scanned along the route of his approach.

Not running into any spotters along the way, Bolan crossed the street and moved up to the masonry wall that enclosed the block around the factory complex. It was nice of the French to make a custom of building tall walls around industrial sites. Not only did it give him cover on the way in, but also in this case, it would serve to keep in the people he was coming for where he could conveniently find them.

Using the detachable periscope feature of his
NVGs, he held the small lens high enough that it was
above the top of the wall and scanned both sides, as
well as the area right on the other side of the bricks.
Nothing. Not wanting to wait until someone stumbled
by and spotted him, he scrambled over the wall and
crouched in the shadows to survey his front. His left
front appeared to be clear, but there was a guard coming up on his right.

Lesson one on securing an interior perimeter came
when the gunman reached Bolan's hiding place.
There was nothing for the guard to see, so he didn't
even pause. Two steps later, Bolan was on his back,
one hand over his mouth jerking his head to the side
while the other hand plunged his Tanto fighting knife
into the hollow of his neck.

The gunman struggled as he swiftly bled out, but
had no strength. Pulling the body back behind a row
of empty oil drums, Bolan keyed his com link.

"I'm inside," he said softly, "and in the clear."

GRIMALDI WAS FLYING with a dozen propane cylin-
ders on board rigged to become FAE—Fuel Air Explosive—bombs when they hit the ground. If one of
them went off at the wrong time, they wouldn't even
find enough of his body to mail home in an envelope.
In terms of HE, he was carrying the equivalent of a
dozen 750-pound bombs.

To make this thing work, he was going to have to
toss his "bombs" out of the chopper while he was in

a high hover. Anything under a thousand feet would catch him in the blast. And even that would be cutting it a bit too close for his tastes. But anything higher would mean that his accuracy, what little there was, would disappear.

He had done some downright wild and crazy flying since he'd signed on with the Stony Man Farm crew, but this was going to be one for his logbook. If his bomb run went as planned, it would give Bolan the cover he needed to get in. If it didn't, at least he'd die at the controls of an airplane.

One way or the other, it was worth trying.

He clicked in his com link. "I'm inbound, ready to rock and roll."

"Bring it on," Bolan replied.

"Look out, baby, 'cause here it comes!"

Taking the cap off the road flare taped to the side of the first propane canister, he scratched to ignite it and tossed it out.

By the time the canister hit the ground, it was moving at over a hundred miles per hour, enough to split the thin case of the cylinder and release the liquefied gas inside. The propane flashed into a gas and was ignited by the road flare. The resulting explosion was satisfying.

A second one soon followed.

Banking, Grimaldi came in on another bomb run and saw the first winking muzzle-flashes aimed into the air, but didn't panic. Been there, done that, bought the T-shirt and wore that sucker out.

THE HOLLOW CRUMP of Grimaldi's first bomb brought Yakov Katzenelenbogen out of a sound sleep. He hadn't quite expected a bomb run, but knowing Jack, he wasn't at all surprised. And from the sound of the detonation, he had a good idea what kind of bombs were being dropped. What would this world be without propane canisters?

It was time for him to get ready to escape or die. At least, though, he'd been given clothing. He'd have hated to die in his shorts. All he needed now was a weapon he could use with one hand, but he'd have to wait for that. Maybe one of his guards would bring him one.

WHEN FARJANI SPED down the side street to the factory, she spotted Belasko's car parked in a neighboring alley and knew she was at the right place. Slamming on her brakes, she parked behind his car and heard Belasko's com link message as she got out. With that confirmation that she was at the right place, she hurried for the factory.

She was across the street from the compound wall when the detonation of Grimaldi's first bomb caught her by surprise. She had no idea what it was, but she knew that it was her guys at work and it was time for her to make her own move.

She was surprised how calm she was. Her heart was pounding and she was breathing fast, but she was determined to do whatever she could to help her friends. She mentally reviewed the basics of shooting as Bronski had showed her, but she was under no illusions about her abilities as a gunfighter. Knowing that she was going to need all the breaks she could get, she decided to use her assets as a combat aid.

She had seen how the men in the Kit Kat Klub had fixated on the naked breasts of the dancers on the stage, and it gave her an idea. In case it might help her tonight, she'd not worn a blouse or bra under the jacket of her black uniform. She'd also not buttoned the jacket all the way up; it was closed only with one button in the middle. As a last prop, she would take her head scarf off and unpin her hair so it hung free.

It wasn't much, but if even one of the enemy paused for an instant because his eyes were telling him that he was seeing a half-naked, long-haired woman, she might be able to kill him first.

First, though, she had to get inside.

Spotting a small gate in the wall, she saw a man standing immediately inside it on guard. She opened her jacket and hurried toward it. A second explosion kept the guard's attention long enough for her to get within easy pistol-shot range.

Catching her approach from the corner of his eye, the guard turned to face her. Seeing her open jacket and long hair, he paused, his weapon at his side, giving her the extra time she needed.

"Hello, big boy," she said in French. "Want to play?"

Before he could answer, she brought up the pistol in both hands as Bronski had taught her and fired three times. Two of her shots hit the target and the man went down.

Stepping wide around the body, she pushed through the gate and headed for the sounds of the gunfire. Belasko would be in the middle of it.

She was acutely aware that she only had two magazines of ammunition for the pistol and the remainder of the box of fifty bullets in her side pocket. She wouldn't be able to shoot for very long before she would have to stop and hide while she put more bullets in her magazines.

When another gunman ran past without seeing her, she shot him twice in the back. She had also learned that niceties had no place in a situation like this.

UNDER THE COVER of Grimaldi's attack, Bolan quickly worked his way toward the main building, but was unmolested. The firing was all directed at the high-flying helicopter. Even experienced troops didn't like to have explosives raining from the sky, and these thugs weren't trained troops. This was giving a new meaning to close air support, though. He had a passive NV marker high on the back of his jacket so the pilot could hopefully spot him on the ground and not drop a propane canister on him.

The two gunmen cowering in the doorway of the main building were so occupied with ducking and covering that they had no time left over to look around. He permanently cured them of their inattentiveness, one with the Beretta and the other with a .44 slug.

Stepping past the bodies, he paused to scope out the inside of the building. As he had feared, the Desert Eagle's roar had awakened someone. Two men raced toward him, their assault rifles on full-auto. Since they weren't well trained in running and shooting at the same time, they were wasting their ammunition.

Again he went for a two-handed solution, the Beretta in burst mode and the Desert Eagle with a double tap. The second .44 slug hadn't really been needed, but it felt good.

Pushing past them, he headed for the small enclosure sticking out from one of the building's interior walls. If Katz was anywhere in there, that's where he would be.

A shot rang out and a bullet sang past his ear. Rolling to the side, he spotted a second muzzle-flash and sent a long burst toward it. He was rewarded by a cry of pain, so he delivered an insurance shot.

Going up to the body, he paused long enough to pat it down for keys, but found none. The face, though, was Oriental, and likely one of Dong's men.

After scanning to make sure that he was now alone, the Executioner carefully approached the boxlike enclosure and called out softly, "Katz?"

"I thought I heard Flying Jack's calling cards falling out there," Katz answered from behind the door.

"His fantasy is to be a bomber pilot." Bolan

grinned in the dark. "Stand clear while I open this door. I couldn't find a key."

"Oh, shit," Katz murmured as he pressed himself against the front wall of his cell and put his hands over both ears.

The Desert Eagle bellowed and the lock shattered, opening the door.

"How are you?" Bolan asked as Katz staggered out. "Can you move out?"

"If I had my fucking arm and a gun," Katz growled, "I'd be right as rain."

"I didn't bring the arm," Bolan said, "but we can get you a gun as soon as we get this harness on you."

He pulled the mountaineering rig out of his assault pack, and it took no time for the two of them to get the nylon web straps in place and cinched down tight. It wasn't quite an issue STABO harness, but it would work for a single short-distance, uncomfortable snatch.

"Where's yours?" Katz asked when he saw that Bolan wasn't wearing a STABO rig.

"Later," Bolan said as he handed him a AK-74 from one of the dead guards. "I'm getting you out of here first."

Katz started to argue, but knew that Striker had his mind made up. Once he got out of this place, though, all bets were off.

The two of them quickly made their way out the other side of the building to what had been a truck loading zone. When it looked clear, Bolan stopped and keyed his com link.

"We're in the clear," he sent to Grimaldi. "North side parking lot and I'm showing the strobe. Bring it on."

"I got your strobe," Grimaldi came back instantly. "Coming in on that side and I'll be there ASAP."

GRIMALDI CAME IN HOT and blacked out. He had a light fuel load on board, so he'd be able to make the snatch as quickly as possible. Weight and lift canceled out each other, and he wanted all the lift the rotors could give him.

On the way in, he dropped a couple more of his propane bombs on the south side to distract the opposition. This time, he saw more muzzle-flashes tracking him, proving that someone down there had finally figured it out. Their chance of hitting him, though, was zip. They were firing at the sound of his turbine.

Vectoring in on Bolan's strobe, he went into a high hover, reached over, unclipped the weighted end of the rope and tossed it out the open door. The red light stick on the end of the line would make it easy for Bolan to spot.

"Line's away."

"I got it," Bolan sent back a second later.

Grimaldi had tied a pair of locking carabiners on the rope with a mountaineering hitch, and Bolan quickly snapped them into the carabiners on Katz's harness.

"Go! Go! Go!" Bolan sent over the com link.

Grimaldi twisted the throttle of the hovering chopper up to a maximum and pulled full pitch on the collective. The turbine howled as the blacked-out chopper lifted straight up, snatching Katz off his feet as if he were on the end of a bungee cord.

With no lights showing in the complex, Grimaldi had a difficult time judging the height through his NVGs and transitioned to forward flight with almost no room for the dangling Katz to clear his feet when he passed over the corner of the building.

CHAPTER TWENTY-FIVE

Napoleon Garza was enraged. When the bombing had started, he and Gao Dong were in the small building at the front side of the compound. Back when the plant had been running, the factory manager's office had been situated well away from the main building to escape the noise, and now it kept them out of the line of fire.

The sound of the retreating helicopter, though, told him that the Chinese agent's plan had failed and their hostage had been taken from them.

"Now what?" he asked Dong.

"I was not the man who picked this place to hold him," Dong replied calmly, his hand hovering by the holster belted around his waist. "I warned you that the Yankee was not an amateur."

Garza was a merciless thug, but in his own mind he was an honest man. Dong had warned him, and he hadn't taken full measure of that warning.

A firefight raged in the yard, and Garza knew that at least one of the Americans had stayed behind to

cover the chopper's retreat. That he had no radio reports that his men had even slowed down the attack,
much less killed any of the commandos, only increased his fury. He was Napoleon Garza, and no one
treated him with such contempt.

Grabbing a radio, a subgun with a magazine carrier
and a pair of Russian night-vision goggles, he rushed
out into the darkened yard. He hadn't gotten where
he was without knowing how to fight.

Gao Dong intended to be long gone before Garza
returned. Yet another vaunted European gang leader
had turned out to be a complete idiot. If only Dong's
people were ruling Europe, men like Garza would be
in unmarked graves.

Now that Katz had been extracted, Bolan started
carefully working his way out of the yard on the side
of the main building. His natural inclination was to
clean out as many of Garza's gunmen as he could
before leaving. From the sirens he was hearing,
though, the detonations of Grimaldi's makeshift
bombs and the gunfire had finally drawn someone's
attention. He'd better take care of business as quickly
as he could and do it on the way out instead of con-
ducting a proper rat hunt.

There was a lot of sustained firing going on in one
area of the yard, and he didn't really know why. The
most likely conclusion was that different groups of
Garza's thugs were out of communication and were
shooting blindly at one another. If that were the case,

it was a game he could play to his benefit, as well, and was worth a short detour.

The field of discarded machinery and crates he was moving through gave him good cover on the flanks, but he kept a sharp eye on the open areas he passed. He was just breaking cover when he spotted a target fleeing the combat and drew a bead on it. His finger was tightening when something in the back of his combat mind tripped and stayed his trigger.

The target had long hair and breasts.

"Jasmine," he called softly over the com link, "off to your right."

When the figure turned to face him, he confirmed his ID. "Over here, I'll cover you."

"Just run the way you're facing. I'm back in the shadows."

Farjani sprinted across the open space, keeping low. "I'm out of bullets," she gasped as she paused to button her jacket.

Bolan didn't bother asking her what in the hell she thought she was doing there. That was obvious, and her being out of ammo explained the firing he'd heard. He pulled out his next-to-last extended mag for his 93-R. It would fit into the butt of her 92 and held twice the rounds.

"Here," he said as he handed it over. "This'll fit, but it sticks out a little."

"Thanks."

She dropped the empty from her pistol, slammed

the longer magazine in place and pulled back on the slide.

"Come on—" he motioned her back into the maze of machinery and crates "—we're pulling out."

The two made only another ten yards before Bolan spotted men moving through the junk toward them. When he tired to break off to the side, he found that way blocked, as well.

Taking Farjani's hand, he pulled her back into cover by what had once been a boiler and led her through a hole that had been cut in the side. The wall was thick enough to stop small-arms fire.

"Stay put."

"I can shoot, too," she said.

"Only if I get hit," he snapped. "Otherwise stay put."

JACK GRIMALDI HEADED for the sports stadium a couple of miles away. No soccer games were scheduled for the evening, and it would be a good place to set down Katz unseen and hopefully unharmed. Once he cleared the bleachers, he went into a low hover. Leaning out the open door, he carefully watched the package on the end of the rope as he feathered his rotors to kill the lift.

When Katz was down, Grimaldi sideslipped the chopper and put it on the ground as far from Katz as he could so as not to get him caught up in the rotor blast. Rolling the throttle down to idle, he left the rotor turning, quickly unbuckled and stepped down.

"You okay?" Grimaldi asked as he ran up to his passenger.

"Get me out of this damn thing," Katz growled as he clawed at the harness with his one hand. "We've got to go back for him."

"He told me to get you clear and that he'd make his own way out."

"I'm going to forget you ever said that." Katz's voice was soft. "And if you say it again, I'm going to have to learn how to fly this damn thing one-handed, because I'm going to kill your sorry ass and take your seat. Got that?"

"Katz!"

"I'm serious. I'm going back, and you're going to fly me there."

"Okay, okay," Grimaldi said as his hands flew over the buckles of the mountaineering harness. "Dammit, man, I was just doing what he told me to do. You know how he gets when you don't do what he wants."

"But he's there and not here, so we're going back."

"I got it."

"And on second thought, hook that harness back up. I'll go down on the rope."

"With one fucking arm?"

"Whatever it takes, I'm going back down there."

Grimaldi hurried to prepare Katz for a one-handed rappel. When he was hooked up, Katz snatched the pilot's MP-5 subgun. "Where's your magazines? I need all the ammo I can carry."

"I got two ten-packs," he replied.

"Give me both of them."

Grimaldi handed them over without comment.

"I'll ride in the back," Katz shouted as he slung the magazine carriers around his neck and the MP-5's sling over his shoulder. "Hook the rope up back there."

With the extraction rope on carabiners, it took but a moment to unclip them and take them back to the cabin.

KATZ STOOD behind the pilot's seat, looking forward through the canopy. "Do a flyover so we can spot him."

"Striker," Grimaldi sent over the com link as he headed toward the factory, "we're inbound—show a light."

"Lev and Jack," Jasmine's voice said, "we're pinned down and he can't talk to you right now."

Katz couldn't believe what he was hearing. "What in the hell are you doing down there?"

"I got a gun and I'm trying to help him, but we're both running out of ammunition."

"Oh, shit. Hang on—we're coming."

Spotting a propane canister Grimaldi hadn't thrown out on his bomb run, Katz grabbed it. "When we find them, arm this thing for me and I'll give them a little fire support."

"With one hand? Oh, Jesus."

KATZ MADE a one-handed rappel with his MP-5 slung over his shoulder. It made him a sitting duck for those few seconds it took him to reach the ground, but he had no other choice. He was halfway down the rope when a burst of fire flashed past him and he released the rope. Almost too late, he hit the brake and barely slowed himself before he slammed into the ground. He was stunned, but not enough for him to forget to punch the release to get clear of rope. The last thing in the world he wanted to do was take another ride.

As soon as Katz shook the rope to let Grimaldi know that he was clear, the pilot broke hover and went back to playing dive-bomber. He only had two propane canister bombs left, but when they were gone, he still had his pistol. Trying to fire it with one hand made flying damn near impossible, but he'd done it before.

"I'm down, Striker," Katz whispered over the com link. "Where the hell are you?"

"Go to where they're making the most noise," Bolan replied. "We're in the middle of it."

"On the way."

Though not as comfortable for him to use as his trusty old Uzi, firing an MP-5 one-handed was a snap. And he had the stump of his right arm to balance it on.

Coming up behind a pair of thugs, Katz swept the

MP-5 from left to right, the sustained burst punching both men facedown on the ground.

With his path clear, he clicked in the com link. "I can use a little air support off to my right."

"On the way."

When the explosion shattered the air, Katz made his move.

"I've got you in sight," Bolan said over his earphone. "Move to your right."

Katz spotted Bolan and raced toward him. The Executioner snapped a long burst to clear the field of fire as Katz reached their hiding place.

"Here," he gasped, ripping an MP-5 magazine out of the carrier and handing it to Farjani. "Strip the ammo out of it and reload your magazines."

Bolan hurriedly loaded his 93-R from another MP-5 mag and slapped the mag into the butt of the pistol. That done, he loaded up his other mags. With that and the half mag he had remaining in the Desert Eagle, he was ready to go back to work.

"I'm up."

"Okay," Katz growled. "Let's get the hell out of here."

With Katz's firepower added to the mix, they started working their way backward, taking the shortest distance to the wall.

NAPOLEON GARZA WAS having a difficult time coordinating his troops. He'd never been in a situation like this before, and his people weren't used to military-style reporting and coordination. Every man was fighting his own battle, and even his subleaders didn't know where their own men were.

Making his way along the inside of the perimeter wall, Garza tried to get around to where the firing seemed to be coming from. He wanted to get some of his men to join him and form a sweep line.

Seeing movement to his side, he called on the radio but got no answer. That was good enough for him. Stepping out, he fired half a magazine from his subgun on full-auto.

BOLAN SAW the muzzle-flash and slammed Katz onto the ground. Farjani was trailing them, and he couldn't get to her in time. She cried out and staggered. Katz reached back for her to pull her under cover while Bolan swung around to face the threat.

GARZA SAW his targets fall and felt that he had scored a hit. He was stepping into the open when he saw one of the figures appear from the shadows. Flame appeared in the figure's hands, and he thought he heard a roar at the same time a stunning blow struck him.

Napoleon Garza died with his chest blown open by a .44 Magnum slug.

"HOW BAD is it?" Bolan asked as he ducked back into cover.

"Not bad at all," Katz said as he tied the ends of

Farjani's camouflaged head scarf around her upper right arm. "It's a light hit."

"Let's go."

THE FIRST THING Katzenelenbogen wanted when he got back to the hotel suite was his artificial arm.

"If you'd brought this thing with you," he said as he checked his artificial arm for damage, "I could have stayed and fought my way out."

"I didn't know if it had been damaged or what shape you were going to be in."

"You should've known that if I wasn't dead, I'd be ready to kick some ass."

Bolan laughed.

Katz slipped into his arm and tightened the straps in place. "Damn, that feels good," he said. "I hate being without my right arm.

"By the way," Katz added, "when are we going to get Dong? I'm tired of dancing around with him."

"It ought to be a little easier to get to him now," Bolan said. "If I was counting right, three of his four sidekicks didn't make it out of the factory."

"That's nice to know, but where do you think he's going next?"

"According to Aaron, an Oriental matching his stats and using a Taiwanese passport took a flight to Berlin."

"Hooking up with the Russian Mafia?"

"It looks that way." Bolan nodded. "And it follows his pattern so far. Following the slavery network.''

''More thugs.''

''First, though, we have to get Jasmine the hell out of here for good.''

''How are you going to do that?'' Katz asked. ''Hand carry her?''

''Exactly.'' Bolan grinned. ''I had one of the young blacksuits flown over to escort her back.''

''She's going to be spitting mad.''

''She's not going to have any choice.''

AGAIN BOLAN CARRIED Jasmine Farjani's baggage as he walked her into the airport terminal. Brognola had sent one of the blacksuits to be her escort on the flight back. He wanted her back in the States, and he wasn't going to take any chances on her getting away again.

''This time I'm staying with you until you get on the plane,'' Bolan told her as he held out her ticket.

Farjani smiled. ''I guess with the wound, I'm not much help to you anymore.''

''You've been all the help in the world, but you've got to give that arm a rest. The doctor said that it'll be as good as new and that a little plastic surgery later will take care of the scar.''

''Never,'' she said. ''I want to keep the scar. That way when I start to think that this was all just a dream, I'll be able to remember what I did.''

''As will Lev and I,'' Bolan said.

Seeing a young, fit American tourist standing by

the gate flash him a recognition sign, Bolan steered the woman toward him.

"This is Dave Brown," he said, introducing the young blacksuit with one of the cover names they used for missions like this. "He'll fly back with you and take care of the formalities in Atlanta."

"I almost think that you don't trust me."

"Let's just say that you have a track record."

She laughed. She was going to miss this man more than she knew.

CHAPTER TWENTY-SIX

Berlin

The divided symbol of the cold war was united once more and taking her rightful place as the jewel of northern Europe. As the capital of the German Federal Republic, Berlin was working hard to be a showcase for the most powerful nation in the EU. Paris and London were both grand cities, but Berlin was more modern and flashier. If something was hot and right-now, it was in Berlin at least a week before Paris, London or even New York had even heard of it. The city had a reputation to uphold, and its citizens were sparing no effort to keep it.

With Berlin's new status, it had also become a dominant financial center once more and was the chic address for European corporate headquarters. With so much going on, it was also the preferred home away from home for many less savory operations, the foremost among them being the Russian Mafia and their allies.

A boom town was always a good place to do business in the illegal and the forbidden. Not much was illegal or forbidden in German society, but that little that was verboten, the Russian Mafia specialized in. Included on that shortlist were young prostitutes who weren't allowed to complain about anything their customers wanted to do to them. Drugs of a number of varieties, mundane and exotic, were also a Russian Mob specialty. With the good times rolling in Berlin, the Russians were making money hand over fist.

DEMITRI SORGE LEANED back in his expansive leather chair, his hand on his chin. He didn't quite know what to think about the Chinese operative sitting in front of him in his opulent downtown Ku'damm office. He knew about Gao Dong's activities, of course, but had never expected to meet the man in person. They were competitors, and in his line of work, he usually garrotted any of his competitors he got his hands on. He would, however, give Dong the honor of a hearing before deciding his fate.

"You have an interesting story," the Russian said in English. Dong's Russian wasn't quite up to speed to handle a delicate conversation. "But I'm not sure that my organization can help you in any way."

"I was thinking more in terms of helping you," Dong replied calmly.

Why was it that the damn Russians were even more bullheaded than the Arabs? If he didn't have the Soldier after him, he would have gone to the United

States and offered his services to the American Mafia. If this bid didn't work out, he still might have to chance it.

"Just what is it you think you can do for me, Mr. Dong?" Sorge asked.

"I can give you an introduction to an entirely new, and very lucrative, enterprise," Dong replied. "As I explained earlier, with Napoleon Garza and his Union Corse no longer in the business, I thought you might be interested in picking up where he left off. I know his networks, so I will be able to help you take them over."

"Were you there when Garza and his people were wiped out?"

In the cyber age, mobsters had the same access to the latest breaking news that anyone had. Sorge made it a point to have his intelligence section keep him informed. Being an ex-KGB officer instead of a street thug, it was second nature to him. The shoot-out in the abandoned factory in Marseilles was front-page news in France. The positive identification of Garza's body hadn't escaped his notice. That was the only reason he was talking to Dong at all.

"I was," Dong answered honestly.

"And who did that to him?"

The French authorities were calling it a gang turf war, just as the two attacks on Italian Mafia holdings had been labeled, but Sorge was withholding judgment. He never made up his mind before all the facts were in.

"That American I mentioned," Dong replied.

"One American?"

"He might have had help," Dong confessed. "There was a helicopter involved."

"And why did the Americans want to do something like that?" Sorge asked. "It seems like a lot of effort for them to make on something that doesn't directly affect them."

"He's not official," Dong said. "He's a cowboy crusader working for reasons of his own."

That was another assessment Sorge would take under advisement. He'd worked against the Yankees for too long to take anything they did as being unofficial.

"But how does that affect my operation?" he asked. "And why should I care?"

"That's the part where I think I can help you," Dong said. "There was an adjunct to Garza's operation you might not have been aware of."

Sorge leaned back in his chair. Now the Chinese was getting to the part where the "rubber met the road" as the Yankees liked to say. He had always prided himself on knowing the latest American slang. It always impressed the shit out of them, as they said.

"And what might that be?"

BOLAN AND KATZ DEPLANED from the Lufthansa Boeing 727 at Templehof airport. Once a marvel in the midthirties it was now the smallest of Berlin's three airports. It had been the center of the postwar

Berlin air lift, but now only handled domestic commuter flights. It was, though, in the center of the city.

Out front, they caught a cab parked by the Luftbruke monument to the Allied Air Bridge, which had saved the cut off city from the Red Army. "The Berlin Hilton," Bolan said.

"You know," Katz said after they were settled into their comfortable suite, "we've got us a real problem here."

"Which one?"

"Well, to start with, this is a big place and we haven't a clue where our guy might be hiding out."

"I think we can rule out him bunking up with his best buddy in the Berlin police barracks."

"That's about the only place we won't find him," Katz agreed. "That and the Reichstag. Back in the good old days of East and West Berlin, it would've been a piece of cake to chase down a Chinese guy. Just have the Berlin cops collect all of the two dozen Oriental guys in town and grill them. Now that the cold war's over, though, the place is crawling with Asians. Before we got out of the terminal, I heard Japanese, Chinese and Vietnamese being spoken."

"What do you suggest?"

"I'll be damned if I know," Katz said. "But the way this has gone, if we look for the biggest white slaver in Berlin, we ought to be able to get a lead on him. He's ran with them so far, and with Beijing putting a price on his head, he's about out of places to hide."

"Sounds like we need to get Aaron on that."

"That's first on my agenda."

"And while you're doing that," Bolan said, "I'm going to contact an old friend."

Katz didn't need to know whom Striker was going to call on. As he himself did, the Executioner had a select circle of people he had crossed paths with over the years. Old friends were always a good thing to have.

Stony Man Farm, Virginia

HAL BROGNOLA WOULD have much preferred to have Bolan and Katz back in the States and had told them so before they had left France. Not unexpectedly, though, Striker had blown him off, so he'd gone to plan B immediately. That was to put Stony Man on the job full-time, presidential approval or not. The sooner that Striker caught up with Dong, the sooner he'd run out of things to do and come home.

Katzenelenbogen's call from Berlin came as no big surprise. "Where's Striker?" was the first question Brognola asked.

"He's talking to old friends," Katz replied. "And he left me to try to get you guys off your ass and doing something useful."

"What do you need?" Brognola asked. "Whatever it is, you've got it."

Katz quickly gave him their conclusions as to where Dong might be hiding out.

"That sounds likely," Brognola said. "We'll start running that info right now. And by the way, tell Striker that Jasmine Farjani arrived here safely and is undergoing a debriefing right now."

"That's great," Katz said. "That's one hard-core woman, Hal. You might want to think about having someone give her a job."

"I'm working on that right now."

"Good," Katz said. "How about patching me through to the Bear?"

"I'm on-line," Kurtzman broke in. "And I've already started looking for your guy along just those lines. Right now, the biggest player in the slave trade is a Russian named Demitri Sorge. He works for one of the big Moscow families. He's ex-KGB, and the Germans are hot after his ass, as well, but they can't pin anything on him. He's covered in layers of cutouts and dummy corporations."

"Sounds like a New Jersey Mafia Don."

"Not quite as humble, though," Kurtzman replied. "He lives large."

"Good," Katz said. "I like going up against a man whose ego outpaces his common sense."

"He has a security force equal to his ego, though," Kurtzman cautioned. "He's got a band of ex-KGB and Stasi toughs swarming around him like flies on a ham sandwich at a Alabama picnic in July."

"You've been talking to T.J. again." Katz laughed. "The man does have a turn of phrase."

"Give me a data dump on this Sorge guy, and I'll start on my Interpol contacts."

"On the way."

Berlin

THE WESTERN SIDE of the reunited Berlin hadn't changed all that much since the Berlin Wall fell. The greatest need for rebuilding had been in the old Communist sector because the West had already been built up nicely. Motze Strasse, one block off Nolendofter Platz, was much the same as it had been in the seventies and eighties. Many of the shops, bars, discos and small restaurants had changed hands, or at least their names, but the apartments in the upper floors of the block-long buildings remained the same.

Bolan had no trouble finding stairwell number 119-126 Motze Strasse. The faded paper tag on the rank of mailboxes in the entryway showed the name he sought. Rather than call ahead, he had decided to call in person, figuring that Dieter Rigmann would most likely be in.

He rang the doorbell at number 24 on the third floor and heard steps slowly approach.

"I haven't seen you in a while, old friend," Rigmann said in accented English as he opened his door wide. "Come in, please.

"What can I get you?" the old German asked as he led Bolan into a small living room decorated in faded but neat fifties style. "Schnapps? *Jaegermeis-*

ter? I have a fine Madeira. Maybe a port? But of course. You're working. I will make coffee.''

"Coffee is fine," Bolan answered with a smile.

"It will take but a moment," he said. "Eva has been gone these many years now, so I have had to learn how to serve my own guests. Not that I have all that many since the fall of the Wall.''

"They've put you out to pasture?" Bolan spoke loud enough that Rigmann could hear in the small kitchen off of the living room.

"More or less, as you say." The German laughed bitterly. "They say that the war is finally over. The Evil Empire, as your Reagan called it, is at last dead. Old men like me are no longer needed because our eyes are too finely attuned to seeing evil under every bed to fit in a society where we let new evils grow unchallenged.''

"It's one of those new evils that I want to talk to you about," Bolan told the old master of intelligence operations. "Specifically the Russian Mafia.''

"I rather thought so," Rigmann said as he came in carrying a tarnished silver tray bearing a coffee service. "It's so good to be able to speak English once again. I was afraid that I had forgotten it.''

Rigmann poured, gave Bolan his cup and sat back down. "Who are you looking for this time?"

"Whoever's the biggest mover of women in Berlin. White slavery.''

"Demitri Sorge," Rigmann answered without even having to stop and consider candidates. "Ex-KGB, late fifties, backgrounded at the German desk but served all over Europe. Known for living the high life and reputed to have been the whoremaster for Lubinka Street. A very nasty piece of work, our man Sorge.''

Rigmann smiled thinly. ''What do you want with him?''

Bolan sipped his strong Turkish coffee. ''Actually I'm looking for a Chinese operative who might be hiding out with him.''

''That is interesting.'' The old spymaster leaned forward in his chair.

Bolan then launched into a briefing on his activities since he had come across a gang rape in progress in L.A. When he was done, he sat back.

''You do come up with interesting problems,'' Rigmann said. ''And how is Katzenelenbogen?''

''He's well and he's in town with me.''

''And your other friends?''

Bolan shook his head. ''No, just him and I this time.''

''That you are still alive, old friend, tells me many things.''

Bolan smiled.

''One of them is that you have not lost your eye nor your belly.''

'' 'Guts' in English,'' Bolan gently corrected him.

''You, of course,'' Rigmann said, ''will want to know where to find Sorge.''

''If you can help me, yes.''

The old German got up from his chair. "Give me a moment, please."

Dieter Rigmann, once a man whose name chilled the blood of Communists and terrorists throughout Europe, shuffled to his "office" in the rear of his apartment.

When he came back, he handed a big envelope stuffed full of paper to Bolan. "This should be what you will need."

"Thanks, Herr Rigmann."

Rigmann stiffened and bowed slightly. "It is the least I can do for someone who has done so much for my city."

"I FOUND Dieter Rigmann," Bolan said when he walked back into the hotel room.

"Damn, is that old Nazi still alive?"

"He is," Bolan said. "And, as you well know, he wasn't a Nazi. He was just one of Galen's brightest young studs at the end of the war."

"I know, I know." Katz glanced at the bulging envelope in his hand. "What did you get from his vault?"

"An ex-KGB officer named Demitri Sorge."

"Damn," Katz looked at his notes. "That's the same guy the Bear came up with."

"And Rigmann doesn't even have a computer."

Katz shook his head. "Who says that good old-fashioned human intelligence has gone out of style."

"Oh," Bolan said as he opened the envelope, "he asked about you. I told him you were well."

Katz didn't even want to go there. "Let's compare notes," he said instead.

Kurtzman's data was extensive, but Rigmann's was more in-depth and went back to the year when Sorge had first come to town as a front man for a mobster back in Moscow. It chronicled his career from bag man to undisputed ruler of a vast criminal enterprise extending from Eastern Europe, through the West to the United States.

Katz finished reading and looked up. "Looks like we need to take a closer look at this guy's home turf."

Bolan looked out the window. "It's a nice day. Let's do that."

THE SHORES of Krumlanke had once been dotted with the minor estate houses of Berlin's old aristocracy. The Nazis had appropriated many of them, as had the Americans in turn after WWII. During the cold war, many clandestine operations had been launched from one particular manor house, Zum Wilden Sau. It was a three-story mansion with enough outbuildings to have been a small village in Bavaria. The entire compound was surrounded by a six-foot stone wall.

When the Americans pulled out of Berlin after the fall of the Wall, Zum Wilden Sau had remained derelict until Demitri Sorge picked it up for a song. It was true that he'd had to dump a ton of his ill-gotten gains into restoring and modernizing it, but it had still been a bargain. Now, except for the Reichstag, it was the most secure location in Berlin. Sorge had spared no expense to make it that way.

It was also one of the most picturesque of Berlin's old mansions. The grounds had been replanted and the wild pigs the house was named after again roamed the fields. With the back side of the compound bordering the lake, ducks and geese wandered the lower grounds and had their nests in the rushes. Even a swan or two called the place home.

"We forgot to bring an army with us, Striker," Yakov Katzenelenbogen said as he studied the manor's lower grounds through his field glasses.

Bolan glanced over as he piloted their small pleasure craft through the wake of one of the larger excursion boats on the popular lake. "That good?"

"Better," Katz said as he made a note on the pad in his lap. "The only thing I can't see is his air-defense system. But," he said, again raising his binoculars, "I know it's there. I can see the radar dish."

"You got everything you need for now?"

"Yeah." Katz put the glasses down. "Let's go back and call the Bear."

CHAPTER TWENTY-SEVEN

Stony Man Farm, Virginia

"I got it, Katz." Kurtzman sounded triumphant as he almost shouted over the phone. "Sorge had to file plans and blueprints for his restoration project with the city building inspectors, and the work he had done was properly inspected. Further, those plans were inputted into their data banks."

"What's the bad news?" Katz asked.

"Like you thought, this place has all the earmarks of a fortress. I can't tell what went in after the inspectors left, but you can see where it was intended to go."

"What's the auxiliary-power situation?"

"Not to your liking, I'm afraid," Kurtzman replied. "He's got a full power setup in the basement. A bank of Honda diesel generators."

"What kind of power?"

"Enough to drive a TV broadcasting station and enough left over for full satellite com network and the world's biggest boom box."

"How about some good news?" Katz sounded weary.

"How about an airborne Ranger battalion?" Kurtzman said bluntly. "That's about what it looks like it's going to take to get in there."

"Let me look around," Katz said drily. "I seemed to have misplaced my Ranger battalion."

"Some of Sorge's other sites aren't that well hardened, though," Kurtzman offered. "He's got a lot of cover places, and you guys might want to try one of them instead of committing suicide."

"How about a list of his business establishments?" Bolan cut into the conversation.

"I've got those, as well, and some of them look pretty soft," Kurtzman replied. "Whorehouses and bars usually aren't too well fortified."

"Send it all."

"On the way."

Berlin

KATZ'S LITTLE PORTABLE printer was smoking by the time he finished printing out Kurtzman's data dump. "We need to get us some better equipment if we're going to keep doing business this way," he grumbled.

"Remember when we did this without all that stuff?"

"I remember." Katz shook his head.

Again the two men split the pile and sat down to read themselves into the situation. For this to work, they'd have to depend on smarts, not surprise, to pull it off.

"Demitri Sorge is a real piece of work," Katz said as he exchanged his half of the pile with Bolan. "We'll be doing Berlin a favor if he should happen to get caught up in the cross fire."

"More than just Berlin." Bolan locked eyes with him. "If these numbers are even close, he's been moving a lot of women, and that needs to stop."

Katz didn't need to reply to that. That was what had brought the Executioner into this in the first place, and the man hated to leave a job only halfway finished.

AFTER THOROUGHLY checking Gao Dong's story through his own sources, Demitri Sorge had decided to keep the Chinese around as long as he was useful. As soon as he wasn't, Sorge intended to "shop" him back to Beijing. Dong, of course, had failed to mention that he had a price on his head, but that was all right with Sorge. If Dong didn't know that he knew, it left him vulnerable. The first rule of staying alive was to never leave anything out when you were turning your coat. To do so made your new master think that you were less than honest. And in Sorge's profession, to be less than honest was a rock-solid death sentence.

He had also checked on this mysterious American agent Dong had reported to have caused all of his problems, but he didn't like what he got back on that query. Such a man did exist, or at least he once had. And he had been known to the KGB by a number of names. None of which was good news. Under any name, that man, if he was the one who had dogged Dong's heels, was the absolute last thing he needed to have to stop to deal with right now.

Sorge had a number of delicate deals in the works, the culmination of months of negotiations with a number of people from several organizations, and he simply didn't need the distraction.

The thought had occurred to him that after getting Garza's operation from Dong, he should shop him to the Americans instead of the Chinese. He wouldn't be paid as well, if he got anything for him at all, but it might take the heat off of him and get him a ''good boy'' badge in the CIA's books. Or it might backfire and raise his profile with them, so he would have to consider that choice carefully. Nonetheless, he'd make that decision when the time came and this wasn't it.

It was time, however, to have Dong lay out the details of the operation he had been running with the Corsican and see how it might fit into his own operational scheme. He had to admit that having Garza six feet underground had saved him a lot of trouble in the future. The Corsicans had been on his shortlist of organizations he wanted gone.

Sorge punched the button on his intercom. ''Send him in.''

Dong was wearing his usual game face when he

walked in and took a seat. Sorge was going to see if he could remove it.

"The price of my protection," he said, "is that you reveal each and every last detail not only about your Corsican operation, but everything else you were doing for China. I have learned that you are a much wanted man and very valuable to the right people. You must become more valuable to me if you wish to stay alive."

Dong didn't let any expression show on his face. He'd never thought that Beijing would have contacted men like Sorge, but it appeared that they had. This meant the end of everything he had worked for and betraying his family all the way back to the first ancestor. The alternative, though, was to kill himself if Sorge would give him that chance.

He had always been willing to die for the mother country, but only in her service. Killing himself to stay out of their hands wasn't the kind of service he had envisioned doing for his ancestors.

"I will do what you want," he said.

"Good." Sorge smiled. He'd halfway expected that Dong would balk. Maybe even try to kill himself, as some of the captured Chinese agents he'd worked on during the old days had done. But not this time apparently.

Sorge leaned back in his chair and let Dong talk about his industrial spying project, the Dragon Egg teams and the sideline he'd help Garza set up to market high-tech items to Third World governments.

"I have to admit that sounds as if it has possibilities," Sorge said. "We will have to explore this further."

Dong was a little surprised at the relief he felt when the Russian said "we," but he didn't allow a trace of it to show on his face. Damn all Western long noses who didn't credit his people with the ability to feel human emotions. The Han felt them, but were usually too disciplined to allow them to be paraded in public as if they were barbarians.

"Let me get you settled in while I have some of my people look over your proposal," Sorge stated, playing gracious host. "And tonight I will show you Berlin. I know that you're well experienced with the West, but Berlin is not like any other city in the world. I think you will enjoy it.

Normally Dong would have rather been flayed alive than have to accompany a Russian on an extended drunken debauch. Most of the Russians he'd known were pigs, and barbaric pigs at that. But this was business and his personal survival was on the line.

"I look forward to it."

WITH A FULL-COURT PRESS in progress at the Farm, the single most critical element was communications intelligence. Brognola was fully aware that Bolan was more than capable of tracking down Dong by himself, but it would take time and he wanted the man back home as soon as possible. He and Katz had been exposed for a long time now, and every day that passed only increased the risks they were taking. The Man would be more than unhappy if Striker got put out of action even temporarily.

He knew, though, that Bolan had the bit in his teeth and wasn't going to back down until Dong was dead. He had never backed down and the day he did would be the end of him.

"How's Carnivore working?" he asked Aaron Kurtzman.

Carnivore was a program worked up by the NRO—National Reconnaissance Office—to supplement their series of spy satellites. Basically it was a hacker's dream and could listen in to any kind of electronic communications system from TV signals to faxes, cell phones, palm pilots, land-line communications and anything else that used electricity. About the only thing it couldn't intercept was two kids talking over tin cans and a string.

"As advertised." Kurtzman spun his chair. "We're zeroing in on exactly which phones Sorge's using."

While Carnivore could, and did, pick up everything, sorting it out was the art that had to be applied to the science. Without that, it was all just electronic garbage.

"How much longer?"

Kurtzman shrugged. "Usually this process takes days, and we're trying to do it in hours. And Sorge is not your average Eurohood—he's got secure modules on most of his stuff."

When he saw that look come over Brognola's face, he quickly added, "But he's using last year's KGB coding and we broke that right after it came out."

"Just get it to Katz, dammit!" Brognola growled.

"Right away, boss."

AFTER DIGESTING Kurtzman's data dump on Sorge's legitimate establishments, Bolan and Katz took a personal recon of the top dozen on the list. They were on the third stop when Katz's cell phone chirped.

He punched it on. "Yeah?"

"We're getting unscrambled intercepts," Kurtzman said, "and several of them are about some kind of affair being set up at one of Sorge's places, the Katrina."

"We haven't scoped that one out yet," Katz replied. "When's it taking place?"

"It looks like he's planning an all-nighter starting at nine," Kurtzman replied. "We've gotten intercepts from the caterers, the other support people and even his security force. There's been several mentions of a 'special visitor,' and that could be your man."

"It could also be someone from Moscow."

"It could be," Kurtzman admitted, "but we know Dong's in town."

"We'll check it out."

Katz put his cell phone back in his pocket. "The Bear's getting Carnivore hits about Sorge setting up a big party at one of his places."

"Which one?"

"Katrina at the Europa Center."

"Let's check it out."

When Bolan pulled onto the Ku'damm, the Katrina was right on the corner of the large mall. "Three story, right?" he asked Katz, who was frantically thumbing through the stack of hard copy he'd brought with him.

"Yep, three story, two elevators and a basement garage. One exit leading into the garage, a service door in the rear and the entrance. That's it."

Bolan eyed the flat-topped building. "How about the roof?"

"Nothing noted."

Bolan spotted a parking space across the street as it came open and beat a Fiat into it. "Let's take a closer look."

Bolan plugged a couple of coins into the meter before entering the mall. At one time, the Europa Center had been Berlin's showplace shopping and dining address. It was a bit dated now, but looked to have been recently refurbished. He remembered the space that Sorge's club now occupied as having once been two separate restaurants with shops on the upper floors.

The entrance to the club was Berlin gaudy, which was to say tasteful. The two hard-eyed guys flanking it were well-dressed, but weren't there for decoration. Sliding his eyes past them, Bolan walked up to the kiosk on the sidewalk, looked at the club's advertisements and scanned the menu posted behind the glass. "Maybe we should have dinner here tonight?"

"Looks good to me," Katz said as he studied the background details of the photos of the acts on the stage. Since this was Berlin, there was more background than there was clothing on the dancers.

Moving on, they entered the atrium and paused for a couple of moments to watch the ice skaters before moving on. They went up the stairs to the shops on the third floor opposite the atrium from Sorge's place.

"No way in from that side," Katz commented.

"Let's take a look at the roof."

There was a small observation tower on the far corner that overlooked the ruined tower of the Kaiser Wilhelm Memorial Church. It also looked down onto the roof of the Katrina one floor below it.

"That looks doable," Bolan commented as his eyes swept the roof below.

"With bolt cutters."

DEMITRI SORGE WAS proud of the Katrina, the flagship of his business enterprises. This was the one club he had that catered to the fashionable Ku'damm crowd. In Berlin, location was still everything if you wanted to be noticed. If you didn't want anyone to see what you were doing, Sorge could also handle that, but not at the Katrina.

"The mayor of Berlin had a reception in here just yesterday," Sorge bragged as he ushered Dong in past his security men. "And a famous Hollywood director is holding a cast party tomorrow. It was only by chance that I wasn't completely booked tonight."

Dong wasn't impressed by capitalist decadence in any form. To him, the Katrina was just another restaurant serving overly prepared food that only a barbarian could enjoy. He let himself be directed to a large table close to the stage and sat beside Sorge as uniformed waiters carrying silver champagne buckets converged on them.

It was going to be a long night, but he would have to get used to it.

BOLAN WAS COMING in from the top and Katz from the bottom. Pulling this off in the middle of downtown Berlin was going to be dicey, but it could be done.

The Executioner came down from the Europa Center's observation tower to the roof of the club. Sorge didn't have security stationed up there because after all, this was the Ku'damm and it would have looked out of place. Bolt cutters and a titanium pry bar got him through the access door leading into the club, and he waited in the laundry service room inside.

IN THE BASEMENT, Katz breezed past the guy in the parking booth and slipped into the elevator at the other end. Taking a titanium lock wedge out of his pocket, he jammed it into the sliding door to block it open. That done, he moved on down to the locked back door leading into the club.

That took a little longer to get through, but he was equipped for the task. He was also prepared for de-

feating the security system covering the door. Had
Sorge placed a guard there, he was prepared for him,
as well, but no human eyes were watching. Being on
the Ku'damm had given Sorge a caveat that had soft-
ened the Russian's instincts. Who would want to attack one of Berlin's premier dining experiences?

"I'm in," he whispered over the com link.

BOLAN DIDN'T BOTHER with the contents of the rooms
on the upper floors as he made his way to the dining
room. The Berlin police could sort out who was doing
what to whom later. His mission was one man in the
dining room, maybe two if the opportunity presented
itself. One shot and his work would be done, two at
the most.

The second-floor landing, though, presented a problem in the form of a pair of security men. Both of
them were looking down onto the dining area and
stage and weren't watching their back.

"Got a light?" he said as he approached them.

The closer goon turned and saw a tall man in evening dress approaching, a cigarette holder in his left
hand. One of the boss's guests.

"You are not..." the guard began right before he
saw a flash and took a silenced 9 mm slug between
the eyes.

His partner spun and collected another bullet. But
in turning he was off balance, and the impact tumbled
him over the railing onto the table below.

Instant chaos broke out in that corner of the room,

and Sorge leaped to his feet. Not knowing what was going on and having no German, Dong looked around at the second-floor open landing and saw a tall black-haired man standing at the railing.

The man smiled as he brought a big pistol from behind his back. The American!

Dong dived under the table, but over the shrieks of the crowd, the pistol roared. The first round tore through the thick wooden table close to his head. The second shot tore into his back before he heard the report. He didn't hear the third shot at all.

KATZ WAITED in the corridor leading to the dining room, his back to the stairwell leading into the base-ment. A flash-bang, the pin pulled, was in his artificial hand, and his good hand was wrapped around the butt of his mini-Uzi, the sound suppressor attached to the muzzle.

The dining room was a scene of chaos. Well-dressed men and women were trampling one another in their rush to get out of the restaurant before more shots were fired. The neatly uniformed waiters had all disappeared, and the only people on their feet were Sorge and his thugs. The Russian shouted and a pair of gunmen raced forward, pistols in their hands.

Katz tossed the flash-bang into the room and turned his head to protect his vision. Since the grenade had landed at the feet of the gunmen, they were down for the count.

"Go!" Bolan said as he came down the stairs behind Katz. "I'll cover you."

Katz split for the stairs, and Bolan stepped out into
the dining room. Since he was on the scene and had
a few seconds to waste, he might as well make a clean
sweep. Rigmann had included a photo of Sorge in his
package, so he knew whom he was hunting for.

Sorge was standing at the back of the room and
shouted as he drew a Stechkin machine pistol from
inside his coat.

Bolan knew the Stechkin climbed badly on full-
auto and didn't drop his stance. He also wasn't giving
Sorge a break. The Desert Eagle roared again, and the
Russian flew backward from the impact right over his
heart. The Stechkin stuttered in Sorge's death grip,
the 9 mm rounds spraying the ceiling.

Bolan backed out and followed Katz down the
stairs to the garage.

KATZ AND BOLAN walked past Kaiser Wilhelm
Church as a cluster of police cars and vans screeched
to a halt in front of the corner of the Europa Center.
Black-clad emergency-alert police stormed out of the
vans, MP-5s in hand, and raced into the club.

"You ready to go home now?" Katz asked.

Bolan glanced over his shoulder. "I'm done here."

James Axler
Outlanders

EQUINOX ZERO

As magistrate-turned-rebel Kane, fellow warrior Grant and archivist Brigid Baptiste face uncertainty in their own ranks, an ancient foe resurfaces in the company of Viking warriors—harnessing ancient prophecies of Ragnarok, the final conflict of fire and ice, to bring his own mad vision of a new apocalypse. To save what's left of the future, Kane's new battlefield is the kingdom of Antarctica, where legend and lore have taken on mythic and deadly proportions.

In the Outlands, the shocking truth is humanity's last hope.

DEATH LANDS®

Destiny's Truth

Available in
December 2002
at your favorite retail outlet.

Emerging from a gateway in New England, Ryan Cawdor and his band of wayfaring survivalists ally themselves with a group of women warriors who join their quest to locate the Illuminated Ones, a mysterious pre-dark sect who may possess secret knowledge of Deathlands. Yet their pursuit becomes treacherous, for their quarry has unleashed a deadly plague in a twisted plot to cleanse the earth. As Ryan's group falls victim, time is running out—for the intrepid survivors…and for humanity itself.

GOLD EAGLE®

James Axler
Outlanders

FAR EMPIRE

Waging a covert war that ranges from a subterranean complex in the desert to a forgotten colony on the moon, former magistrate Kane, brother-in-arms Grant and archivist-turned-warrior Brigid Baptiste find themselves pawns in a stunning strategy of evil. A beautiful hybrid carries an unborn child—a blueprint for hope in a dark world. She seeks Kane's help, unwittingly leading them into a trap from which there may be no escape....

In the Outlands, the shocking truth is humanity's last hope.